OUTBACK SKIES

Suzanne Cass

S C

STORM CLOUD
PRESS

Outback Skies

Storm Cloud Press, Perth Australia

Copyright © 2022 by Suzanne Cass

Edits by Tanya Saari

Cover by Vikncharlie

All rights reserved.

To all my beta and ARC readers who loved this series and helped to make it a success.

CHAPTER ONE

Finn Stevenson brought the motorcycle to a skidding stop, red dust flying in plumes around him. Cattle streamed in a steady line across the dry plain to his left, driven by the mustering team toward the holding yards. They were nearly back at camp. The long day was almost at an end. Finn lifted his helmet visor so he could wipe the sweat from his eyes. This heat was a killer.

"Watch out!" The call came from behind him. He turned to see an enormous bull bearing down on him at a dead run. Finn barely had time to twist the accelerator, the back wheel spitting dirt in a wide spray as he gunned the motorcycle and got out of the charging animal's path just in time.

"You need to keep your wits about you," a woman atop a brown horse yelled at him as she sped past in pursuit of the rogue bull, a kelpie dog at the horse's heels. Indy Solomon on her horse Gypsy.

Finn's heart was beating like a drum. Shit, that'd been close. Indy was right, he'd let his concentration slip. After a long day mustering cattle in the Queensland heat, he was hot, thirsty, and tired, longing for that first swig of cold beer back in camp and not focusing.

Putting the motorcycle back in gear, he took off after the

bull and Indy. Following as close as he dared, he watched as she zigzagged through scrubby stands of acacia, trying to get alongside the animal and turn him toward the main herd.

He'd only met Indy for the first time around the campfire last night, but she'd definitely made an impression. One of the ringers employed full time at Stormcloud Station, unlike himself, who was a contract musterer, brought in to help with the yearly round-up. She was right at home amongst the cattle and living at a muster camp, and today, her superior horse skills had taken her up another few notches in his estimation; he wasn't sure he'd seen a better rider anywhere. And don't forget those chocolate-brown eyes that could melt a man into a puddle of desire at ten paces; sultry and dark beneath her Akubra. She was a petite little firecracker in a pair of blue jeans and cowboy boots. He had to admit, he was a tad intrigued.

Indy and the bull disappeared, swallowed up by more patches of tall, leggy acacia bushes. There were places her horse could go where his motorcycle couldn't. He could see why some of the staff preferred their four-legged friends over a mechanical beast. Instead of following her into the bushes, he waited, patrolling the perimeter, watching carefully.

A noise alerted him just before the bull burst from the shrubs, heading back out onto the plain, searching for his freedom. Finn took off on his motorcycle, not waiting to see if Indy was on the bull's tail. The animal put on a good turn of speed, now that he could smell liberty. This was a micky bull, a young, wild, unmarked male that'd been missed in last year's muster. They were highly unpredictable and dangerous. He directed the motorcycle in a wide arc away from the bull's trajectory, but then rounded in an arc to head it off. His bike bounced beneath him as he hit hidden potholes and dips in the earth. He stood up on the pedals, using his knees and thighs as shock absorbers to balance on the bucking machine. Gaining on the bull, he came in at an angle. The animal never turned its head or acknowledged his presence. Damn, was this bull going to get free after all? He revved the engine and put the bike on a direct course that meant they'd collide if they continued on their chosen paths. Finn held his breath.

At the last second, the bull lowered his massive head, then swung in a half-circle, slowing his breakneck charge to a lumbering trot, snorting his displeasure loudly, foam dripping from his muzzle. Finn took a long look at the sharp tips on the bull's horns and was quietly glad he'd decided to comply in the end.

Now that the bull was cooperating, Finn had no trouble herding him back toward his buddies. Indy jogged toward him on her horse as he watched the micky bull trot up and join the growing group of cattle headed toward the camp, just over the next rise.

"Good work. Thanks." Indy's horse propped to a standstill beside him. "Sorry, Gypsy got turned around in the scrub." She patted the brown mare's neck. "It took us a while to bash our way out. But you seemed to have that bloody bull handled nicely."

"No probs," Finn replied, lifting his visor to get a better look at the woman atop her horse. Her kelpie popped up onto the pommel of her saddle and rested there, long tongue lolling from his endeavors.

She swiped a hand across her forehead, leaving a streak of ochre behind. Her light-blue Stormcloud shirt and denim jeans were also covered in a film of red dust. This woman worked hard, and it seemed she wasn't afraid of anything. A real pro when it came to mustering and living on the land. Finn again found himself impressed. She lifted what looked to be an old-fashioned canvas water container from a small saddlebag attached to the rear of her saddle and took a long drink. Finn watched her throat work as she swigged the water. Even covered in dust, her long, graceful neck had him mesmerized.

"Want a drink?" She offered him her bag.

"Nah, I'm good, thanks." He patted a water bottle strapped to the front tank of his bike in a leather holder.

"Your name's Finn, right?" she asked. "Sorry, there were so many new names and faces to learn last night."

"Yeah, that's right." It was true, the first night at a new camp was always full of meeting people and remembering faces. But he'd remembered her face, all right. The second he'd laid eyes on her, he'd felt as if there were an undertow pulling him toward her. Something about the flash of her dark eyes in the firelight and her gorgeous smile made it almost impossible to tear his gaze away.

Which was stupid, because he was here to do an important job. One that didn't allow for dalliances with a woman. No matter how pretty, or how gutsy, she was.

"Just gotta get them yarded now," she said. "See you back at camp." Indy touched her horse's flank and Gypsy leaped forward, away after another group of cattle who'd decided to make a break for it.

Finn watched her go. A strange thought that in another life she might've made a great cop suddenly flittered through his mind. With her sharp intellect and her own brand of courage, she'd make a brilliant detective. He laughed at his own stupidity before lowering his visor and taking off in a plume of dust. He wasn't here to pick out new police recruits for his team; he was here to do a job.

Half an hour later, Finn cut the engine on his motorcycle and removed his helmet with a sigh. All the cattle were yarded. They still needed to be sorted, branded and loaded onto the big rig road trains—double-trailer trucks that took the cattle out to the nearest dockyard to be shipped out for the live trade, or sent to the slaughterhouse. But that was tomorrow's job. He needed to wash all this dust off. But that could wait, too. Finn grabbed his folding chair and ambled toward the big tent in the center of the camp. The mess tent was the main hub of the camp, where everyone gathered to eat and sit and talk about their day. The amazing Stormcloud camp cook, Bindi, crafted some of the best meals he'd ever tasted. Most of the team was assembling around the campfire, which Dale, the owner's stepson and leading hand, was building up with a couple of large logs in readiness for tonight.

The Stormcloud helicopter pilot who'd helped bring the mob in today had already returned to the lodge. Finn had learned the pilot, Aaron, was the boyfriend of one of the owner's daughters, and was new to the task. But he thought Aaron had done a mighty fine job, if he truly was still learning the profession. He'd flown that little helicopter like a pro, dipping and swooping it close to the ground, to scare up the cattle and get them moving. He took it back to the lodge before nightfall, to refuel and sleep next to his lady.

"Helluva first day," Dave drawled, raising his can of beer in Finn's direction. "Did you see Carrot get charged by that angry heifer?" Dave asked with his boisterous laugh. "He jumped off Ryder to free the heifer from a tangle of wire, and she repaid him by trying to gore him," Dave continued, sloshing beer on the ground as he waved his arms around, re-enacting Carrot's tussle with the cow.

"Nope," Finn replied, snagging himself a can from the cooler. The last station they'd mustered had been a dry camp, which meant no alcohol, not even one well-deserved beer after a hard day's work. Finn understood why the rules were in place, but he was terribly glad that Stormcloud's owner, Steve Clements, ran a slightly less military-style camp. As long as everyone drank responsibly and got out of their swags in time to put in a full day in the saddle, then Steve was lenient on his riders. Finn didn't doubt if anyone got too far out of line, that may well change, however.

Carrot—his real name was Hugh, but with all those freckles and shock of red hair, the nickname had been formed from an early age—appeared around the back of the mess tent and followed Finn's lead, digging his hand into the ice for a beer. "Yeah, the bloody bitch. Lucky her horns were just starting to grow in, or she would've stuck me like a squealing pig."

"I'm pretty sure I *did* hear you squeal like a pig," Dave shot back.

"Nah, mate, you were hearing things," Carrot retorted. "Or else it was Indy screaming, because she was worried about me."

Indy must still be up at the yards and so wasn't around to defend herself. The men bantered back and forth between themselves while Finn took a few long swallows of his beer.

Finn had joined Dave and Carrot two months ago. They ran their own contract mustering business, and it'd been just the two of them for the past three years. But they'd been in high demand due to the good season last year, leading to high cattle numbers, and they'd needed someone to join their venture. Finn had been extra keen to get in with this pair; his research showed they worked well together, had no outstanding warrants, and weren't heavy drinkers. He may have stretched the truth about his experience working with horses and cattle to get the job, but he was a fast learner, and he did have some experience working as a jackaroo, even if it'd been nearly ten years ago. They didn't even mind that he preferred to ride a motorcycle. They owned a fleet of horses themselves, but it wasn't hard for Finn to procure a used cross-country dirt bike that was up to the task.

The two ringers had given him a one-month trial period,

which he'd just completed, and while he still had a lot to learn, they'd been happy for him to stay on. This was only their second job of the season, with three or four more already lined up. Living out of a stock camp sure took some getting used to. As did traveling around in a sixteen-wheeler truck, with all the horses and equipment they needed for months in the outback crammed into it. But he needed this job. Needed Dave and Carrot to help him achieve his goal. So, he was going to have to get used to sleeping in a cramped folding camp bed, eating dinner by a campfire, and checking his boots for snakes every morning.

Finn set out his chair and sat with a sigh. His gaze roamed out over the flat land of the plains. It was full-on dusk, the golden orb had already sunk below the horizon, leaving pink clouds in its wake. The sky had lost its brilliant blue and was slowly going a darker indigo. A lone hill rose in the near distance, the only outcrop to break the flat monotony. Stormcloud stock camp was a permanent site; they used it every year, and so it was set up well. There was a permanent water source, a natural billabong a few hundred meters away, which was being inundated by bird life settling into the gum trees for the night. The symphony of the birds and night insects was a wonderful backdrop to the encroaching evening.

Except for the dratted crows, who were sitting in the tree nearest the mess tent, nearly drowning out the sound of the other birds. Finn wasn't sure, but the crows were possibly worse here than at the last camp. There were always crows. The carrion eaters of the world, they hung around wherever people resided, hoping to pick through the detritus left behind. But Dale made sure this camp was kept clean, which is why it surprised Finn the crows were so plentiful here.

Indy appeared out of the dusk, the other station ringer, Mack, right beside her. Mack walked with a slight limp, and someone had mentioned that he used to be a bull-riding champion, and had suffered a bad fall. But then he'd also had a tussle with someone who wanted him dead because of his connection to the bull riding, which'd left him with a broken ankle. Sounded like he was lucky to be alive; perhaps he had nine lives. The guy was an American cowboy, with a cocky grin and playboy looks, but he seemed to fit in okay with the team, and that was all that mattered. Indy and Mack were discussing whether the cattle had enough water to get them through the night. The Stormcloud crew were a tight team, and Finn watched as Dale joined them and they all put their heads together to discuss the water problem, a tad envious of their connection. Steve had given Dale the responsibility of running this stock camp by himself for the first time, and Dale was taking his job seriously. Bindi lifted her head from the gas stove and frowned, as if she'd like to be included in the conversation. It seemed that while Bindi was a great cook, she also played a role in the stock side of things, as well. Finn liked to observe people; it was a necessary part of his job, but he also had a deep-seated curiosity, wanting to know why people did what they did. This was an interesting crew, with a good dynamic. He had a positive gut feeling about them. They were good people. He was pretty sure they weren't involved with the group he was looking for.

Finn found his gaze resting a little too long on the petite form of Indy and forced his eyes away. Wouldn't do to get caught staring. Turning his head, he saw his mate, Dave's eyes fixed on Indy, too. Seemed like he wasn't the only one who found the woman fascinating. Finn tamped down on the flash of heat that surged through his gut. He had absolutely no call to feel jealous. Indy wasn't for him. No woman was for him, at the moment.

Then, he suddenly had no choice but to look at her, when she unfolded her chair next to him and took a seat. She crossed her booted feet out in front and relaxed into the chair. He sat up a little straighter.

"Big day, huh?" Removing her Akubra, she dropped it on the ground and ran her hands through her shoulder-length, auburn hair, pulling it out of the short ponytail.

"Yeah." Finn flicked her a glance, enjoying the flash of her chocolate-colored eyes in the firelight. Enjoying the notion that she'd chosen to sit next to him. The buzz of her proximity sending a tingle up his forearm. "You guys run a tight ship here. I can see why Dave and Carrot were eager to work with you. Your cattle are in great condition, too."

"Thanks," Indy replied, sitting back and tilting her head sideways toward him. "I only joined Stormcloud five months ago, but it sometimes feels like I've been here forever. They certainly made me feel welcome, and Steve's a great boss. As is Dale," she added quickly.

Hmm, another interesting tidbit about Indy. She was right, he would've guessed she'd been with the team much longer. He stored the information away for further dissection later.

"Where did you work before Stormcloud?" he asked conversationally.

"Ah… Mountvey Downs. Over in the Kimberly." She said no more, and Finn was left wondering why she'd clammed up so suddenly.

He changed the topic. "Where's your dog? The little kelpie you had with you today?"

"You mean Barbie?" Indy smiled, and he knew he'd chosen the right subject. "I tie my dogs up at night. To keep them safe. Barbie is my old faithful. I've had her for six years. Then I've got Digger, a red male. He's only two, and boy, does he live up to his name." Indy laughed and Finn let the happy sound sink into his bones. Two dogs. That wasn't unusual, but it added to his growing respect. "Dogs are the way of the future," Indy said, a tad wistfully. "Mustering with dogs is way less stressful on the cattle. A team of them can move a mob of cattle more efficiently and quietly than a whole crowd of noisy ringers," she went on. It sounded like this was a topic she was passionate about.

Finn was about to ask more, when he looked up to see Brian and Rosie join the group. A husband-and-wife contract mustering team. He and Indy nodded their welcome to the couple. They looked like they were fresh from the shower, changed into clean clothes, and Finn suddenly felt every speck of dust covering his body.

Just as the couple set up their chairs, Bindi called "Grub's up," and everyone surged forward, eager to pile their plates high with the slow-cooked beef brisket, and jacket potatoes roasted in the fire that'd been assaulting their olfactory senses for the past half hour.

Finn was happy to see Indy join him again once her plate was full. This time, she had a beer, as well, and she settled happily into her chair and they both ate with gusto. Chasing cattle all day made a person hungry enough to eat an elephant, Finn decided.

Through mouthfuls of food, Finn asked Indy about the brown mare she'd been riding today, another topic he knew she was passionate about.

"Gypsy is such a beautiful girl," she replied, her face going a tad wistful. "I got her as a barely weaned foal from some ringer over at a station farther east five years ago. He was selling off most of his stock horses because he couldn't afford to keep them due to the drought, so I got her cheap. I've got another horse, a gelding, Beethoven. He's a lot older, and I left him back at the station for this muster. Between me and Beethoven, we got Gypsy broken in and trained her up to be a brilliant muster horse. She's the most sure-footed horse I think I've ever ridden," Indy told him. "Poor old Beethoven, I don't think he really minds being left behind. I'm sure he's being pampered like he's a king by the girls at Stormcloud while I'm away."

Finn savored her conversation almost as much as he savored Bindi's food, which was delicious. Her face lit up when she talked about her dogs and her horses and her life at Stormcloud, and he watched her with growing fascination. An interesting life, indeed. He wondered if he should broach the topic as to whether there was someone special in her life, when she suddenly stopped speaking and sat back in her chair.

"Are you married?" she asked, her gaze fixed on the gold band on his finger, as if she'd only just noticed it.

"Oh, ah…" Funny, he'd almost forgotten he was wearing it. A sudden urge to tell her the truth had him tongue-tied for a second. But he finally said, "Yes, I am."

"Oh." Indy seemed to withdraw from him, her eyes losing their sparkle. "Where's your wife?"

"She, ah… She works down in Brisbane."

"Right," Indy replied, a little too sharply. "And she doesn't mind that you spend months at a time up here? Away from her?"

"No. Well, yes. But no. We need the money. She understands that." Finn needed to stick to the story. It was a good one, and it hadn't failed him so far. Why was he suddenly baulking at telling Indy the same thing he'd told countless people over the past month?

"Yeah, I guess you're not the only guy up here who lives that way." She picked up her plate and stood. "I'm going to hit the shower. See you tomorrow." And she was gone, leaving Finn feeling like he'd just said something wrong. That she'd rejected him. And that was crazy; he wasn't here to hook up with anyone.

She was correct, he wasn't the only married man up here who was just trying to eke out a living; who left a wife and sometimes kids behind in an effort to make a buck. There were the odd few, like Brian and Rosie Wagner, who made it work as a couple, and seemed as happy as two cats who'd got the cream. Said they were saving for a property of their own, and this might be their final year on the road before they settled down for good. They were fortunate they could make it work.

Finn turned to Brian and took up a conversation about how much rain this area had had over the last wet season. But his heart wasn't in it, now that Indy had gone. His gaze kept drifting in the direction of the large water tanks at the edge of the camp, where the shower had been built to utilize the bore water in the tanks. An hour passed, while Finn chatted to everyone around the campfire, getting to know his new workmates better. Apart from Dave and Carrot, Brian and Rosie, there was another contract team working for Stormcloud this season. Mick Scanlon—Scanner to his mates —and his two daughters, Beth and Maddie. There had been three daughters, but the oldest, Sue, had met a guy and got pregnant and was now too fat to join them, according to Beth. Scanner had been doing this contracting thing the longest of all of them, and he regaled them with tales of blood and carnage from his many days as a ringer in his younger days. Finn watched his mates out of the corner of his eye. Dave and Carrot had met the Scanlons during last year's muster. They seemed to pick up right where they left off, Dave with his eye on Beth and Carrot with his eye on Maddie. And Scanner with his eye on all four of them.

Finn gave a quiet chuckle.

After another five minutes of watching the interplay, he stood and folded his chair, ready to head back to the tent before either of his mates.

"I'm knackered." He stretched his arms above his head and yawned. That part, at least, was true. "I'm off to bed."

"Yeah, be there soon," Dave said, his eyes never leaving Beth's face.

While Dave and Carrot remained at the campfire, enjoying their last drink, Finn made his way to their shared tent. It was a large, square canvas thing, only one room, but plenty large enough for the three of them and all their stuff. Finn rummaged through his bag until he reached the bottom, then fumbled with the false bottom and dug out his satellite phone from the hidden compartment. Reaching farther into the pocket, he felt around until he found the reassuring shape of his field weapon, wrapped in a T-shirt. He'd tossed up whether to take his handgun into the desert—if anyone found it, he'd be up shit's creek—but he felt more secure knowing it was there, even if he never had to use it.

He wandered into the dark desert. If anyone spotted him, he'd just say he was out relieving himself and looking at the stars. Which were absolutely amazing. In the past month, he'd become well acquainted with the northern Queensland sky, and its myriad of celestial bodies.

Once he was far enough away from camp that he wasn't afraid of being heard, he turned on the sat phone and waited to get reception. Then he pushed the pre-programmed button and listened for the ring tone.

"Good evening, Carmody. How's it going in the new camp?" His boss's voice was deep and gravelly. He was getting so used to his undercover identity, it felt strange to hear his real name, and it took him a second to respond.

"Good, thanks, Sarge." Finn tipped his head back to stare at the stars, while he relayed the day's events to his boss, Detective Sergeant Mike Rogers. "This new station seems a little more relaxed with the rules around camp than Pullman's."

"That's good." Rogers only paused for a microsecond before he dove into the important stuff. "I have some intel.

We received a tip-off today. We think the drugs may be hidden in cattle trucks. If you think about it, it's a perfect way to move large quantities of drugs. There must be plenty of places you could secrete kilos of the stuff in the body of a truck. We need you to take a good look at any cattle trucks that come through. Are there any at camp right now?"

"Yes, two trucks came in late this evening," Finn confirmed. The two men had joined them at the fire, and were probably still there. "The truckers will stay the night and load up at dawn tomorrow morning, then get on the road."

"Good. That should give you time to check the trucks. Can you get near them without being seen?"

Finn thought about it for a second. The truckers were sitting around the fire with the remaining crew. Both of them slept in their trucks in a little compartment behind the driver's seat. He'd have to go now if he were to make any attempt at a search.

"I'll give it a try, Sarge. I'll report any findings tomorrow."

"Good. But be careful. Don't do anything reckless. You're ideally placed to—"

"What are you doing out here?" an accusing voice drifted through the trees. Finn pushed the end button on the phone, cutting his boss off mid-sentence. He raised his head and searched the surrounding bushland, the moon lending enough light to make out shapes and movement.

Indy appeared between the trunks of two ghost gums; he'd know her petite form anywhere.

Oh, shit. Had he just blown his cover?

CHAPTER TWO

Indy had tossed and turned in her swag, sleep staying annoyingly just out of reach, and now it was nearly morning. Her conversation with Finn playing over and over in her mind. She was sure she'd heard him use the word *Sarge*, which was odd, because that was a police reference. What the hell was a contract musterer doing talking to a cop? And Finn's lame excuse that it was the pet name he used when he was talking to his wife didn't wash with her. No one called their wife Sarge. At least not to their face.

Indy liked to look at the stars before she went to bed. A nighttime ritual. It soothed her, so she could sleep easier. Looking up into all that great vastness made her feel like her own problems were small and insignificant. It put her world into perspective. The stars out here were just as spectacular as they'd been back in the Kimberly, but seen from a different reference point, they were even more intriguing. Back at Stormcloud Lodge, she'd liked to watch the evening star rise up over the escarpment, appearing as if by magic above the large, red cliffs. And out here, it was different again. This was her first time seeing the stock camp, and she enjoyed the way the moon sat atop the distant hill, like a glowing ball dropped by a thoughtless child of the gods from somewhere up high.

Wandering through the outskirts of the camp, she'd heard someone talking, and curiosity drew her toward the sound. In the moonlight, she could see it was Finn, the new ringer, and he was talking on a phone. It had to be a sat phone, because that's the only way he'd get reception out here. Which was a little odd. He was clearly trying to keep his conversation private, if he'd come this far away from camp. She'd been about to turn away, deciding the man's conversation was none of her business, when she heard him say *Sarge*, and alarm bells started ringing.

Finn had shut the phone down as soon as she'd confronted him, and acted all friendly and casual, like she hadn't just caught him doing something odd. Said that he was talking to his wife, like he did every night—trying to earn brownie points, she'd thought cynically—and he must've wandered farther away from camp than he realized as he chatted. Indy couldn't argue with that, and so they'd walked back to camp together, an awkward silence hanging between them.

Indy wasn't sure how she felt about Finn. He seemed a little...different from the other musterers, but she couldn't put her finger on exactly what made him so. She'd appreciated chatting to him around the fire. He was cute. Actually, more than cute, he was damned good-looking, in a square-jawed, fiercely blue-eyed way. A layer of designer stubble set off his strong face nicely; no scruffy, unkempt beard for this man. He wasn't overly cocky or rude, like his partners, Dave and Carrot. There was a confidence, a seriousness to him, that Indy found terribly attractive. Perhaps that was it. He was more refined than the rest of them. Slightly less rough around the edges, and she'd begun to relax in his presence.

That was, until she'd noticed his wedding ring. She'd almost doubled over as a sharp pain had sliced through her stomach at the discovery. Married men weren't to be trusted.

She should know.

Should she mention her eavesdropping to Dale? Or perhaps wait and tell Nash when she got back to the lodge? The local Senior Constable was a regular fixture at Stormcloud, as his fiancée, Skylar, was the resort chef. She'd got to know Nash well over the past few months, and he wouldn't mock her for reporting it. He was a good guy, a good cop, probably the only one Indy even came close to trusting. But still. She wasn't exactly sure what she'd overheard. Perhaps she should keep it to herself.

She worried over these thoughts until finally, the sun touched the sky with fingers of pink and Indy got out of bed and dressed quickly. The outback might be scorching during the day, but temperatures often dipped dramatically at night.

Bindi was already up, Indy could see the gas lamps burning in the mess tent. The camp cook was always first up to make sure breakfast was ready when the hard-working hordes descended before they went out for the day.

"Morning," she called, heading for the large steel kettle on the stove to pour herself the first coffee of the day.

"Morning," Bindi replied, looking up briefly from where she was frying up a pile of bacon. "Did you sleep well?"

"Mmm," Indy replied, noncommittally. No point in burdening Bindi with her lack of sleep woes.

Dale would be around somewhere, too. Steve had entrusted the stock camp to Dale this year for the first time, and he was taking his role to heart. She guessed he would already have stoked the fire for Bindi and got the water she needed for the coffee and to boil the eggs. They carried all the drinking water with them out to camp, as the bore water here wasn't fit to drink. Indy added a dash of milk and took a few cautious sips. Ahhhh, that was better.

"I can do the toast, if you like." Indy grabbed a loaf of bread and headed for the fire, where a wire grill was already set up over the low flames. She'd done the same task yesterday morning, and found it gave her a chance to help, while also sipping on her much-needed coffee.

"Thanks, that'd be wonderful," Bindi sang out, flashing her a bright grin.

Bindi had a great work ethic, and she really seemed to love what she did. Indy liked her immensely. As a matter of fact, Indy got on well with everyone at Stormcloud. Her decision to move from Western Australia to Queensland had been a good one, and she was glad she'd landed here, where the staff welcomed her with open arms and the boss had a reputation of being fair and affable. A nice change from her previous one, she thought darkly.

Indy didn't want to think about Patrick, it just made her sad. And then she got mad. At him and at herself. How could she have been so stupid? So gullible?

"Morning, gorgeous." Indy spun her head to see Mack slide his hand around Bindi's waist and kiss her full on the lips. Those two were so in love. If they weren't so adorable, it might turn Indy's stomach. Mack was one cocky bloke, and he liked to dress to impress, but he was a hard worker and underneath all that flashy exterior, he had a heart of gold. And Bindi brought out that side of him every time she glanced in his direction. Bindi was sweet, with large, brown eyes, and a wicked smile. It was no wonder Mack was hooked on her. She looked away, not wanting to intrude on their intimate moment. They were still murmuring sweet nothings to each other, and she had to resist the urge to block her ears. Opening the packet of bread, she slid four slices onto the wire rack to toast.

Come to think of it, all the Stormcloud staff seemed to be loved up and paired off. Dale had married his gorgeous wife Daisy back in December; they'd actually been off on their honeymoon when she'd arrived to take up her position at

Stormcloud. Rumors abounded—mainly started by Bindi and the receptionist, Sasha—that Skylar and Nash would be next to tie the knot. They were living together in a rambling, old, colonial house halfway between town and the station. But Indy kept reminding Bindi and Sasha that Nash needed to propose first. Bindi waved that minor problem away as if it were a foregone conclusion.

Steve's daughter, Julie, was totally in love with Aaron, the sexy, Adonis-like, helicopter pilot. Julie was one of Indy's favorites, she could make anyone smile with a word or a hug —she was such a warm personality. Indy secretly had her money on Aaron popping the question to Julie before Nash asked Skylar. Then there was Alek, the Polish activities manager, who seemed to be the only unattached male at the station. But he only had eyes for Sasha, any fool could see that. Indy liked the status quo. No one bothered her, and no one took her fancy. She was free to be single and alone, which was how she wanted it.

"Good morning." It was Finn, wrapped in a warm jacket, his hair still tousled from sleep. "Can I give you a hand?"

She regarded him for two beats. Talking about someone to take her fancy. She ignored that thought and said, "Sure. Could you please grab a large plate and a few clean dish towels from Bindi?" Was he trying to get back in her good books? Not that he was in her bad books, but it was clear they could both feel the slight tension buzzing between them left over from last night.

"Will do." He flashed her a warm smile. She watched as he walked to the mess tent, unconsciously drawn to the way his blue jeans hugged his nice backside. He was just as delicious from the back as he was from the front. Her gaze wandered up to those broad shoulders, filling out his sheepskin jacket. With his athletic build and chiseled cheekbones, it was hard not to stare. The man was hot. She was surprised for a moment that she'd actually noticed. It'd been five long months since she'd left Mountvey Downs. Five long months since she'd even considered another man in any kind of romantic capacity.

The smell of toasting bread brought her back to reality with a snap, and she only just caught the bread before it burned, flipping the pieces over with a set of tongs. Toast was a tricky thing, especially over an open fire. You couldn't get distracted, or it'd burn quicker than you could blink. And Finn was a distraction, that much was for sure. A distraction she didn't need. Her battered heart wasn't ready for anything more than feeling sorry for herself right now. And he was married, for God's sake. Why was she even looking at him?

He returned just as she checked the other side of the toast. It was done. He held out the plate, she dropped it on, and he covered it with the cloth to keep it warm while she cooked up some more. He got down on his haunches next to her, eyes trained on the fire, cup of coffee in one hand, plate of toast in the other. It was nice of him to offer to help. Most of the other ringers left the cooking and camp duties to Bindi and the Stormcloud crew. They were here to muster, and they did their job well, worked bloody hard during the day. But they didn't think it was their job to do any more than that. Finn obviously took a different view. She'd noticed that about him, right from the start. He was keen to jump in and help wherever he was needed; it didn't matter who was supposed to do the job.

He was a good man, she could feel it deep in her bones.

Right then, she made the decision to keep Finn's odd nocturnal phone call to herself. For now. Whatever he was up to, she didn't think it was malicious.

She looked at him and smiled. He smiled back and the tension suddenly evaporated between them.

Someone called out and she and Finn turned as one, to see

Swampy puffing noisily into camp. Swampy was one of the two truck drivers who'd arrived last night and shared a meal and a yarn with the musterers. Truckies often stayed overnight in camp. It meant they could get the cattle loaded early, and be off on their long drive north sooner, rather than later. Swampy was a big guy, he reminded Indy a little of a wannabe biker, with a long beard and tattoos all over his body. Truckies were a tough breed, they had to be, to live most of their lives on the road.

"He's gone." Swampy looked from Indy and Finn beside the fire, to Mack and Bindi in the tent.

Finn stood and asked, "Who's gone?"

"Wombat. He's not in his truck. And he's not around camp, neither."

Finn's eyes narrowed as he glanced at Mack. It looked as if he wanted to say more, but he let Mack take the lead.

Mack shrugged and said, "He's probably just gone off into the bush for a little...alone time." Indy silently agreed with Mack. The camp had a bush dunny situated a few hundred meters from the perimeter of the camp. But at least half the truckies and contract crew would rather take their own personal trowel and roll of paper and find a nice tree to squat behind.

"Nah, mate," Swampy shook his bald, tattooed head. "I've been up for an hour, and I checked his truck then because he asked me to make sure he was up; he sometimes sleeps through his alarm." Indy wasn't surprised to hear that after the amount of beer the man had consumed last night. "But he's still not back. It's not like him. I've worked with Wombat before. He might be a bit of a cowboy, but he always likes to check his truck before he takes on a load, he's pretty fussy about it."

Indy had taken a quiet dislike to Wombat. Something about his beady little eyes that were just a tad too close together. He was jovial and loved to tell loud, bawdy jokes, while watching the women with his piggy eyes to gauge their reaction. But to hear the man was missing made the hair on the back of her neck stand up.

Dale strode around the side of the tent and they all looked at him expectantly. "What?" he asked, coming to a sudden halt.

Swampy repeated what he'd said, and Dale pursed his lips in exasperation as the story unfolded.

"Bloody hell," Dale swore quietly. "Get everyone out of their swags. We need to go look for him."

Indy was surprised, at first. But she guessed Dale couldn't very well get on with the day's work if a man was truly missing. The outback was unforgiving. If he'd wandered off somewhere, he wouldn't last long once the sun got up to scorch the earth. She felt a pang of sorrow for the cattle, who were supposed to be loaded onto the trucks this morning. Instead, they'd be left penned up in the growing heat of the day. She hoped they found this idiot soon, so they could get on with their proper work.

"I'll go get Dave and Carrot," Finn said, placing the plate of toast on the folding table at the front of the tent. He cast her a worried glance, blue eyes piercing and sharp, and rushed off. Indy was a tad surprised at his haste. The guy was taking this all a bit too seriously, wasn't he? The truckie had probably got himself turned around while he was out there taking a dump. They'd find him soon enough.

"I'll organize us all into search parties while we eat," Dale called out.

Good idea, a crew always worked better on a full stomach. And by the way Dale rolled his eyes, Indy guessed he was hoping the wayward truckie might wander back into camp before they even got searching.

"I'll rouse Brian and Rosie and the Scanlons," Indy

volunteered. Most likely they'd all be awake anyway, they just needed a hurry along.

Ten minutes later, the whole group was eating breakfast while standing in a semicircle around the fire, listening to Dale give them directions. He was breaking them into pairs and each pair was given an area to search in a grid-like pattern, starting off at the perimeter of the camp and with each arc getting slowly farther away. The search groups were Brian and Rosie, Beth and Maddie, Mack and Dale, Indy and Finn, Dale and Carrot, and Mick and Swampy. Indy stiffened slightly as Dale gave them their assignments. Did she really want to be paired with Finn? She guessed she didn't really have a choice.

Aaron had just arrived in his helicopter, so he would also join the search, flying in concentric circles around the camp. Aaron was an ex-bodyguard, and he'd joined the Stormcloud crew last year when he'd been called in to protect Julie from a crazed stalker. They'd fallen in love and he'd stayed on, exchanging his career as a bodyguard for one equally full of adrenaline; the resort's new helicopter pilot. When Aaron heard the news, he narrowed his eyes—Indy was still getting used to his one blue eye and one brown, but everyone else was totally blasé about his multicolored gaze—and drew his broad shoulders up to his full height. It was Aaron's tense reaction that made Indy wonder if the lost truckie was indeed perhaps something more alarming than she believed.

Bindi was to stay at camp and let them know if he turned up. That allowed her to continue to organize lunch. If they hadn't found anything by lunchtime, they were to meet back at camp and Dale would call in extra backup. If they hadn't found anything by lunchtime, it meant something sinister might be afoot. All the vehicles around camp had been accounted for, just in case Wombat had taken it into his head to steal an ATV or a motorcycle and hightail it out of there.

Which would've been highly unlikely.

There was some discussion as to whether they should go on horseback or motorcycle. Dale decided that horseback was preferable, as their slower pace allowed for a better scrutiny of the search area. But there weren't enough horses for everyone. Brian and Rosie had their horses, as did Dale and Mack, and Dave and Carrot, but the Scanlons all used four-wheel-drive vehicles. It was decided to give Finn's motorcycle to Swampy, and Finn said he'd ride one of Dale's spare horses. They always brought three or four spares in case of accident or injury.

"You can ride, I assume?" Indy asked over her shoulder as she saddled Gypsy a few minutes later. Others were also saddling their horses around them, and there was the hum of light conversation and the snort of horses impatient to be away.

"Of course, I can," Finn replied with a wounded look. "Might be a bit rusty, though. It's been a while since I've been on a horse." He lifted the borrowed saddle over the palomino mare's whither and bent to grab the girth, tightening it with practiced ease. He was riding Sahara today, Bindi's preferred horse, and Indy guessed Bindi was probably watching the saddling yard wistfully from the mess tent. "I just prefer motorcycles. They're faster," he added with a mischievous grin.

"No, they're not," she retorted. "Well, maybe over a piece of flat, open ground," she acquiesced. "But certainly not over the potholed floodplains where we muster the cattle. I guarantee Gypsy would beat your motorcycle hands down, if you ever want to race."

"Is that a threat, or a promise?" he asked, as he swung a leg into his stirrup and was in the saddle in one easy motion.

Finn had swapped his bike helmet for a light-brown Akubra. It suited him. Suited him so much, Indy had to look away before he caught her staring. His snug jeans defined his muscular thighs even better when he was astride a horse. And he'd removed his sheepskin jacket and rolled up his shirt sleeves, to reveal nicely tanned forearms. Finn made one damn sexy cowboy. She just needed to keep reminding herself he was married, and to stop drooling over him like some lovesick teenager.

"This way." She swung into her own saddle and guided Gypsy in a northerly direction to the search area Dale had given them. "Good luck," she called back to the rest of the group.

"Let us know via the two-way if you find anything," Dale reminded her, as he, too, swung up onto his horse, Dante.

"Will do," both she and Finn replied in chorus.

Indy whistled up Barbie and Digger from where they'd been investigating a pile of horse dung. Great, she was probably going to have to wash both of them later on. There was nothing Digger loved better than to roll in the freshest horse poo he could find. It was one of the reasons she usually left him tied up back at camp; he was still young and did immature, stupid things. The dogs were at Gypsy's heels in an instant. She was hoping they might help her locate the missing truckie with their superior sense of smell. They were far from trained search and rescue dogs, but if they smelled something different or interesting, they might lead them to him.

They walked their horses side by side toward the big, old gum tree that marked the start of their search area, a silence falling easily between them. She watched Finn surreptitiously out of the corner of her eye. He had a natural seat in the saddle, easy and long-legged, hands held lightly above Sahara's mane. It seemed he hadn't been lying when he said he could ride. Their knees bumped gently, and she directed Gypsy farther away with a light touch to her flank, ignoring the jolt of heat his touch sent up her thigh.

"Right, let's find this guy." Finn's light bantering mood from earlier seemed to have disappeared. He was now focussed, taking this job seriously. His eyes took on a sharp, intense glow as he surveyed the surrounding area. If Indy didn't know any better, she might even think Finn had a vested interest in finding this guy. "I think we should stay around twenty meters apart," he said. "That way we can keep a good eye on the ground between us, as well as cover a corridor about the same distance away on the other side." Indy shrugged one shoulder. If the guy wanted to take charge, she wasn't about to argue. The gravel road leading into the stock camp was to be the boundary to their search area on their right, and Indy used that as a rough guide to help her sort out their grid pattern.

They moved apart, and Indy sent her dogs out to range on her far side. They bounded off, bright-eyed, into the scrub. Barbie would stay close, but she'd need to monitor Digger. If he found a bunny trail or something equally interesting, he might well disappear. Walking in parallel as much as the terrain would allow, they set off in their pre-ordained direction. Indy sighed in frustration. This was such a waste of their time. It'd put the whole muster a day behind schedule. She silently cursed Wombat and his odd disappearance.

"What do you think happened to Wombat?" he asked, after a few moment's silence, never taking his eyes off the ground in front. His question surprised her for a second.

"I don't know," she replied carefully. "Why? What do you think happened to him?"

He raised an eyebrow and stared at her, speculation swimming in his eyes. Speculation and something else. Something like misgiving. Or unease. Or both. Did Finn know something he wasn't telling her? "I don't know," he finally replied. "But you have to admit, this is very odd. Have you ever known someone to go missing from a stock camp before?"

She thought about it for a while. "Not like this, no. Not without some sort of clue, like a missing vehicle. Or a fight with a co-worker." She had to agree with him, it was very peculiar. A strange feeling of apprehension skittered over her skin.

They continued their search, conversation sparse, and eyes locked on the ground. She stopped to take a drink of water occasionally. At one stage they came upon a cattle watering station, and both her dogs hopped into the concrete trough and lapped thirstily, enjoying the cooling sensation of the water.

They were about half-way through their search transect when Digger barked. Indy checked to see that Barbie was trotting at Gypsy's heels. What had that dog found now? Indy called him back to her, but he ignored her, continuing to bark. It was unusual. Even though Digger was unruly, he always came when he was called, and he rarely barked unless he was chasing a rabbit, or something had scared him.

"Shall we see what your dog's so worked up about?" Finn called.

"I guess so." Indy touched Gypsy's side with her heel and they trotted off in the direction of the barking.

Digger was around a hundred meters ahead of their current search area, near the gravel road that was their right-hand boundary. They would've searched this area in the next two or three sweeps, but he'd led them straight to a spot overlooking the edge of a ravine.

"What's got into you?" Indy asked, half impatiently.

Digger stopped barking and looked up at her expectantly, tongue lolling happily. Then he looked back down into the ravine, which was really a shallow culvert cut out by last year's heavy rains. Finn pulled Sahara up beside her, and they peered as one into the depression.

"Oh, shit," Indy breathed. "Is that...?" She didn't finish her question as Finn leaped off his horse and scrambled down the short incline.

"Stay there," he commanded. As if she was going anywhere near that...mess. It looked like they'd found Wombat. But he was certainly dead. With all that blood, there was no doubt. Indy recoiled and covered her mouth. She might be sick. "Don't look," Finn called back over his shoulder. "It's...nasty."

Finn picked his way carefully down the ravine and crouched over the body, reaching in and checking for a pulse, even though he knew it would be useless. Who would do something like this? Indy finally averted her eyes as Finn had told her to do, not wanting to look at the mound of clothes and flesh that'd once been a man. Someone had used a knife, or something sharp to cut Wombat up like he was a piece of steak.

"Call this in, will you?" Finn commanded. And Indy pulled her radio from her shoulder holster before she thought to wonder at how Finn had suddenly taken charge. And why wasn't he repulsed by the body, like she was?

Indy thought back to Finn's arched eyebrow and skeptical look an hour earlier. It was almost like he'd known what they were going to find.

CHAPTER THREE

Finn ran a hand through his hair, watching Senior Constable Nash King survey the crime scene from his spot at the edge of the ravine. "Shit. Shit. Shit." He tipped his head back to glare at the branches of the enormous gum tree above. This was all he needed.

"You all right?" Indy was standing a few feet away, and she looked at him sharply.

He felt a twinge of guilt. He should be the one asking her that question. While he didn't see this kind of thing on the job too often, and it wasn't something anyone could really get used to, he was at least partly immune to the scene. Her face was still incredibly pale, but at least she'd stopped shaking. It wasn't every day you found a mutilated body by the side of the road, and he knew she was probably suffering shock; although she was hiding it well, behind her resolute demeanor.

"Yeah, sorry. This is just a shitshow, that's all. What about you?" He leaned in closer and touched her arm. A move meant to convey compassion, but her eyes widened at his touch and so he withdrew his hand. She studied him from beneath the brim of her hat.

"I'm not sure how I'm feeling," she finally admitted. "I

mean, I've seen some nasty things in my time as a jillaroo working on a station. Cows and their calves mauled by dingoes, cattle dying from disease and drought, hunters shooting so many roos in a single night just for fun that it makes you sick. Death is a constant when you live on a station. But this is…" She bit her lip and her chin wobbled slightly. "This is like nothing I could've imagined." Indy looked so lost and alone in that moment that Finn had to resist the urge to place his arm around her shoulders. She hadn't appreciated it when he'd touched her arm and so he presumed she would take to him embracing her even less. Her beautiful, brown eyes shimmered with emotion. This was a different Indy he was seeing. Gone were all her sass and confidence, replaced by distress and apprehension. He hated seeing her like this and his heart went out to her, wishing he could wipe the sadness from her eyes.

"It is terrible," he admitted. "And if you need to talk about it, I'm here. Talking is good. It stops you bottling things up inside." He bent his knees slightly so he could look directly in her eyes. "Promise me you'll talk to someone about this. Me, or Bindi, or Steve. There are professionals out there you can talk to, as well." Finn knew he was pushing the point, but he also knew firsthand how easily these things could become a problem. Especially with country people, they often weren't keen to talk about their feelings.

She nodded, her gaze warming slightly, and his stomach tightened as she continued to hold his stare.

There was a commotion behind them, and Finn turned on his heel to look at the growing crowd assembling on the roadside fifty meters away as the crew from the camp milled around beyond the police tape, watching from a distance, wanting answers. One of their own had been murdered in cold blood, and they were all understandably worried.

Finn was worried, too, but for a completely different

reason. After his sarge's intel last night, telling Finn he thought it was the cattle trucks moving the drugs, this was all-too-real evidence that Rogers had been right. The most annoying part was that after Indy had sprung him on his sat phone, he'd decided to leave checking out the trucks to another day, not wanting to arouse any more suspicion.

But if his boss's intel was true, then this looked like a murder with one aim in mind. It was meant to send a message. Don't fuck with the syndicate, or you'll end up dead.

What had Wombat done to piss off the traffickers? Had he been skimming off the top? Selling drugs to his mates on the side? Or could it be as simple as he'd refused to take the bribes the drug gang was offering? Finn knew he shouldn't judge, but he didn't think the latter was true. Wombat had looked a tad seedy, not the kind of guy to take the moral high ground. Whatever it was, the drug traffickers were taking a huge risk, if they were willing to kill someone. It might mean things were escalating.

But these were all minor questions, compared to the one burning through Finn's mind right now. If Wombat's murder was related to his undercover investigation, should he reveal his true identity? At least to the Senior Constable? The information he had might be vital to helping them solve this murder. Without his input, they might never know what Wombat had really been up to. The problem was, this investigation was way bigger than just one murdered truckie.

His team had been working on this case for over a year now, had put in thousands of man-hours. They were trying to break up a methamphetamine trafficking racket. There were two other detectives deep undercover in other parts of Queensland, all trying to bring this international drug ring down. They had strong clues to link this group to an Italian-based group of businessmen. Very rich, very influential businessmen who jet-setted between Australia and Italy, as well as across half the globe. If they could find out how the drugs were being shipped, trace it back to the big player—or players—in the game, they might take this all the way to the top and put a stop to this particular crime cartel for good. Which would mean hundreds, maybe thousands of hits off the streets. Save countless lives. Finn had personal experience of how the scourge of addiction to this powerful drug could ruin lives and families; even whole communities.

Garrett's face appeared in his mind's eye. They must've only been around thirteen years old, and their mother had taken them to the beach. Garrett had challenged Finn to a hundred-meter sprint up the sand, and he'd been so ecstatic when he'd won—by a hairsbreadth, mind you—that he'd turned, punched Finn in the arm and let out a whoop of joy. His face had been so lit up. Innocent and happy. Things had changed soon after that, when their father, a firefighter, was killed in the line of duty, and Garrett had never been the same since. He'd lost that wild enthusiasm, turned in on himself, let dark thoughts claim him. That's when Garrett had let drugs into his life and he and Finn had lost their bond. Their brotherly connection—the biggest thing in Finn's life up until then—was broken beyond repair.

Finn looked down to find that he was twirling his wedding ring, an old habit that he couldn't seem to break now he had the ring on again for his undercover persona. The ring reminded him of Chloe. And Kayleigh. Fleetingly, he wondered how they were doing, what Kayleigh might be up to at this very moment. Did she have a favorite new toy? Her preferred choice seemed to change from day to day, which made it so hard to decide what to send her as a present.

His introspection was severed when the senior constable spoke. "Whoever did this, didn't even bother to try to hide the body." The police officer spun around and beckoned to

Finn and Indy to come closer.

"Did either of you touch the body?" King asked.

"No. Oh, God, no." Indy recoiled from the mere idea of it. "Finn went down and checked he was really dead." She tipped her head in Finn's direction. "I stayed up here with the horses."

"Right." King wrote something in his notebook. King's offsider, Constable Willow, stood guard in the ravine, around ten feet away from the body. Young and clean-cut, he had his back half-turned away, as if not wanting to see the gruesome image. Possibly the first murder he'd had to cover, Finn mused. But then the constable turned a hard gaze in his direction, and Finn reassessed the man. Young, but definitely not as green as he first looked.

"I wanted to cover the body," Indy blurted, looking away from the terrible sight below. "But Finn wouldn't let me. He said we needed to preserve the crime scene." She shuddered slightly.

"Is that right?" King turned a probing gaze in Finn's direction.

"Yes. I've heard you shouldn't touch anything if you find a dead person." Finn feigned naïveté. "You know, from watching all those cop shows on the telly," he added with a half-grin. "I hope I did the right thing, Senior Constable."

"Hmm. Yes," the cop mused, his searching gaze still fixed on Finn's face. "Call me Nash," he added. "Everyone else does." Finn had noticed that most of the Stormcloud crew were on a first-name basis with both of the local police officers. There was obviously some connection there, but he was yet to figure it out.

Finn shifted his feet, then stopped himself. No point in showing his agitation. He needed to talk to Mike before he made any rash decisions. His supervisor had always said that it was ultimately up to him if he ever needed to reveal his true persona. If he ever felt like his life was in danger, or anyone else's life, for that matter, then he should just get out. But Finn didn't want to jeopardize all the work he and the rest of the team had put into this investigation.

"Homicide are on their way. And I'm sure they'll be bringing a forensics team out for this one, as well. Once they get here, I'd like to talk to everyone back at camp. Take your statements. Who was the last to speak to this man?" Nash asked.

"I think it was the other trucker, Swampy." Indy pointed a finger at the tattooed man standing slightly to the side of the group on the road.

"Right." He looked squarely at Indy for a second. "How are you holding up?" he asked, voice softening. "I know this must be traumatic for you." He placed a hand on her arm, but this time, Indy didn't seem to mind.

A spike of jealous heat surged through Finn's gut. He quickly tamped down on the surprising emotion. Who was this guy, and what did he mean to Indy? There was a familiarity that spoke of more than a vague acquaintance. Nash was good-looking, in a blond, surfer-dude type of way, with sky-blue eyes that seemed to see everything at once. Finn was sure he did well with the ladies.

"Skylar would want to know that you're holding up okay. And Julie, too. All the women at Stormcloud would break my balls if they thought I wasn't concerned about you," Nash added.

Finn wracked his brain. He'd heard that name before. Skylar was the resort chef, and the owner's daughter, if he wasn't mistaken. Was Nash involved with Skylar? A little of the tension leeched from Finn's shoulders.

Indy gave Nash a wan smile. "You can tell Skylar that it was a shock to see a body like that, but I'm tough. I'll cope. I always do."

"I'll make sure she's okay," Finn said, trying to keep the possessive tone out of his voice.

Nash dropped his hand from Indy's arm and glanced at Finn. Again, his gaze was penetrating, and it was all Finn could do not to look away.

"Right. Would you mind getting everyone back to camp, please?" Nash's tone took on a no-nonsense edge again. "I'll come over as soon as the homicide boys get here to take over the crime scene."

"Will do," Finn promised, leading Indy toward the road. She seemed eager to get back to camp, and he didn't blame her.

"What's Nash saying?" Dale asked, coming forward to meet them.

Indy didn't answer straight away, and Finn jumped into the silence. "We'll tell you when we get back to camp. Let's get everyone moving," he directed.

The murder scene was around a kilometer from their camp. Far enough for none of them to have heard anything, but close enough to wonder at the gall of the murderer to take a chance this close to such a large bunch of people. Some of the crew had ridden their horses up to the crime scene, and some had driven up in their vehicles. Indy and Finn untied their mounts from the shade of a large tree where they'd left them, and people mounted up or returned to their cars as he ushered them back down the road toward camp.

Glancing back only once, he followed at the rear of the slow-moving crowd. He'd love to know what Nash thought about this whole scene. Would love to talk it over, professional to professional, to get his insights. And he'd also love to stay and watch the homicide boys work the scene, to see what clues, if any, they turned up. But if he were to stay undercover, then he needed to act as ignorant as the rest of them, so he didn't arouse any suspicion.

Everyone drifted into camp in an aimless wave. He knew how they felt. Instead of being out mustering cattle all day, their work had been disrupted, and they were all at a loss for what to do next. Most people took a seat around the campfire, which had been left to burn down to glowing coals. Dale took the initiative, and stacked a few longs on the embers, while Bindi turned on the gas stove to heat the big, steel kettle.

"I'll get lunch going," Bindi called to no one in particular.

It was too early for lunch, but they'd all missed smoko, and most people would be hungry. And Bindi clearly needed something to keep her busy. Although, Finn's stomach was churning so badly, he didn't think he could eat. He'd also like to get Mike's take on this disaster. But without his boss's input, he had to play it cool. Think on his feet and make his own decisions. This wasn't the first time things had gone south while he'd been undercover. This was what he was trained for.

"I'll help," Mack chimed in, but Finn wondered if his sudden urge to assist was more out of a need to stay close to Bindi. People were on edge and jumpy. And they had every right to be. They may not have guessed it yet, but Wombat's killer could possibly be hiding in plain sight. The murderer might be part of this crew, and the very idea had Finn's skin crawling.

Talk around the campfire was subdued, everyone overawed by the reality of death. Brian and Rosie huddled close to each other in their seats on the other side of the fire, talking quietly. Rosie's face was ashen, and it looked like she'd been crying. Brian had an arm around her shoulder, comforting her. The Scanlon team stood near the entrance to the mess tent, talking to Dale. Their gazes constantly darted around the camp, and Beth kept biting her lip, also looking as if she were close to tears. Dave and Carrot sat staring into the fire, not saying much, as if trying to process what'd just happened.

Just as he began to worry that Indy was taking a long time tying up her dogs, she returned and flopped down into a chair next to him.

"How you holding up?" he asked.

"I'm okay." But her words belied the listless slump of her shoulders. "I just can't believe that a human being could do that to another human," she said softly. She was probably reliving the image of Wombat. The murderer had sliced him over and over with what looked to have been a very large, very sharp knife. Finn just hoped the wounds had been inflicted post-mortem, but he had a horrible feeling that they hadn't been, not with all that blood. The man had his mouth taped up and his hands tied behind his back. He would've been as helpless as a sacrificial lamb.

"I know," he replied. "It was shocking. I'm sorry you had to see that."

Indy's normally vivacious brown eyes had lost their sparkle, and Finn wished there was something he could do to bring it back.

"Thank you. I don't know what I would've done if you hadn't been there." Her small hand briefly rested on his arm, sending a tingle of awareness up his shoulder. "You were so calm. Almost like…" She brushed a stray lock of hair from her eyes and tilted her head to stare at him.

Like what? he wanted to ask. But he was afraid of her answer. She was too perceptive for her own good, this lady.

Swampy stomped into camp, breaking their moment. "I told yous all there was something wrong," the bearded man growled, snatching a handful of biscuits in one hand and a coffee in the other from the table where Bindi had set up a makeshift smoko. He took a seat. "Now he's bloody turned up dead." Coffee slopped over the edge of his mug as Swampy waved it in the air to punctuate his words. "What kind of half-assed camp you running out here?" The tattooed man turned to glare at Dale.

"What do you mean?" Dale took a step forward.

"I mean that my schedule is all fucked-up, now. I'm supposed to be on my way to Townsville with a truck full of cattle right now. Which means I'll be late for my next job."

"Well, I'm sorry that Wombat's death is such an inconvenience for you." Dale raised his voice. "But we're all just as shocked and as put out by this mess. And I don't think I like what you're implying." His fists were now clenched by his side, and he stared daggers at the truck driver.

Just as Finn was about to stand and intervene, Scanner lay a warning hand on Dale's arm. They were all wrought up, and emotions were running high. Dale drew in a visible breath and shook his arm free.

"This has put a spanner in the works for everyone," he said, voice slightly calmer. "We'll make sure we do everything in our power to get you back on schedule as soon as is humanly possible. But some things are out of our hands."

The sound of an approaching vehicle cut through any retort Swampy might've been about to throw in Dale's direction. A Land Cruiser barrelled down the gravel road and pulled to a dusty halt next to the small trailer Bindi used as her base to store her foodstuff and do some of the cooking.

"It's about time," Dale muttered. He shot Swampy another hard glare, then went to welcome the newcomers.

Finn had briefly met Steve on the first night of the muster, before he'd headed back to the lodge and left Dale in charge, and so he recognized the owner of Stormcloud when he stepped out of the four-wheel-drive. A smartly dressed lady that Finn guessed was his partner, Daniella, quickly followed suit. But the easygoing, affable man he'd met the other night was nowhere to be seen today. A dark frown lined the owner's face as he stalked toward them.

"Mum. Steve." Dale acknowledged them with a nod of his head.

"Dale," Steve returned the nod.

But Daniella came up and touched her son's arm, a worried frown playing over her features.

"How is everyone?" Steve lifted his gaze, encompassing the whole crew with his question. Finn couldn't help but be impressed. It was the sign of a good leader that Steve was more worried about his staff than about the dead man found on his property.

There were murmurs of *okay*, and *fine*, from the group. A typical reply from a group of staunch country folk, and Finn had to suppress a smile. The replies might've been a lot different if this were a group of city slickers.

Apart from Swampy, of course, who stood and glowered at Steve. "I need to get going. With or without your damn cattle. When can I leave?" he asked.

This guy was certainly in a rush to get out of here. Finn narrowed his eyes and studied him.

Steve regarded him for a few silent seconds. "Nash says he's going to send Constable Willow over soon to check the trucks. Once that's done, he'll allow us to load up Swampy's truck," Steve said.

"Thank Christ for small mercies," Swampy muttered.

"But Wombat's truck will have to stay right where it is. And no one is to go near the trucks until then," Steve added with lowered eyebrows.

Shit. Finn needed to get to that truck before the constable did. Being spooked by Indy last night and not checking the trucks might come back to bite him in the butt. It now seemed more than likely that Wombat, at least, was involved with the drug gang. And perhaps Swampy was, too. Was that why he was so fired up about getting moving? Or was it more sinister than that? Could Swampy be the murderer? Had the two men had a fight over the drugs? A turf war, where Swampy was asserting his dominance?

Finn pretended to study the flames while trying to figure out a way to get over to that truck. But they were parked right out in plain view, over on the perimeter of the camp. There was no way he could even take a nonchalant wander over there without being seen, let alone crawl underneath looking for hidden drug stashes, like he wanted to.

Constable Willow would check the trucks for clues, but would he even know what to look for? Then forensics would give it a more thorough going-over once they'd finished with the body. Even if Willow didn't find the drugs, forensics might.

Shit. He needed to warn Mike, so he could get on the phone and see if he could stop these bozos from blowing this whole investigation sky high. He might not be able to sneak over and snoop around the trucks, but he could excuse himself and make a call on his sat phone. It was risky, but he didn't see any other option.

"And no one is to leave the camp until Constable Willow has spoken to you," Steve added with pursed lips.

Finn saw the moment comprehension sunk in, as some of the other crew turned to look at Steve.

"What?" Rosie surged from her chair. "Surely you're not saying we're all suspects?" she demanded.

But that was exactly what Steve was saying. Or, at least, what Senior Constable King had told him.

"Settle down, love." Brian pulled Rosie back to her seat and talked to her in a low voice.

Finn thought he heard Rosie say, "I want to get out of here..." before Brian cut her off, making soothing noises and stroking her hair. Rosie was freaked out, and Finn didn't blame her.

"Do you think they'll let us get back to work anytime soon?" Dave asked, always the pragmatic one.

Steve nodded. "I'm hoping things will get back to normal tomorrow. But for now, you guys all need to sit tight and take the rest of the day off." He lifted an eyebrow in Indy's direction and then motioned for Dale and Daniella to follow him into the tent, where he gathered with Mack, Bindi and Aaron in the back corner. Indy grimaced at Finn as if in apology, but got up and followed them into the shade. Steve was obviously checking on his valued staff, as well as debriefing them on their morning so far.

Perhaps Finn should take this opportunity while it presented itself. Steve had told them not to leave the campsite, but a short trip into the surrounding bush to *relieve himself* wouldn't take too long.

"I'm off to the dunny," Finn said quietly to Dave and Carrot, who merely lifted a hand in reply.

After a quick stop by his tent to grab his sat phone, Finn headed into the floodplain on the opposite side of the camp, hoping the large trucks would block his progress from view until he was far enough out for the trees to cover him completely.

When he was sure he was out of sight, he pulled out the phone and pushed the button, hoping like hell that Mike wasn't in a meeting or something and could take this call. Finn was breaking protocol by calling in the middle of the day, but Mike would understand once Finn told him why.

Mike answered on the sixth ring.

"Are you somewhere we can talk?" Finn asked urgently.

"Yes, I've stepped outside," Mike replied. "Go ahead." His boss didn't waste any breath on the niceties.

Finn relayed the morning's events, and Mike listened without comment.

"It's an interesting development," Mike said after Finn had

eventually wound down. "I know it might feel bad to you right this second, but this might be the break-through we've been waiting for."

Finn considered his boss's words. It was true. The murder was a terrible thing for Wombat. But if it was connected to the drug gang, and Finn had a gut feeling it was, it also meant that someone in the drug syndicate was getting sloppy. Or arrogant. Or both. And perhaps it meant they were closer to figuring this thing out than they'd thought.

"It's frustrating that the local cops are now involved," Mike went on. "But if we can collaborate with them, they might actually be of some help." Finn was dubious. He'd had dealings with local police before and they tended to go at things like a bull at a gate, ham-fisted, without any finesse, or attention to detail. That was the reason Finn had been recruited to this particular Special Drug Squad in the first place. Mike Rogers had studied Finn as a young and upcoming detective and liked his attention to detail, his organization skills, and his ambition, and hired him on the spot.

"I'll get on the phone and talk to the Senior Sergeant Johnson in charge over in Cairns, see if I can stop them from going apeshit if they find drugs in Wombat's truck and tipping off the drug lords that we're after them," Mike continued. "I think it's time to reveal yourself to this Senior Constable King. Do you think we can trust him?"

Finn sighed. It looked like he'd be dealing with the local force, whether he liked it or not. He considered the question for a few seconds. Corruption could be an issue inside the Queensland Police Force. The drug ring had endless money and a long reach when it came to bribing susceptible cops. But Finn didn't think Nash was one of those cops. It was always impossible to tell one-hundred percent, but if the rest of the Stormcloud crew thought he was good, then Finn would have to, as well.

"Yes. I believe so," Finn replied.

"And what are the odds that this is an inside job?" Mike asked crisply.

Finn didn't know how to answer that. Because it meant someone he worked with could be the murderer. He was pretty sure Dave and Carrot weren't involved. He slept in the same tent as them. Surely, if one of them had crept out in the dead of night, Finn would've heard something. But come to think of it, Dave *had* got up to relieve himself last night. Had Finn heard him come back, or had sleep reclaimed him beforehand? He couldn't be sure. There was Scanner and his girls. Yesterday, Finn wouldn't have questioned if they could be involved. Certainly not in a murder as violent as Wombat's. But human beings were complex creatures, and Finn had come across stranger things than this in his line of work.

"It's a possibility, Sarge," Finn admitted.

A twig snapped, and Finn lifted his head, then took the phone away from his mouth.

"Finn, is that you? Who are you talking to? And don't you tell me it's your bloody wife."

Shit, not again.

Indy was stalking through the bush toward him.

CHAPTER FOUR

Finn glared at Indy, blue eyes like chips of ice, and Indy suddenly wondered if she'd misjudged him. Had she been a fool to follow him out into the floodplains alone? What if he were the murderer? And she'd just presented herself up like a sacrificial lamb.

Clenching her fists into balls by her side, she stopped walking. Perhaps she hadn't thought this through properly. She'd watched Finn slip out of the camp, even while she'd been talking to Steve and the others about Wombat. When her curiosity had become too much to bear, she'd excused herself and followed Finn's wraithlike figure through the scrub. He was being careful, not wanting to be seen, and that cemented the idea in her head that he was up to something dodgy. And she needed to know what. Maybe she should've told Dale about Finn's nocturnal activities last night, after all. It suddenly occurred to her he could be involved in the murder. Perhaps he'd been calling in backup to help him deal with the cops, or to get him out of here. But it was too late for any of that. Finn was striding toward her.

"What's going on?" she demanded. "If you don't tell me what you're up to, I'm going to go straight to Nash and tell him you're acting strange."

A spike of adrenaline made her stomach flutter as he came right up to her. But she stood her ground as he towered over her, a frown marring his handsome face. *Never show your fear.* It was something she lived by. He lowered his gaze and those bright-blue eyes pierced into hers.

"Shit, Indy," Finn said, running a hand through his hair and taking a step back. She released a shaky breath. "Why do you have to be so..."

"So what?" she demanded.

"So bloody annoying," he retorted. He huffed out an exhalation, and seemed to be considering her, phone still dangling in one hand. "I'm assuming that if I ask you really nicely not to tell anyone what you overheard, you're not going to agree?"

"Not unless you give me a really good reason," she shot back.

"Shit," he said again and took her by the arm to lead her deeper into the scrub. "Come with me, then."

She shook him off. "You're not taking me anywhere." She glanced over her shoulder; she was still close enough to camp that if she screamed, they might hear her.

Finn dropped her arm and held up his hands in supplication. "Shit, sorry. Look, it's not what you think. I'm not going to hurt you."

Something deep inside Indy always knew he would never hurt her, but it was good to hear the words come out of his mouth, nonetheless.

He stared at her, his jaw working, the cords of his neck standing out, but he finally seemed to come to some decision.

Sighing, he said, "I'm an undercover cop, okay?"

She stared at him, unbelieving. Of all the schemes and reasons she'd concocted in her head for Finn's strange behavior, this was not one of them.

A laugh broke free from her throat. "No, you're not," she

said through her chuckle. "That's hilarious, Finn. You're not a cop," she scoffed, shaking her head.

"I'm glad you think this is all so funny."

She stopped laughing. Now that she thought about it, Finn *could* be a cop. He was certainly assertive enough. Officious enough. She considered him as she stood there in his jeans and shirt, tall and strapping. Bold enough. Muscular enough. Her mind flitted back to how Finn had taken control at the murder scene.

"Oh, shit." It was her turn to swear.

"So, you believe me?" he asked, tone mildly mocking.

"If you're a cop, what are you doing here? In some two-bit, isolated, little out-of-the-way stock camp?" she asked, her mind scrambling to catch up. Nothing ever happened out here. Well, not normally. Not until a man was killed in cold blood this morning.

"We're investigating an international drug ring. They're bringing in methamphetamine and transporting it all over Queensland and down into New South Wales. I'm trying to discover how they're transporting the goods. We had a tip-off that some of the drugs were filtering through these North Queensland stock camps, so I infiltrated Dave and Carrot's team as a way to get in."

"You infiltrated them?" she asked softly. Who the hell was this guy? And what was he saying? Drug gangs? Out here in the desert? No way.

"Yes," he replied, his voice softening. "I'm going to talk to Senior Constable King in a minute and reveal my true identity. I don't want to, but Wombat's murder has brought things to a head, and I need to know what the local cops know. Plus, I don't want one of them getting the wrong idea and locking me up in jail because someone on the mustering crew tells them I'm acting shady." He smiled at this, but she was still too shocked to reply.

She turned to stare at the camp and then back at the surrounding bushland. In the harsh light of midday in the desert, this all seemed a little surreal.

"Indy, look at me." He was up in her face again, gaze intense, standing so close she could feel the heat of his body seeping into hers. "You have to promise you won't tell a soul." He used a finger to tip her hat back so he could see her face properly. She laid a hand on his chest, perhaps to push him away, but then she looked up, and was snared like a bird in a net by those intelligent, light-blue eyes. "My life is literally now in your hands."

Indy suddenly understood the huge risk Finn had taken by telling her who he was. And she'd forced him to take such a risk. It was both thrilling and terrifying, all at once. She made a pact with herself that she would keep him safe. Something about Finn—or whatever his name was—reached out to her, spoke to her inner-self. He was good-looking, but it was more than that. It was the person he was inside, principled and unafraid. She'd like to get to know the true Finn better. Speaking of true identities…

"What's your real name, then?" she demanded. She deserved to know that much, at least.

"Griffin Carmody," he replied.

Ah, so not Finn Stevenson, after all. "But Finn is a derivative of Griffin, isn't it?" she blurted out the first thing that came to her mind.

"Yes, but I'm known as Griff in the real world. Hardly anyone calls me Finn, so it seemed like a safe bet."

That made sense. Indy mulled his name over in her head. There were so many things she wanted to know about the real Finn. Then he shifted slightly, and she remembered she still had her hand on his chest. Could feel the contours of his muscular pecs beneath her fingers. Was breathing in his musky scent. Suddenly, she dared not meet his gaze, but instead watched the tanned skin of his throat as he swallowed. A buzz of anticipation hung between them, and she was unable to break away. As if some kind of force kept them suspended together. The few times Finn had tried to touch her, she'd pulled away, and now she knew it was because she was afraid of this electric reaction each time they came in contact.

His hand came up to cover hers. "I know we've only worked together for a few days, but I believe I can trust you, Indy."

She was suddenly struck dumb. By his words, by his trust in her, by his presence. She tilted her head back and looked up into his face. Then wet her lips, which were suddenly dry. His eyes traced her mouth, watching as she sucked in a breath. Was he just as affected as she was by whatever was humming between them?

He deserved an answer, but it was hard to form the words in her dry mouth. "I promise, your secret is safe with me," she murmured.

"Thank you." Finn closed his eyes for a moment, and Indy suddenly realized how much on edge he'd been waiting for her answer. As if she could've promised anything else. "We need to get back to camp before we're missed," he added softly.

"Oh, yes. Right." Indy gathered herself and took a step back, pulling the brim of her hat firmly back into place. They walked quickly side by side through the bush in silence. She had so many questions, but they'd all have to wait. He was correct. The last thing they needed was for someone to notice they were missing. That might make them number one suspects in this murder.

At the edge of the camp, they separated without a word, each knowing instinctively they shouldn't be seen together. Indy headed for her tent, which was set up slightly away from the rest of the camp in the shade of a large gum, so she could keep her dogs away from everyone. Quickly untying both dogs, she sauntered back into the camp. She could pretend she'd been filling their water bowls, if anyone asked.

Seating herself unobtrusively around the fire, she told the dogs to lie down and be quiet. They both obeyed, delighted to be allowed into the main camp. Most of the crew were seated around the fire and the conversation still encompassed Wombat and how he'd ended up in the ravine.

Indy relaxed into her chair. It didn't seem like she'd been missed.

Then Bindi banged the bottom of a large metal saucepan, the sign lunch was ready, and everyone surged forward, glad of something to take their minds off their confronting morning. Large piles of cold cuts, cheese, and salad adorned the table, as well as hunks of homemade bread on a platter, all of it awaiting the ravenous horde. Indy was glad she'd made it back just in time. Grabbing a plate from the stack, she joined the line of hungry people, catching sight of Finn as he slipped around the side of the tent and took his place at the end of the line. Did he look different somehow? Now she knew the truth? She made a concerted effort not to look in his direction for the rest of lunchtime.

Less than half an hour later, just as they were finishing their meal, Nash arrived, and the mood sobered again. He was here to take everyone's statements. Indy quickly went over the facts in her head. She had nothing to hide, so she'd tell the truth. Steve offered Nash the small caravan as an interview space, and Daniella slipped him a beef sandwich as he went off to set up, which he accepted with a smile. Daniella wasn't normally the mothering type, but Indy knew she had a special soft spot for Nash, who'd come along at a particularly vulnerable time in Skylar's life, and now they were such an amazing couple.

Indy offered to help Bindi with washing the dishes; she needed something to keep her mind off what was going on inside the little van. Dish towel in hand, Indy dried the plates and cutlery and Mack put them away for her.

"Indy, can I have a word?" Daniella asked, appearing at her shoulder as if from nowhere.

"Yes, certainly." Indy handed the dish towel to Mack and followed Daniella around the back of the tent, where they could have some privacy.

"Don't worry, this has nothing to do with the..." Daniella waved her hand in the air, furrowing her brow in a frown, showing her distaste for the whole murder scenario. "I didn't want to bring this up in front of anyone else," Daniella went on. "But I've had two calls from your ex-employer over the past few days. He seems desperate to get in touch with you."

"Patrick?" Indy exclaimed. What the hell would Patrick want with her?

"Yes, Patrick Mountvey. That's him." Daniella smoothed back a non-existent stray strand of hair. "He said it's urgent. He's sent you quite a few messages, but you're not replying."

"Well, of course not." Indy looked around and shrugged. There was no cell phone reception out here.

"Anyway, I promised I'd pass on the message to you." Daniella regarded Indy for a second. "He seemed rather... demanding. Is everything all right? I know Steve said Patrick wrote you glowing references for this position."

Indy heard the *but*, even though Daniella didn't say it. The last thing she needed was Daniella worrying that she'd done something wrong in her last job. Indy's heart squeezed as she thought about Patrick. That bastard had no right to contact her.

"I'm sure it's nothing," she assured Daniella. "I'll check my messages when I can, and get back to him." There must be somewhere she could get reception, even if she had to take a car and drive halfway back to civilization.

The rest of the day passed in a hazy blur of restrained impatience. The crew wasn't used to sitting around all day with nothing to do. It was too hot in camp to sit near the fire in the midday sun, and people retreated to the shade of the surrounding trees, or to their tents. Indy watched from her spot beneath her tree as Finn was called into the van by Nash. Her heart was in her mouth as she wondered about the conversation going on in there right now.

A reprieve from their inactivity came in the form of Constable Willow, when he told Steve they could load up Swampy's truck and he could be on his way. It only took two people, three at the most, to load a truck, but they all wandered over to watch the proceedings and help where they could.

Swampy looked like a bald, bearded thundercloud, growling at anyone who came near him. Indy couldn't figure out if it was because he was now on the police list as a person of interest, or whether it was as simple as the fact his next job had probably now been cancelled because he was running late. Whatever the case, Swampy was desperate to get out of this stock camp, and Indy was just as happy to see the back of him.

They all stood around the holding yards and watched the large truck with the double trailers grind up through its gears in a haze of dust as it slowly wound down the gravel road.

"I've organized for another truck to be here tomorrow morning," Steve said to the assembled crew. Which meant the poor cattle had to spend another night in the holding yards. But it was the best Steve could do, under the circumstances.

"Indy." She looked up to see who called her name. It was Mack, striding toward her. "Your turn," he said with a grim smile and her heart leaped into her throat.

"Thanks." She nodded, biting her lip.

"It's not a problem," Mack said in a low voice. "Just tell them the truth."

"I know," she agreed, but her feet felt like lead weights as she slowly walked toward the van. Why did she suddenly feel this way? Like Mack said, all she had to do was tell the truth. Just because she and Finn had found the body didn't mean anything. It didn't mean she was a suspect. Nope. Her feeling of dread came from the fact she now knew Finn's true identity. Wondering what Finn had said to Nash. Wondering what she should say to Nash.

Two steps led up to the door of the van, which was open, and Indy took them slowly.

"Come in," Nash said, standing up in the cramped surroundings to offer her a chair in the corner. It was hot in here, despite the caravan being parked in the shade and the electric fan rotating slowly on the countertop.

She removed her hat and took the proffered seat.

Nash sat and shuffled some papers on the counter, which was serving as a makeshift desk. He lifted his head and smiled at her, and some of the tightness loosened in her chest. She knew Nash. He knew her. They were friends. Or at the very least, good acquaintances. This was all going to be okay.

"This is just routine," he said. "You can relax. You've already been through the worst of it when you found the body."

She grimaced and then dropped her shoulders. Was it that obvious she was so nervous? He was right. She'd already been through this with him when he arrived. This was just a formality. She looked up to meet his bright-blue eyes. Skylar was one lucky lady, because Nash really was a catch. Curly, blond hair, tall, surfer good looks. She'd often thought he'd look more at home on a tropical beach than he did here in the outback. But then Nash's face became serious, and she remembered he was also a cop with a job to do. He had a reputation as a good, fair police officer, but that didn't make this any easier.

"Before we start, I can confirm that Finn has spoken to me. We are now working together to solve this case."

Indy gave a relieved sigh. Finn had told Nash everything, then.

"He's asked me to reiterate to you how important it is to keep his secret."

"Yes. I know that," Indy replied.

"Right. Can you walk me through how you found the body again, step by step, please?"

"Sure." Indy drew in a deep breath and turned her mind back to this morning. If only they could truly go back in time to this morning. Before they'd found the body, and before she knew the truth about Finn. Because it now weighed heavy around her shoulders. She suddenly didn't want to be the owner of such a secret.

* * *

Indy glanced over her shoulder to the only hill breaking the monotony of the flat landscape, and could just make out the spike of the repeater tower jutting into the air from the top. The repeater tower was there to help strengthen the transmission of the UHF radios everyone used out on muster. But it wasn't the tower that interested her. It was because the hill was the highest point for miles around, and there was mobile reception up there, or so Bindi had told her.

She needed to get up there and see if Bindi was correct. She needed to read those messages Patrick had sent her. The gall of the man. Her blood boiled at the mere idea he'd called Stormcloud. How dare he?

It was now late afternoon, and Nash had finished his interviews. They'd been given permission to resume the muster tomorrow morning, and everyone was now taking it easy for the rest of the day. Some of the crew, like Brian and

Rosie, were attending to small jobs, such as repairing horse tack and sorting through bills that needed to be paid. Others, like Dave and Carrot, were snoozing in the shade of an ironbark. It was the perfect time for Indy to take a quick trip to the top of the hill.

Steve and Daniella had returned to Stormcloud once Nash had finished his interviews, leaving Dale in charge once more. And Aaron had flown out soon after, buzzing his red helicopter over the camp, raising a haze of dust as he went. They still had a lodge to run, with at least twenty guests to keep occupied, and they couldn't leave Skylar and her half-sister Julie to do it all. Even with Alek and Sasha's help, they'd be run off their feet. The owners would make it back just in time to help with dinner service.

Indy went to find Dale, who was sitting in the mess tent, chatting to Mack and Bindi, as Bindi prepped the evening meal.

"Dale, is it okay if I take a quick ride up to the repeater tower?" she asked. "Bindi says I can get cell phone reception, and I'd like to check my messages, if that's okay?"

Before Dale could even open his mouth to reply, Finn appeared around the side of the tent, carrying what looked like a load of laundry.

"Did I hear someone say there was cell reception around here?" He looked like an eager puppy who'd just been thrown a bone.

"Yes, and yes," Dale replied with a slight chuckle. "Why don't you take the new guy with you, Indy? I'd be happier if you didn't go alone. Not with all that's going on around here."

A chill went down Indy's spine. She hadn't even considered that she might be putting herself in danger by going off alone. Surely, she wasn't at risk. Was she?

When she cast an uneasy glance at Dale, he shrugged and

said, "We can't be too careful. Not until the police have caught the person...or people...who did this."

"But I'll take my dogs. They can protect me, and..." she started to argue. This was something she wanted to do alone. If Patrick had been sending her messages, she didn't want anyone around as a witness to her private hell. And she certainly didn't want that person to be Finn. One look at Dale's serious face, however, told her she wasn't going to get her way.

"Fine," she said, trying to keep the slightly sulky tone out of her voice. "Thanks, Dale." She turned on her heel without meeting Finn's eye and headed toward the saddling yard. "I'll get the horses ready," she said over her shoulder.

"Take a UHF with you, as well. Just in case," Dale called after them.

Her spirits picked up again ten minutes later, as she kicked Gypsy into a fast trot, with Finn riding Sahara close by. She was aware of Finn beside her, without even having to look. As if his presence were a magnet, calling to her sub-conscience. It was nice to break free of the sombre mood that'd descended over the camp, even for half an hour. Everyone was on edge and withdrawn. Indy thought she could be imagining it, but she might've even seen Dave sending suspicious glances toward Scanner when he thought he wasn't looking. Was everyone starting to have suspicious thoughts about everyone else in the crew, now? It wasn't a nice thought, and it wouldn't bode well for their work environment if they didn't trust one another.

"Thanks for letting me tag along," Finn said brightly. She guessed he might have an ulterior motive for wanting to come with her. He might have information for her. And maybe this was the chance she needed to ply him for the answers to fill in some of the gaping holes in her knowledge about Finn and what his undercover job encompassed.

"No problem," she replied, then whistled up Digger, who was heading away from them at a dead run, probably on the trail of a kangaroo.

With the horse's ground-eating jog, it only took them another ten minutes to reach the base of the hill. The climb was a little slower, as there was no real track. But once they reached the top—Gypsy blowing slightly from the exertion—Indy drew in a breath at the spectacular view. Who would've guessed they'd be able to see so far in every direction from this small mound? It just went to show how flat and never-ending these floodplains really were.

"I wasn't expecting this," Finn said, dismounting and letting Sahara's reins drop. Both horses were well-trained, they'd graze any feed nearby, but wouldn't wander too far.

"Me, either," she agreed. "This puts it all into a different perspective, doesn't it?"

Indy also dismounted and turned a full circle to get her bearings. The repeater tower was off to their left, casting a long shadow over the ground. The stock camp was below, and Indy took a few moments to orient herself, picking out the mess tent, the cooking caravan, then her own little tent beneath the ironbark. She told her dogs to stay close. They both lay in the shade, tongues lolling after their fast climb up the hill.

"At least the forensics boys have left," Finn said. "But homicide is still there."

She shifted her focus to follow the road away from the camp until she saw a group of police cruisers parked at the edge of the track. Nash's Land Cruiser was still there, as well.

"Will they stay there all night?" Indy asked, a little incredulous.

"Nah. They'll probably wrap it up soon. I'd say forensics have taken the body back to Cairns with them." Finn shrugged and took off his Akubra, then swiped a hand through his sweaty hair. "But they'll definitely leave a guard or two out here tonight. And perhaps even over the next few days. Until they're sure they've covered every inch of ground around the crime scene."

"Oh." It was all Indy could find to say. Who knew these things took this long to process? It all seemed to happen much quicker on those police procedural shows she sometimes watched. It was comforting, in a strange sort of way, to have Finn explain all this to her.

Her gaze drifted away from the outlook below, not really wanting to be reminded of the gruesome scene from this morning.

"Stormcloud must be over there." She raised a finger and pointed at a smudge of red hills in the far distance. The lodge rested in the foothills of the Mount Mulligan escarpment, part of a conglomeration of mountains called the Featherbed Ranges.

"Ah. I've never been." Finn shaded his eyes and followed her line of sight. "I hear it's pretty nice. Maybe I could come for a visit one day." He stepped closer, and their shoulders touched.

"Maybe," she replied perfunctorily. She didn't really want Finn at Stormcloud. His presence out here was distracting enough.

Indy walked toward the towering metal tower, and suddenly her phone pinged. Once. Twice. Three times.

"You got reception?" Finn was at her side in a microsecond. He flicked the button on his shirt pocket and pulled his phone out. She was a little slower to follow suit, suddenly unwilling to see these messages Patrick had supposedly sent her.

Finn quickly became distracted by his phone, head bent over the screen, trying to shade it from the sun and read it at the same time. Indy wandered slowly away, also pulling her phone from her pocket.

She drew in a breath. Better to get this over with. Swiping up her screen, she was greeted by a host of messages and three missed calls from Patrick. What was he doing? She'd told him never to contact her. The day she'd left Mountvey Downs in tears was the last day she ever hoped to see his face, or hear his voice again.

She quickly scanned through the messages. What the hell…?

She didn't need to read them all in their entirety to get the gist of his words.

I miss you… Please come back… Sheila left me… I need you back in my life…

That complete asshole. A lump formed in her throat. Memories of the two of them together assaulted her mind. He couldn't do this to her. Not now. She'd gotten over Patrick and his conniving ways. He'd broken her heart into a million pieces and then stomped on it. She was still surprised at how easily she'd fallen for his shit.

Indy swore and nearly threw her phone down the hill.

"Are you okay?"

She'd almost forgotten Finn was there for a second.

No, she wasn't okay. She felt like screaming. Or bursting into tears. Or falling into a heap on the ground, never to get up. Or all of the above.

CHAPTER FIVE

Finn looked up from his phone to see Indy's pale face, her eyes swimming with unshed tears. His mind switched gears, pulling him out of his phone and back into the real world. He'd been looking at the photos Chloe had sent him of Kayleigh, laughing as she sat on a swing. His heart had nearly burst at the sight. Kayleigh was getting so big now. But then Indy had made a noise, like an animal in great pain. The photos would have to wait until a more suitable time.

"Are you okay?" It looked like she'd just received terrible news. He slipped his phone back in his pocket, his own personal problems forgotten in the path of Indy's obvious distress.

She looked up, as if only just remembering he was there.

"That bastard. How dare he?" she ground out between clenched teeth. But her harsh words belied the look in her eyes. One of pain and anguish. "He can't do this to me." This time her chin wobbled as she spoke and then she leaned over and placed her hands on her knees, dragging in deep breaths. It sounded like she was hyperventilating.

"Come and sit down," Finn suggested, suddenly worried she might fall over. She let him lead her, as if on autopilot, to a rock formation a little way down the slope, where they could sit in the shade. He sat close, in case she needed him, but not touching. His proximity didn't seem to worry her, like it had before, and she actually leaned against his shoulder, as if she needed the support.

He set his Akubra in the dirt and did the same for her, carefully removing her hat and placing it beside her. But she didn't seem to notice, her eyes were focussed into the distance, as if she were seeing something that wasn't really there.

It hurt Finn to see this strong, amazing woman breaking down in front of him.

"Do you want to talk about it?" he asked softly. He wasn't the world's best communicator—Chloe could attest loud and long to that fact—but the least he could do was try to comfort Indy, if that's what she needed. He was beginning to think of her as a friend, and he hated to see her so wrought up.

"No," she snapped, still staring into space. One of her dogs, the black-and-tan female, came up and nuzzled Indy's hand, but she ignored the animal, so she proceeded to curl up beside her mistress. Finn wasn't surprised at the little dog offering comfort. Kelpies were renowned for their loyalty and intelligence, and Barbie would feel her mistress's unhappiness.

"Okay." He was fine with just sitting here until she recovered her equilibrium.

Silence settled over them both. He studied the land spread out below them. It really was quite amazing how much just this small elevation allowed a person to see such a long distance. Red dirt stretched out as far as the eye could see, covered with scattered scrubby bushes, the odd bottle tree, or ironbark. It was strangely, starkly beautiful.

Finn had been born in Ireland, and then his father had moved them all to Sydney when Finn was two years old to take up a position at the Seven Hills Fire Station. Finn had loved growing up in Sydney—he was definitely a city boy—but a part of him had always longed to explore this wide, brown country. When he was fifteen, his mother had sent both him and Garrett off to spend their school holidays on a working farm to give her some peace and quiet; she could no longer cope with two boisterous teenage boys, when her own grief at losing her husband still sat so heavily on her. Garrett had hated it and couldn't wait to get home. But that farm had started Finn's love affair with the Australian landscape. He kept returning at every possible holiday. When he'd finished school, he'd taken a gap year, and travelled up and down the whole eastern side of Australia, taking odd jobs on farms as a jackaroo, or picking fruit, or as a handyman. It'd been hard, soul-cleansing work. He always knew he was going to come back and join the police force afterwards. But that year had given him some valuable lessons, and, without that experience, he would never have fitted in so well to this undercover mission.

Indy stirred beside him, breaking his introspection.

Her voice was so quiet, he almost missed her words. "I thought I was over him. I thought I was over this whole thing. I never even cried over him. He wasn't worth it. But now…" A tear rolled down her cheek, and she dashed it away.

She'd obviously had her heart broken by some asshole, but without all the facts, Finn wasn't sure where to start. If she really hadn't cried when they broke up, then this sounded like she might be having a delayed reaction. She might've stayed determinedly strong when she left this man, but it looked like the waterworks were coming now.

He couldn't let her sit there, suffering, without offering her comfort. So, he reached an arm around her back and tucked her under his shoulder. She was so small beside him, almost waif-like. He half-expected her to push him away, but instead, she lay her head against his collarbone.

"I had an affair with the married owner on the last station I worked at," Indy blurted, her tears running freely now.

Oh, wow. He hadn't been expecting that. Indy seemed like such a person of principle. He assumed there were extenuating circumstances. He didn't think she would be easily enticed into such an illicit affair. But it certainly explained why she'd withdrawn from him when she'd thought he was married. He didn't let his surprise show, however. Merely kept his arm around her shoulder and murmured encouraging noises.

"He told me he was going to leave his wife. That we would be together."

Mm-hmm, didn't they always? Finn kept this thought to himself, saying instead, "But I'm guessing he didn't leave her?"

"No." Her sniffles were becoming sobs. "Patrick started it. He was the one who seduced me. I would never… But he was so persistent, so charming. It was a small station, with few other staff. We spent a lot of time together."

It sounded so stereotypical that Finn had to hold back his cynical grunt of annoyance. She'd obviously been lonely, and this other man sounded like he'd pursued her with his charisma. In some ways, Finn didn't blame the man. Indy was gorgeous.

"I r-r-resisted him for m-months, and then one night, he kissed me and I thought, why the hell not? I was l-l-lonely, I guess," she said through her sobs.

Yes, he'd already guessed that part. He could feel his shirt becoming damp from her tears, but he let her go on crying. It was cathartic, perhaps just what she needed. He wasn't sure why she was telling him all this, but in a way, he was glad he could be here for her.

"But in the end, I knew I n-n-needed to leave. So, when

Stormcloud advertised a p-position, I jumped at it."

"That's good," he murmured. "A clean break."

"Yes. But n-now he's telling me that his w-w-wife has left him. And he wants me to come back. I c-c-can't go back. Not ever. I won't," she wailed. This time she broke down completely, sobbing uncontrollably, her words becoming incoherent noises of pain and sadness.

"You don't have to," he soothed. "You're safe here. We'll look after you. I'll look after you."

He let her cry. Her little dog put her snout in Indy's lap, casting worried glances up at Finn with her liquid brown eyes. He patted the dog on the head, telling her she was a good girl, hoping that Indy was receiving some small comfort from her doggy pal. Then Digger appeared from out of the bushes and came to curl up next to the female. He was touched by their faithful devotion to Indy. He'd always wanted a dog of his own, but it wouldn't have been fair given his long hours spent at work. There was nothing in this world like a canine's unconditional love.

Pulling Indy closer, he rested his chin on top of her head, smoothing her hair with one hand, and letting her run through the gauntlet of her overwrought emotions. The sun was slowly setting behind them, but they still had at least an hour left before it got dark. The landscape turned slowly from ochre to a deep, rich red as the sunlight disappeared and the sky became dusky.

Indy's sobs slowly became less and less. He wished he had a handkerchief, or something to offer her, but his shirt would have to do to soak up her tears, for now. Finally, she turned her head slightly, gaze fixed out on the floodplains, as her tears subsided.

"This is why I didn't want you to come up here with me." Her words surprised him, and he sat up a little straighter. "Because I didn't want you to see me like this," she sniffled into his shirt.

Finn's heart went out to this woman, who thought she had to do everything alone. Who thought she had to stay strong all the time. He wanted to let her know she wasn't alone; that he cared.

"It's not a burden, Indy. To bear witness to your tears. I'm *glad* I was here for you."

"Well, thank you," she replied, drawing back just a little.

"I know some people. I could send someone over to make it clear that bastard needs to leave you alone," he added, with what he hoped was enough humor to soften his words.

Indy raised a watery smile. "Thanks, but I'm not sure police intimidation is the right way to solve this problem."

He grimaced. "Maybe not. But sometimes it's the only thing these types of men understand." He stared down into her tear-streaked face. On instinct, he brought up his hand, using his thumb to wipe away the tears on her cheek. Her skin was soft beneath the pad of his thumb. Brown eyes, full of liquid warmth, stared up at him, widening slightly at his touch. Those sultry, dark eyes that'd mesmerized him from the first moment he'd seen her.

She didn't look away, and neither did he. The silence stretched out between them. Her body was soft and pliant against his. Lips, velvety pink. And enticing.

Before he knew quite what he was doing, he'd dropped his head and his mouth was on hers. For a second, she kept her lips firmly pressed together, and then it was as if all her resistance melted away and she welcomed him in. He told himself that all he wanted was to make her feel better, to take away the pain, replace it with something good for a few seconds.

But his heart knew this was much more than that.

God, she tasted so sweet. More than he could ever have imagined, her mouth moulding to his in a perfect fit. He'd thought about kissing Indy, but never really dreamed it would become a reality. Was he taking advantage of her? Maybe, but there was nothing he could do to stop himself now. He was too far gone.

She tilted her head back, angling it slightly for better access, and he grabbed the back of her neck, wanting to never let her go. Without releasing her mouth, he lifted her into his lap, and she snuggled against him, her hands running over his shoulders and grabbing hold of his biceps to hold herself steady.

He was rock hard in an instant. His mind just about blown by the intensity of this kiss. His tongue delved deep into her mouth, and she gave a small moan of pleasure. It wasn't just kissing he wanted to do with Indy. He wanted more of her. All of her.

Suddenly, Digger jumped on them both, licking and whining, as if he wanted to be involved in the fun. Indy spluttered and pushed the wriggling dog away.

"Digger, get down, boy," she said with a laugh. Smiling, she looked up at Finn and licked her lips, leaning in to continue where they'd left off. All of a sudden, the smile fled from her face.

"Oh, shit." She withdrew sharply. "I just remembered you're married. Fuck, I just kissed another married man." Indy got to her feet in a flurry of dust, the dogs bounding around her legs. "I can't believe I was that stupid."

"Wait." Finn was on his feet now, too. Oh, crap, why hadn't he seen this coming? "It's not what you think."

"You told me before that you were married," Indy said, bending down to pick up her hat and placing it forcibly on her head. "Is that true?" Her cheeks were still flushed pink from their kiss, her eyes still puffy from crying.

"That was part of my undercover persona," he told her, a tad desperately.

"So, you're not married, then?" Indy's face was a mask of confusion.

Finn's chest grew tight, and he dragged in a deep breath to try and ease the tension. "It's...complicated."

"What the fuck does that mean?"

"It means...it's complicated." He wished now they'd had this conversation before he'd been stupid enough to kiss her. Of course, he should've expected this kind of reaction from her. After she'd been fucked over by another married man. This was the worst thing he could've done to her.

"Are you married, or not? And I mean in real life. Not in your stupid make-believe life." She was breathing hard, and her dark hair had come loose to fall about her face. Eyes flashing with anger, she was perhaps even more beautiful now.

He raised his head to look her straight in the eye. She deserved the truth. "Yes. I'm married."

CHAPTER SIX

Married. The bastard was married. And she'd let him kiss her. Had enjoyed him kissing her. Had wanted to do more than kiss him. She was still seething, even though she should be concentrating on moving the cattle. Reining Gypsy around to the right, she heeled her into a fast jog, sending Digger out in a wide arc, just to make sure there were no cattle hiding in the acacia thicket over to the left. It was good to be back at work. At least, it gave her wayward mind something else to concentrate on. Thankfully, Nash had said there was no reason they couldn't continue with the muster. They'd impounded Wombat's truck and searched the site where it was parked, and the perimeter of the campsite thoroughly. Now, it seemed they were leaving it up to the forensics guys. Which was a little surprising, but Indy knew nothing of police procedure, so she assumed they'd come back to them if they had any more questions.

Aaron had arrived in the little helicopter just as the sun touched the sky this morning, his brow still pinched with worry over the ongoing investigation. But when he'd seen that everything had pretty much gone back to normal, he'd relaxed a little. He'd done a good job of leading the muster crew to the mob to be gathered up today, then circling and harrying the bush cattle into a large group, and now they were just collecting up the stragglers before they took them all back to camp. But her mind kept going back to her conversation with Finn at the top of the hill yesterday evening, working over the memories as if they were a sore tooth.

Finn had tried to talk to her twice after their...argument, if she could call it that, on the hill. Once last night, he'd caught her elbow as she made her way from the fire to her tent for the night and asked if he could explain. She'd shaken him off with an angry yank of her arm, telling him she had all the facts she needed to know, thank you very much. Her growled exclamation that she would call for help if he didn't leave her alone was enough to send him away with a grimace. Then again, this morning, he'd cornered her in the saddling yard, pleading for her to hear him out. Luckily, Rosie had walked in carrying her saddle, and Indy had been saved from giving an answer.

He clearly had more to say on the subject, but Indy was too angry to hear his pathetic excuses. Even when he turned those bright-blue eyes flecked with green, that reminded her of the aqua-colored water of a tropical island, in her direction. So blue, she almost forgot what she was thinking as she tried to decide where the green flecks ended and the electric blue started.

After he'd admitted that he was married in real life, Indy had jumped onto Gypsy's back and ridden down the hill at speed, letting him follow as he liked. All she could think was how stupid could one woman be to get involved with *another* married man. She thought she'd learned her lesson after Patrick. She *had* learned her lesson. Which was why she was steering well clear of Finn Stevenson, or whatever his bloody name was.

Indy couldn't believe she'd told Finn all her problems with

Patrick. It was like he'd had the key that unlocked a set of floodgates holding it all back. At least she still had one secret that not even he knew. She'd managed to keep that little gem under wraps. Thank God. What would Finn think of her, if he knew she'd been pregnant with Patrick's child? Indy's hand came up unconsciously to cover her belly.

The look on Patrick's face when she'd told him that she was carrying his baby remained seared into her brain. One of distaste and indignation. It was gone in a flash, but she'd still seen it. Afterwards, he'd been solicitous and fawning, telling her they needed to look at all their options before they made any decisions. Although he'd never said the words, she knew he thought she'd done it on purpose to trap him. But nothing had been further from the truth. In her heart of hearts, she'd known it was time to move on from Mountvey, but then she'd missed her period and she'd been so scared, so unsure of what to do. She must've only been three or four weeks along, but pregnancy tests were getting more and more sensitive, and this one hadn't lied. After seeing Patrick's expression when she'd finally found the courage to tell him, Indy had made a vow that she'd raise her baby on her own. If Patrick didn't want them, then she'd take her child far away, and they'd live happily together, just the two of them.

Because it would be just the two of them. Indy had no family left. Both her parents were dead. She'd been an only child, spawned in a desperate attempt by her mother to keep her marriage together. It'd worked, because her father had stuck around, but her parents never tried for any more children. Then her father had died in a mining accident at work while she was only nine, and what had been left of her mother's love dried up and blew away with her husband's ashes. They'd never really had much of a mother-daughter relationship, but after her father's death it was as if Indy were a ghost in her own home, her mother barely noticed her, no matter what Indy did or said. Indy had left home at sixteen, taking a job as an apprentice jillaroo on a northern cattle station—as far away from home, and her mother, as she could possibly get—and never looked back. Two years later, Indy's mother died from an unexpected brain aneurysm and that was that. Indy had never known a true family, and she thought maybe this pregnancy would help her fix that gaping hole in her life.

So, when she'd lost the baby two weeks later, it felt like her whole world had come crashing down. It hadn't been much worse than a really heavy period, with severe cramps, but she knew. Even though she'd only been six weeks pregnant—some women may not have even realized they were carrying a baby at that stage—she'd felt the loss of something so precious. But at least one good thing had come from the miscarriage. She'd finally been released from her stupid fantasy that Patrick would change. That he'd learn to love her and their child. That he'd leave his wife and marry her, instead. What a delusion she'd lived under for so many months. Her gut churned at the idea she'd been so moronic.

She'd fled Mountvey with her horses and her dogs. Blackmailing Patrick into giving her a glowing reference—which she knew she deserved, but didn't trust him to give otherwise—so she could gain the coveted job at Stormcloud.

The buzz of a motorcycle engine caught her attention, and she lifted her head to see Finn with a trail of dust rising behind him on the tail of a young heifer that was heading away from the mob and onto the open plain. She should go and help him. Gathering up her reins, she hesitated. From over to her left, Dave charged after Finn on his rangy pinto gelding, Amigo. She offered a silent thank you to the powers that be. She knew she shouldn't let this thing between them affect her work, but she still wasn't ready to face Finn.

Digger returned, and with a happy bark reported that there

were no cattle hiding in the acacia thicket. Barbie, who'd been on Gypsy's heels all along, hopped up onto the horse's withers for a rest, and Digger followed suit, crouching behind the saddle on Gypsy's hindquarters. Indy had trained her horse to put up with her dogs clambering all over her, and they had a good animal friendship going on. She hoped Skylar and Steve were taking good care of Beethoven back at the lodge. She missed her chestnut gelding, but she'd make sure to give him lots of love when she returned to the station. Steve had promised to ride him occasionally, when he took out a group of guests on a day tour. Indy trusted Steve implicitly to be gentle with her beloved horse.

She turned Gypsy back toward the flank of the large mob, helping to push them along at a slow pace, not hurrying them or stressing the animals, as some farmers might.

Scanner came up behind her on his ATV, careful not to get too close to her horse. "Dale says to tell you we'll keep pushing this mob for home and have a late lunch once we get there. Okay?"

Indy gave him a thumbs-up, and he roared off in a cloud of dust farther up the flank, staying well clear of the meandering cattle. Scanner could have just radioed her the information, but he was a man who liked to keep mobile, and it looked like he was off to give his daughter, Maddie, the same news.

It made sense. They were so close to camp now. It'd be silly to stop for lunch and then have to get the mob moving again. But her stomach rumbled in protest; it'd been a long time since smoko. She wouldn't be the only one eager to bring this mob in and get something to eat. Getting the mob in early would mean they'd have time to do some sorting, branding, worming and ear tagging this afternoon. Dale would normally stay behind in camp with either Mack or one of the other guys to give him a hand, while the rest of them brought in another mob. This time, they could all help out, and get the job done in half the time.

Indy's gaze fell on Finn again as he and Dave chased the runaway bull into the back of the mob. The sad part was, she'd spilled her guts to Finn, but she hardly knew anything about him. She hadn't given him a chance to tell her anything about his life, because she'd been too busy moaning about her own. Now that she knew he was an undercover cop, she wanted to understand more about him. Why had he chosen this profession? What was it like to work undercover? Was it dangerous? And why was his marriage so complicated?

She sighed. Perhaps she owed him the time to at least give her the bare facts about himself.

Finn stopped his motorcycle and lifted his visor on his helmet. He was too far away for her to see his eyes, but he was looking in her direction. Sitting upright on his bike, long legs splayed out on either side to balance himself, blue chambray shirt stretched across strong shoulders. She could attest to just how strong those shoulders were, because her brain kept reminding her how they'd felt beneath her palms last night.

Bugger. Why did she have to be so attracted to this man?

It was another hour and a half before Indy could finally tame her stomach's rumblings as she gratefully sat down with a plate full of pasta salad and some large slices of corned beef. She'd almost piled on two pieces of the delicious-looking chocolate cake, as well, but had decided that would be plain gluttonous, and she could go back later for dessert.

Finn unfolded his chair next to hers and sat down. She almost rolled her eyes. He'd caught her unawares, too busy stuffing her face to notice he was approaching. Not that there was a lot she could do about it, everyone would be watching if she made a scene.

"I'm starving," Finn said to no one in particular.

"Yeah, that was a long time in the saddle without sustenance," Carrot agreed from Finn's other side. Indy raised her eyebrow in Finn's direction and continued to eat. He gave her a smile, the corner of his mouth hooked up with the hint of a question. He was trying to make an effort to heal their rift, and she should probably let him. It wouldn't do to make it too obvious to the rest of the crew that they'd had a fight. She didn't want any awkward questions from Dale or Bindi. Or the rest of the crew, for that matter, who were now all finding a spot to sit with their plates of food.

"Yep, I'm starving, too," Indy finally said.

Finn's face lit up, clearly recognizing an olive branch when he saw one. "They serve some bloody good grub at this camp," Finn replied, holding up a slab of meat. "I don't think I eat this well at home."

"Me neither," she giggled, and the tension that'd been hovering between them all day subsided a little. "But it's one of the things Stormcloud pride themselves on. Skylar is the best gourmet cook in the state. Or so I've been told. She does all the cooking for the guests back at the lodge, and she taught Bindi everything she knows. So, the crew eat nearly as well as the guests," she continued.

"I'm definitely not complaining," Finn replied, licking his lips and rubbing his belly in a comedic show of humor.

Indy giggled again and found herself staring into Finn's blue eyes.

It suddenly hit her. She liked Finn Stevenson—Griffin Carmody, whatever his name was. And she was going to have to accept that fact. He was a nice guy. Easy to talk to, a bit of a joker, but serious when he needed to be. And so good-looking, she could hardly tear her gaze away from his face. Even streaked with dust and covered with three-day stubble —which was possibly sexier than him being clean-shaven— she liked the way his eyes crinkled at the corners when he smiled, and the way his lips firmed in a strong, straight line when he was pondering a question.

The crows cawed loudly from their roost in the big eucalyptus, breaking her thought bubble. She glanced up at the annoying black birds, wishing they'd go and bother another stock camp. But it was part of mustering; crows came as part and parcel of life in the outback, always on the lookout for scraps and carrion.

"Wonder if the coppers have found Wombat's murderer yet?" Carrot said through a mouthful of corned beef, breaking her bubble of self-introspection.

"Don't be ridiculous," Dave snorted. "Of course, they haven't. They've got all sorts of investigating to do before they find the killer. Hell, they might not ever find him. This case could stay open for months, years even." Dave looked down his nose at his red-haired mate, as if he were the expert here on police procedure, and Carrot was an idiot. "Don't you know anything? Murder investigations take time and patience. Those coppers will have to follow up every lead, look at every clue. It's not like the killer is going to put up his hand and say, *here I am*."

Indy stifled a smirk and cast Finn a quick glance. If only they knew.

She wondered if Finn would say anything, but he kept chewing his food and looking interested in what Dave had to say. Indy admired his restraint. He was good at this undercover thing. She'd be useless at it. She already wanted to blurt out to Dave and Carrot that she had a secret. That she knew more about this murder than she was letting on. That it might be somehow connected to a large, international drug gang.

Indy stuffed a large forkful of pasta salad into her mouth, just to be on the safe side.

Dave and Carrot bickered back and forth about the

intricacies of how a murder investigation should be conducted, and soon enough, Scanner, Maddie, and Beth joined in the discussion.

Indy leaned in to Finn and said, "At least no one else went missing today." She meant it as a joke, but Finn didn't smile, and she suddenly wished she could take back her comment. It probably was in bad taste, with everything going on right now.

"No, you're right about that. But you need to keep your eyes and ears open, Indy." His voice had dropped to a low murmur, so that only she could hear him over the other men's conversation. "One person was murdered out here, and we don't know why, or by whom, yet."

"What are you saying?" she asked, keeping her voice as low as his.

"Just don't get complacent." His eyes flickered around the camp, continuously moving, as if he were searching for something. Or someone.

Was he telling her that she couldn't trust anyone? Did she know something that he wasn't telling her? No. Surely if he suspected the murderer was amongst them, he'd at least warn her. She'd always thought that perhaps Nash might be looking at Swampy as the main suspect. But now her mind did a double-take. Could it be someone here? Someone she worked closely with?

She stared at everyone around the fire. Everyone looked so...normal. Everything was just as it should be. Next to her and Finn in the circle around the fire, Dave and Carrot were still squabbling, with Scanner adding his two-cents' worth when he could get a word in. Maddie and Beth had swapped their conversation over to join Dale and Aaron on their right. Indy couldn't hear it all, but she thought they were discussing their favorite country and western singer—which had to be James Blundell, of course. Brian and Rosie were the last in the semi-circle, huddled together around six feet away from her, staring morosely into their empty plates. Bindi was clanging her pots in the mess tent. It was all perfectly normal.

Staring out past the tents, the mid-afternoon sun was causing a heat-haze to rise over on the outskirts of the camp, where the cattle had just been yarded. The sun beat down on her Akubra, but a sudden cold shiver went through her.

"Anyway, I'm glad we got the cattle in so early," Finn said, more loudly this time so others could hear him. "It gives us more time back in camp."

"Oh. Right," she mumbled in reply, wondering exactly what he meant by his cryptic remark. She was kicking herself now that she hadn't taken more time to find out what his next move as the undercover Finn might be. She had no idea what his mission really entailed, or what he would normally do to uncover a killer. But if it were her, she guessed she'd be assessing the crew. Working out if they had any connection to the murder, or to the drugs. Perhaps that's why he was keen to spend more time in camp, so he could surreptitiously check for clues.

She decided she needed to get Finn alone and drill him for answers. This whole cloak and dagger thing was driving her crazy.

Dale stood and stretched, banging his tin plate to get everyone's attention. "Righto, you lot. We've got work to do. Indy and Mack, you can help me sort the weaners out. Dave and Carrot, can you handle the ear tagging and drenching? And Scanner, can your crew take care of the branding?"

Dale was keen to get going, it seemed. Indy guessed he was still trying to impress Steve, to show his stepfather that his trust was well-placed by letting him run the stock camp. And apart from the homicide, Dale was doing a pretty good job so far.

The rest of the afternoon was spent wrestling the jittery

cattle into the correct yards. Separating the weaners from the breeding cows, which were set free to roam again and fatten up until the next breeding season once they'd had their ear tags and brands checked. Her dogs were good at keeping the cattle yarded up and moving in the right direction, and Dale made a few comments on how well-trained they were and how perhaps they'd get her to train up a few of their dogs, as well. A couple of micky bulls stampeded and nearly broke through a fence and an angry heifer charged at Dave, knocking him down and sending him sprawling in the dust. Lucky for him, he was only left with a few bruises where the cow had trampled over him in her rush for freedom.

Indy got no chance to speak to Finn alone, but she figured she could do it later that evening, after dinner.

The evening meal was later than normal, because lunch had been delayed. They didn't sit down to eat until well after the sun had set, and it made it harder to see the food on their plates using only the light from the fire to see by. Indy had just finished her last mouthful and leaned back in her chair with a sigh, when the low drone of a vehicle reached her ears. She wasn't the only one to sit up and turn around. Headlights could be seen flashing wildly through the trees, as two, no three, cars drove toward camp down the gravel road.

Who the hell could this be?

Dale stood and walked over to the vehicles as they all pulled up beside the cooking van, Mack flanking his left-hand side.

Indy could now see clearly, these were three police cars. Nash stepped out of his Land Cruiser, Constable Willow, from the other side. Two uniformed police officers got out of a police cruiser behind them. She didn't recognize these two, but they could possibly be from the large armada of cops who'd swarmed the place yesterday. A detective she remembered from the murder scene was last to emerge from an unmarked station wagon at the end of the line, wearing civilian clothes.

"What's going on, Nash?" Dale asked, going up and shaking Nash's hand in greeting.

Everyone was now standing around the fire, craning their necks to hear what was being said.

"Sorry, Dale." Nash gave a small grimace. "This is police procedure. It's out of my hands."

The detective came up behind Nash and asked, "Are you Dale Williams?"

"Yes, sir." Dale squared his shoulders.

"Dale Williams, my name is Detective Warwick Sampson. I have a warrant to search all domiciles, vehicles, buildings, and structures that make up this..." The detective hesitated and waved his hand in the air.

"You mean the stock camp?" Dale asked warily.

"Yes. Stock camp. All the details are in there," Detective Sampson replied, never losing his air of aloof arrogance. He handed Dale a wad of papers. "Now please move aside and let my men do what they need to do."

"I thought you'd already searched the camp?" Dale addressed Nash, ignoring the other detective.

"We searched the surrounding bushland and the areas in between your accommodations. But this will be a more thorough search," Nash replied. He kept his shoulders back and looked Dale directly in the eye, but Indy could see the regret etched in the lines around his face.

She wondered how hard this must be for Nash. He and Dale were friends. He was going to marry Dale's sister. He was part of the Stormcloud family. Indy guessed that many small-town cops had this problem, as it was hard not to become emotionally involved with people in a community.

Dale's gaze hardened, but he stepped back and let the police officers and the detective go past.

"What are they doing here?" Rosie asked, her voice thin and wavering.

"It's going to be okay, love," Indy heard Brian murmur to his wife.

"I'm sorry," Dale spoke loudly enough for everyone to hear. "It seems the police want to search everyone's tents and trucks. Please, just all do as they ask, and we can get this over with quickly."

"No. They can't do that," Rosie protested, turning to her husband. "Can they do that?" Rosie seemed especially perturbed by the idea of a search.

"Yes, they can," Brian replied with a grimace.

Others around the fire began to make sounds of dissent. Dave and Carrot descended on Dale and Mack and demanded they do something to stop this blatant invasion of privacy. Dale and Mack were hurriedly reading the warrant by the light on their phones.

"You'd think they all had something to hide." Finn said quietly, sidling up beside Indy. "It will go much easier if they just let the cops do their jobs."

"Hmm." Indy probably agreed, but she understood why the rest of the crew felt violated. The camp had already been searched as far as everyone was concerned. "What do you think they're looking for?" she asked, not taking her eyes off the gruff Detective Sampson, who strode about as if he owned the place, in his ironed jeans and dark windbreaker jacket. A sudden thought struck her. Was this what Finn looked like when he wasn't undercover? All authoritarian and supercilious?

"They're probably looking for the murder weapon, would be my guess," Finn muttered into her ear.

Indy gasped. She hadn't thought of that. Then she turned to eye Finn suspiciously. Had he known this raid was coming? And if he had, why hadn't he warned them?

CHAPTER SEVEN

Finn watched the figure of Detective Sampson disappear into the mess tent, directing the two officers under his command to start searching at the back of the large tent. This new turn of events was annoying, to say the least. Because it undercut Finn's clandestine efforts to do exactly the same thing. He'd been conducting covert searches of the camp himself, but so far had come up empty-handed. Which was why he'd been glad when they returned early to camp this afternoon. It gave him a chance to clamber beneath the Scanlon's big truck and check it out, while everyone was busy grading the cattle. Looking for hidden compartments, suspicious lock-boxes, anything that looked out of place or wasn't supposed to be there. But Finn understood why this Detective Sampson would fast-track a search warrant. They still hadn't found the murder weapon, and it'd only been a matter of time before they came back to make an official search of the camp. It would've been nice if someone could've warned him it was happening. He hadn't had time to check in with Mike today, and that was probably why he'd heard nothing about this surprise visit.

Nash and Constable Willow stood talking in low voices to Dale and Mack, as everyone else hovered in an anxious semi-circle around them. Dale probably didn't realize it yet, but Nash and Willow were here to take part in the search, as well. It was part of the job. A shitty part of the job, but a part, nonetheless. Nash could ask to be removed from the case due to his intimate relationships with some of the members of Stormcloud. But he probably thought he was doing his best to protect his friends the chief way he knew how. Finn was surprised that Nash's supervisor hadn't already asked him to step down. Finn didn't know Nash at all, but he guessed the man had fought to stay on the case. It was what he would've done if he'd been in the same situation. Things could change in an instant, however, depending on what this search turned up tonight. Nash could still be pulled. Almost as if the Senior Constable could read his thoughts, he flicked his gaze up to meet Finn's. Hinting at many unspoken emotions in that gaze, Nash quickly looked back to where Dale was pointing out something in the warrant, but Finn could feel the other man's regret and frustration.

"Did you know this was going to happen?" Indy hissed into his ear as she turned accusing eyes on him.

"What? No!" He took her by the hand to lead her away from the others. If she didn't keep her voice down, she was going to blow his cover.

As soon as they were far enough away, hidden by the dark shroud of night, he said, "Sorry, I know this is upsetting. But blaming me for something I have no control over isn't going to help." But more than half of his concentration was on the way Indy hadn't let go of his hand straight away, clinging to it as if for support. Small and warm, work-roughened but fine-boned, her hand sat in his like it'd always meant to be there.

"So, you didn't know the search warrant had been issued?" she asked, pulling his focus back to her.

They were just outside the circle of light cast by the fire, and he could barely make out the contours of her face. She was all soft lines and hidden depths in the muted dimness. His mind took him back to last night when he kissed her. And she'd kissed him back. The feel of her lips beneath his, inviting him in.

"Well, did you?" she demanded.

"No, I didn't." It was the truth. But Indy was still staring up at him, and even in the dark, he could see the confusion and anger on her face. She needed more from him. "But it was only a matter of time before they came back," he sighed. "They need to find that murder weapon." Or some sort of clue, or connection, that might lead them to the murderer. And the stock camp was the only thing they had right now.

She was silent for many long moments. "And what if they do?" Indy eventually whispered. "What if someone in this camp…?" she didn't finish her sentence. Didn't have to. She was finally getting it. And he knew it was a painful conclusion to come to. That someone in this camp could very well be responsible for Wombat's murder. At the very least, were connected to the drugs somehow. Which was exactly what he was trying to uncover.

"Come back to camp," he said gently. They couldn't be seen off whispering together, it'd look highly suspicious. "Do you want me to be with you when they search your tent?" he asked.

She nodded mutely, raising dark eyes to his. He understood how scary this could be to someone who'd never encountered it before. People often felt violated and irritated that someone else could so casually go through their stuff.

Her small hand was still in his as he led her back to the campfire, and for a second, he considered holding onto it. Liked so much how it felt to be connected this way to Indy that he almost let protocol fly out the window. But it wouldn't do for anyone to see how close he and Indy were becoming, so he gently let her go just as they re-entered the veil of light.

* * *

Finn stifled a yawn. It'd been a long night, and now the morning was dragging by as slow as if he were swimming in treacle. He stopped his motorcycle and flicked up his visor to take a drink. The water was lukewarm, but wet, and that was all that mattered. Thankfully, it was nearly lunchtime. A trail of dust rose over the thicket of gum trees in the distance, heralding Bindi's arrival in her Land Cruiser, which would be laden with their midday meal. His stomach rumbled with anticipation. Finn dearly hoped Bindi had also brought her enormous thermos full of coffee, because he needed a mugful badly. Preferably more than one. As did most of the rest of the crew, judging by their tired expressions.

Detective Sampson had come up empty-handed. Apart from a small stash of dope in Dave's bag, which Finn already knew about, but had kept his mouth shut. Because it was for personal use, Dave was only slapped with a stern warning from the detective. Then there was the unregistered handgun found hidden in the cab of Brian's truck and immediately impounded. Which was a little more concerning, but Brian tried to explain it away as needing protection for himself and Rosie as they were on the road so much. It wasn't unusual for country folk to have a firearm stashed somewhere on their property, and a lot of them remained unlicensed. Nash intervened when it looked like the detective was going to become overly officious about the whole thing, and argued that because Wombat's murder hadn't involved a gun, Brian should be let off with a lesser charge. It would still mean an appearance in court, which would most likely end with a fine. Rosie had dissolved in a puddle of near-hysterical tears until Indy and Beth had gone up and comforted her. And no one had made it to bed until well after midnight.

Finn silently thanked the powers that be, that the cops

hadn't discovered the false bottom in his bag, where he stashed his gun and the sat phone. If they had, he would've had no choice but to reveal himself to them all. But at least his identity was still kept between himself and Nash. And Sampson, who'd been let in on the undercover op by Mike. For now. His undercover mission could continue unhindered, as long as the rest of the mustering crew were ignorant of who he was and what he was looking for.

All of this had left Finn feeling both relieved and disappointed. Disappointed, because if they'd managed to uncover the murder weapon, this case might be on the way to being closed. But mostly, he was relieved. Which was weird, because he should want this case to be over, so he could get back to his real life in Sydney. But that'd mean he'd no longer get to see Indy. And he knew he'd miss her, as stupid as that sounded. He'd only met her three days ago. But she'd already wormed her way into his subconscious.

Finn pushed his visor down and put the bike into gear. This helmet was damn hot and sweaty, but at least it kept the dust and the flies away from his face. Heading toward Bindi's car, which was pulling up beneath the shade of two large ironbarks, Finn wondered if he'd be able to eat straight away, or if he'd have to wait. Dale said he'd split the team in half and rotate them through lunch, leaving a skeleton crew to make sure the cattle didn't drift away and scatter while they ate.

He was in luck; Dale called his name for first seating and Finn went forward gratefully to get a plate of food. A nice big slab of quiche and a pile of potato salad were on the menu today. Finn's mouth watered as he eyed the large tray of brownies on the back table. He'd grab one of those on his way out, too.

Chairs had already been set up in a semi-circle in the shade, and he took a seat opposite Indy, who was conversing with Beth over which website was best to buy clothes online. Finn listened as he ate, learning for the first time how hard it was for country women to get the items they needed. It was often the luck of the draw with sizing when you ordered stuff online, and it could sometimes take months for packages to arrive.

"Time to swap," Dale called, just as Finn stuffed the last bite of potato salad into his mouth. He snagged a brownie and bit into it as he made his way to his motorcycle, as the others did the same to their respective steeds. Goddamn, the gooey, chocolate dessert was delicious. His mood picked up, perhaps because of the food, or possibly the two mugs of coffee he'd slammed down.

It was a typical outback Queensland day. Hot—the temperature was probably hovering around thirty degrees Celsius, very dry, with a sky as blue as a cornflower. And flies. Millions of flies. It amazed Finn that they were heading into winter, and it was still as hot as a furnace out here. The top end of Australia didn't have the normal four seasons most other regions had, they merely had the wet and the dry. Winter was dry and slightly cooler, and summer was wet, hotter, and terribly humid by all accounts. He was glad he was experiencing the dry right now; he could just imagine all this fine, red dust turning to ochre mud when it got wet.

Finn trundled along in the lowest gear at the back of the mob with his visor open. There was no urgency for the next twenty minutes, while the other half of the crew ate. The cattle were allowed to drift along at their own pace; all he was here to do was to make sure they didn't go in the wrong direction, or split up. Someone always took point, to lead the cattle. Today, that was Mack. The others were scattered around the mob, one or two at the rear, driving them forward, and at least one person on each flank to make sure they didn't head sideways.

His mind drifted back to his conversation with his boss, Mike, over the sat phone last night. Mike had confirmed he'd heard about the search warrant exactly five minutes before the cops arrived at the camp. He wasn't happy, and Finn could imagine the earful Detective Sampson would've received once he made it back to his office that morning. Finn reported everything he knew about what they'd found during the raid.

Mike had at least given him one scrap of good news. After going over Wombat's impounded truck with a fine-toothed comb, the police in Cairns had found two likely spots where drugs could be hidden beneath the chassis of the truck. A fake spare tailpipe had been welded on at the rear. And a rusty old lockbox had been inserted into a void next to a rear tire. This was good, as it proved their theory that the gang were using the cattle trucks to transport their ill-gotten wares. The interesting news was that a small stash of methamphetamines had been found in the second hiding place. But it wasn't anywhere close to the huge quantities of drugs this gang was shipping. This news merely deepened the mystery. What'd happened to the rest of the drugs, if they'd even been there to start with? Did it confirm what Finn already thought, that Wombat had perhaps been skimming off the top? Selling some of the drugs on the side to bolster his wages? Was that why he'd been murdered?

Just as Finn had been ready to end the call, Mike had said, "Oh, by the way, Griff."

"Yeah, Sarge?" Finn had stiffened, hearing the underlying tension enter his boss's voice.

"I've heard more chatter. The rumors are getting harder to ignore. Garrett may be more involved in this than we first thought."

Fuck. Finn forced down the ball of anxiety that formed in his gut. This wasn't what he needed to hear, right now.

Mike's voice was devoid of emotion as he said, "You already know I'm unhappy with you working on a case where your brother might be associated. If these rumors are proven to be true, I might have to pull you."

Shit. That was exactly what Finn was afraid of.

"Right. Thanks for the info, Sarge." Finn had ended the call, not needing to hear the rest of it. Mike knew about his brother's connections to the underworld. Finn had revealed his brother's history when he'd first made detective, knowing that keeping a secret like that could jeopardize his job. When Garrett's name had been flagged regarding the international drug syndicate they were investigating, Mike had been upfront with Finn, telling him that working this case may well be a conflict of interest. But the rumors were yet to be confirmed, so Mike had let it slide. For now.

Finn turned and landed his fist in the nearest tree trunk. Fuck.

His mother always lamented that he and Garrett had turned out so differently, taken such divergent paths in life, especially after they'd been inseparable in their younger years. It'd all started when their father had died. Both brothers had reacted differently in their grief. Finn had vowed to take up the mantle of his father's memory and do something good with his life, something where he could be of service to others. Garrett had taken his grief and allowed it to swallow him up, take him to a dark place, where he mixed with the wrong crowd and used drugs and alcohol to drown his feelings. Finn had never told their mother all that he knew about Garrett. She was still blissfully unaware that one of her sons was deep into dealing drugs and criminal activities. So far, Garrett had been able to avoid getting caught, so he could continue the lie to their mother that he worked as a courier and led a normal life. She knew her two sons were no longer close, and she brought up that fact every time she saw Finn.

But he kept the exact details of how deep their estrangement truly ran from her. Little did she know that her two sons were on completely opposite sides of the law. And in the end, only one of them would emerge victorious.

Finn hadn't seen his brother in nearly four years. He'd come to visit when Kayleigh was born, holding out a present as he stood in the doorway, a hesitant grin on his face. There was no way Finn was letting Garrett anywhere near his new-born baby, and he'd told Garrett to keep the proffered present wrapped in pink tissue paper, because it would only end up in the rubbish bin. Finn had made it crystal clear he wasn't welcome at their house and Garrett had left, striding down their front path, his face set in stony hostility, the look in his eyes one of murderous intent. In hindsight, perhaps Finn should've taken the proffered olive branch. For his mother's sake, more than his own. But it was too late for that now. Even if that swift expression of hurt and utter betrayal that'd flashed across his brother's face when Finn told him to keep the present, kept replaying in his mind. His brother had made his choices. And so had Finn.

Lost in his own world of what to do about his brother, he was startled when a horse suddenly appeared in his peripheral vision. He hadn't been paying attention.

"Hello," Indy said.

"Hiya," he replied, gaze traveling the length of her legs, up her jean-clad thighs to where her hand rested easily on the pommel. Her eyes were directed forward at the cattle, and he sketched the profile of her cute, ski-jump nose and high cheekbones. He'd spent the best part of half an hour with Indy last night, standing next to her as the police searched her tent, lending his moral support. She'd watched with wary eyes as they pulled her camp bed apart and searched through her large duffle bag containing all her clothes. Both her dogs had growled and snapped at the intrusion, and Indy had a hard time calming them. Detective Sampson gave the dogs a wide berth but ordered one of his other officers to search the area around the animal's bedding. Which was a smart decision. If Finn had wanted to hide something, that'd be the first place he'd do it. No one was going to approach those dogs without Indy knowing about it. But the inspection team came up with nothing. Even though it was exactly what Finn had been expecting, he was still relieved.

"How are you doing today?" He meant, was she still rattled by last night's raid?

But she surprised him by asking something on a completely different tangent. "I want to know about your complicated marriage."

It took him a few seconds to get his head around her request.

"You said it was complicated. But I didn't give you a chance to explain. So, I'd like to know now. Tell me why I shouldn't feel terribly guilty that I kissed a married man," she said, refusing to meet his gaze.

"Oh. Right." He wondered if she'd been stewing on this question all day. Where to start with the mess that was him and Chloe? If he was going to tell her the truth, then she needed to know all of it. "Let me show you something." He stopped his bike and pulled out his cell phone. Flicking through his photos, he came to the one he wanted and handed it up to Indy, watching her face closely for her reaction.

"Oh, God. You have a daughter?" she asked faintly. "That just makes it ten times worse," she groaned, handing his phone back, and gathering her reins as if to ride off.

"Wait, Indy," he commanded. "You said you wanted an explanation. So, you have to stay to hear the full story."

She cast him such a wounded look that Finn wondered if he'd done the right thing by showing her the photo of

Kayleigh. But it had to be done. If she wanted the truth, then the truth was, he had a daughter. A beautiful, vibrant, funny, four-year-old daughter.

"Fine," she said stiffly. "But let's keep up with the cattle." She whistled her two dogs up, telling them to stay at the rear, but keep the cattle moving forward. The dogs could practically do Finn and Indy's jobs for them; they were that good.

The mob had drifted away, and Finn put his bike back into gear, so that he trundled alongside Indy on her horse. For the first time, he felt at a slight disadvantage on the motorcycle. Indy was a good three or four feet taller than him on Gypsy, and he had to turn his head up to see her face and gauge her reactions.

"Chloe and I got married seven years ago. She was three years younger than me, but at the time, that age gap didn't seem to matter." He'd been twenty-four, and she was only twenty-one. Young, ambitious, and full of life's possibilities. "She was traveling around Australia on a gap year, when we met in a bar in Sydney. She told me she was from Ireland, and we hit it off straight away, because I was also born in Ireland."

"You were?" she asked, pursing her lips and staring down at him, as if reassessing everything she knew about him.

"Yes. My family moved to Sydney from Dublin when I was two, so I don't really remember much. But I like to stay in touch with my heritage. So, when I met Chloe, I was drawn to her…Irishness, if you like."

Indy nodded for him to continue.

"Chloe stayed in Australia, and we got married a year later." It was a typical love story. Boy meets girl, boy falls in love with girl, girl gives up her dreams and marries boy because they are so right for each other. "But she always missed Ireland and her family. Family is a big thing to most

Irish people. And Chloe came from a large one, with two brothers and three sisters."

"Gosh," Indy gave a low whistle.

Finn shrugged. Six siblings weren't unusual in an Irish Family. Add in all the aunts, uncles, and cousins, and it quickly became almost too big to keep count.

"Don't you have any brothers or sisters?" he asked, interest piqued by her obvious surprise at the size of Chloe's family.

"No." She shook her head, casting him a slightly belligerent glance as if to say, *and so what if I don't?* "And before you ask, both my parents are dead, too. But we're not talking about my family. We're talking about yours. So, please, go on."

She was an only child. And had no family to speak of. Finn was shocked. He learned something new about this woman every day. That she was tough and independent. And perhaps a little alone. He had a brother and a younger sister of his own, and couldn't imagine growing up as an only child. He filed it all away for further contemplation, this was a big thing, her not having any family to speak of, but he went on with his story.

"We visited Ireland twice after we were married, and Chloe went back once on her own. Then she got pregnant, and she became..." How did Finn explain this? "She really started to miss her home." It hurt that she still called Ireland home. "She never really accepted Australia. And after Kayleigh was born, all she wanted was her mother to help her out with the baby." Finn believed Chloe had undiagnosed post-natal depression, but she put it down to homesickness, and maybe the two things were interwoven.

"Wait a second." Indy kicked Gypsy into a trot and rode a wide arc out to the right, to head off two heifers who had wandered too far from the main group. Barbie and Digger were still quietly doing the jobs they'd been bred to do at the rear of the mob, tongues hanging out, their faces bright with happiness. A few minutes later, she was back by his side and he picked up where he'd left off.

"Chloe's mother came to Sydney after Kayleigh's birth, and she stayed for over four months. But she couldn't stay forever, and eventually, she had to go back to Ireland." Finn remembered the months after Chloe's mother had left. Chloe had slowly withdrawn into herself. She cared for Kayleigh, but it seemed their daughter was the only thing keeping her anchored to this world. Their relationship deteriorated. Finn tried hard to understand how she was feeling. But he also spent long hours at work, building up a fledgling career, heading toward becoming a detective.

"It sounds like your wife wasn't coping too well." Indy gave him a sympathetic glance.

"No, she wasn't," he agreed. "She begged me to let her go back to Ireland for six months, just while Kayleigh was still young, so she could have her family's support." Finn remembered the night he'd finally given into Chloe's request. She'd been hysterical, screaming that she was a bad mother and a bad wife, and the world would be better off without her. It was at that moment he'd finally understood the depth of her depression. He'd had no choice. Chloe was on an airplane two days later, with their nine-month-old daughter bundled in front of her.

"I let her go. We both thought it would be for a few months, no more." But Chloe never came home. The excuses kept coming, until she ran out of excuses and begged him to move to Ireland, instead.

"I'm guessing she stayed." Indy's voice was so quiet, Finn hardly heard her over the bawling cattle.

"Yes. I flew over two years ago, so we could try to work it out. But…" He shrugged. He loved his daughter like nothing else, but his life was in Australia. And for Chloe and his daughter, it seemed like their life was in Ireland. It was a twisted mess, one that Finn couldn't see a clear path out of.

"I haven't been back since."

Indy gasped. "You mean you haven't seen your daughter for two years?" she asked, dismay etched into her dark eyes.

"No," he didn't try and keep the sadness out of his voice. "I talk to her over the phone, and over Skype. And Chloe sends me pictures, of course."

"Oh, Finn, I'm so sorry." Indy looked like she might lean down from her saddle to touch his shoulder, but the crackle of the two-way radio broke their preoccupation.

"Hey, you two, stop jawboning and get those cattle over there." It was Mack, calling them on the UHF from his position up at point.

"Shit," Indy hissed, and she and Gypsy were off like a rocket after a group of four young bulls, trying to make a break for it.

"Shit." Finn echoed her sentiment, because he hadn't got to tell her the most important part. That Chloe had filed for divorce three months ago. The papers were still sitting on his desk at home, waiting to be signed.

CHAPTER EIGHT

Indy stared at her phone, willing the messages from Patrick to disappear. No such luck. They stared back at her, his words swirling together to form a tangle of black and white on her screen. She hadn't replied to any of them. The other night, up on the hill, she'd been too distraught, and other complications, such as the nighttime police search, had kept her preoccupied for the past few days. She sighed and glanced over at the main camp, where people were beginning to assemble, ready to relax after their long day in the saddle. Dinner was probably still an hour away, but Bindi had some cheese and crackers out for a snack. Indy had walked over to stand beside the little van Bindi used to cook in so she could examine her phone and think about what she wanted to say to Patrick.

What she should do, was ride back up that hill right now and fire off a message to Patrick to tell him it was well and truly over, and to leave her the hell alone. That she didn't care if Sheila had left him, and he deserved to be alone and lonely. But it all felt too hard. She knew she would never go back to him. But…

She needed to think about something else for a while, before she let that prick overwhelm her thoughts.

The second thing top of her mind right now was Finn's revelations about his wife and daughter, and that was just as much of a convoluted mess as her own life seemed to be.

He had a child. A little daughter. And she was so cute. When he'd showed her that picture, the knowledge had hit like a punch to the solar plexus. Why were all men so full of treachery? Not only was he married, but he had a kid. A responsibility. It complicated things even more. At least Patrick didn't have any children. All Indy had wanted to do when she'd seen that photo was to ride away from Finn and never look at him again. Not let the pain of his betrayal show on her face.

But then Finn had opened up about his marriage to Chloe. How they'd lived separate lives for nearly three years. It didn't sound like Chloe was coming back to Australia. And Finn had said his life was here. So where exactly did that leave their marriage? She didn't think Finn knew the answer to that. She was glad she'd listened, and glad she knew the truth now. But it didn't help disentangle her feelings for him. In fact, it just made them worse. She liked Finn. She had to admit she was deeply attracted to him. But neither of those reasons was good enough to get involved with a man and his complicated life. If she even wanted to get involved with another man. After her ordeal with Patrick, she needed something simple and carefree. The exact opposite to Finn Stevenson. Or should she call him Griff Carmody? Even knowing what to call him was confusing.

A couple of crows landed in the branches above her, cawing loudly, as if having an argument. Indy sighed and tried to ignore them. Even though Dale was vigilant about keeping this camp's garbage well sealed, the black birds had seemed to grow in numbers over the past few days.

She turned her phone over in her hands and tried to decide if right now was a good time to ride up the hill and end this thing with Patrick. She had the time before dinner. She should just do it. Get it over with.

The cawing from the group above her became louder and so annoying she looked up. Some sort of crow dispute was going on up there. She could see half a dozen of them now, as she squinted into the tree, hopping from branch to branch. They all seemed to be chasing one particular crow, who had something in its beak. And they all wanted a part of whatever the first crow had.

Anger and frustration got the better of her. All she wanted was a few peaceful minutes to mull over her problems, and these birds wouldn't leave her alone. Indy bent down and picked up a small stone.

Throwing it high into the branches, she yelled, "Scram!"

The birds flew up in a cacophony of angry cries. But as they went, something dropped to the ground at Indy's feet.

She took a step backward. "Ew." What was that? Bending down to get a closer look, she recoiled in shock. Oh, shit. Was that really what she thought it was?

"Finn, Dale, get over here. Now!" she called. Not letting her gaze leave the thing lying in the dust, she called out again. "Finn. Anybody? Come and look at this." Her voice rose to a tremulous squeak.

She lifted her gaze long enough to see Finn get up from his chair around the campfire and stride toward her.

"Look," she said, pointing at the thing, her mouth twisted with revulsion. "Is that…is that what I think it is?"

Finn hunkered down on his haunches and picked up a stick, poking carefully at the glob of fleshy substance lying in the dust.

"Fuck." The curse was so quiet, Indy almost missed it.

Dale appeared at her shoulder and peered down. "What's going on?" he asked. "Oh, holy shit. Is that…?" Dale reared back in a similar reaction to Indy's when she'd first seen it.

"I'm afraid so," Finn replied calmly. "It's a human eyeball."

"Are you sure?" Indy wanted him to be wrong. "I mean, it could be from a cow, or a... I don't know, a kangaroo, maybe?"

"Nope. I'm pretty sure it's human." Finn stopped prodding the eyeball. "Where did it come from?" he asked, turning to look up at Indy.

"A crow dropped it." As soon as she said the words, she knew how crazy they sounded. "It's true," she said, rounding on Dale with beseeching eyes. "I was just leaning against this tree and the crows were fighting over something, so I threw a rock at them, and this landed on the ground." She couldn't help the way her mouth twisted with distaste.

"If it really is human, then where did it come from?" Dale asked the question that was hovering on all their lips.

A few of the crew began to wander over, wondering what all the commotion was about.

"You'd better keep them away," Finn said to Dale. "This might be another crime scene. We don't want people messing with it."

"What?" Dale blinked and looked up, as if trying to clear the image of the eyeball, all gory and covered in dust, out of his mind. "Oh, yeah, right." Dale turned to the approaching crowd and waved them all back. "Go back to the camp, guys. I'll fill you in soon."

Indy stood as if rooted to the spot while Finn took over, yet again. This was becoming an all-too-common occurrence. She shook herself and tried to get her mind into gear.

"I'll go call Nash on the sat phone," she said decisively. "But I'm not sure he's gonna believe me," she added, taking one more look at the human organ lying on the ground. She shivered. Where the hell could that have come from?

She met Finn's gaze, and it was as if he read her mind. He looked up into the sky to where the flock of crows was still circling. As if on cue, the birds took off, winging their way toward the repeater hill. Narrowing his eyes, he watched them disappear into the late afternoon sun.

"I think we need to find out where those crows are going."

Dale looked at him sharply. "What do you mean?"

"Crows are carrion birds, aren't they?" Finn asked.

"Yes. They're renowned for eating roadkill or dead cattle. Anything they can get their disgusting little beaks into." Dale shuddered.

"Well, maybe they found a different type of carrion." Finn stood and put his hands on his hips, still watching the birds, which were fast turning into little black dots on the horizon.

Indy turned to follow his gaze. Could there really be a dead person out there somewhere? Another dead body? What were the chances? Then she turned to stare at Finn. A lot of things she'd never thought possible had happened in the past few days. And if Finn were here to uncover a clandestine drug ring, then perhaps anything was possible.

"I want to go after those birds," Finn said.

"I'm coming with you," Indy shot back.

"Wait." Dale held a hand up. "Exactly what do you think you're going to find?"

"I don't know," Finn replied. "But we've only got around an hour of sunlight left, so I say we need to get going fast, whatever we do." He stared at Dale, waiting for an answer. Indy could see how agitated Finn was, but if he were to keep his undercover persona intact, he had to defer to Dale, who was supposedly his boss. If only Dale knew the truth. "It'll be well after dark by the time the cops get here. They won't be able to do anything until morning," he prompted, when Dale still didn't answer.

Dale's broad shoulders seemed to straighten as he came to a decision. "Righto. I want Mack to go with you. Take a sat phone and UHF radios. And if you haven't found anything by nightfall, I want you back here. Agreed?"

"Agreed," Finn and Indy said in unison.

Finn sprinted toward the fire to tell Mack what was up, and Indy headed for the mess tent and the sat phone to call Nash. Less than five minutes later, they were on their way, the rest of the muster crew staring after them in bewilderment. Dale would fill them in soon enough. He was still standing guard over the eyeball, making sure nothing or no-one touched it before Nash got there.

Finn had wanted to take his motorcycle, but when both Mack and Indy insisted the horses would be better over the rough terrain, he'd conceded and saddled up Sahara. Indy had tossed up whether to take her dogs, but had left them tied to their kennels. They might help them sniff out whatever it was they were looking for, but she wasn't sure what they'd find out there, and instinct told her to leave them safely tied up. The trio followed the trajectory the birds had taken, and in less than fifteen minutes, they'd crested the low saddle of the hill over a small rise. Finn reined in Sahara and they all stopped to stare at the country opening up on the other side of the hill below. Squinting into the distance, Indy let her gaze drift over the dry countryside, not sure exactly what they were looking for. The floodplain was very similar on this side as it was on the camp side. Open country, dotted with the odd bottle tree, interspersed with clumps of acacia, and stands of gum trees. The last swathes of grass, brown and desiccated, ran in patchworks around the trees and followed ravines and other low contours in the gravelly ground.

"Over there." She extended her arm to point at a haze of birds circling in the air around a mile away, over the top of a line of trees that was perhaps following an empty water course.

Both men turned to stare in that direction.

"What do you think it is?" she asked.

"I don't know," Mack replied. "But I guess we're about to find out."

She slotted Gypsy in between Mack, who took the lead, and Finn in the rear. A shiver of unease slid down her spine. No one said a thing as their horses jogged toward the birds still circling in the sky. The light was failing now, as the sun sank over the horizon and dusk descended. Indy figured they only had about half an hour of light left. Suddenly, she didn't want to be out here after dark.

The horses ate up the distance, and within fifteen minutes, the tree line came into view just ahead. Most of the crows had either settled into the branches of the trees or were hopping around on the ground. As they got closer, Indy could see a rudimentary camp of some sort, set up in the low creek bed, almost hidden from view until you were directly upon it. There was a camouflage tarp strung between two tree trunks, some overturned chairs, and a small table. It could be hunters; they sometimes came out here to shoot roos and dingoes. It was deathly quiet, as if the camp were deserted.

"What is this?" she asked, then reined in Gypsy sharply when Finn raised a finger to his lips.

She clamped her mouth shut and watched mutely as Finn slid silently from his saddle and handed her his reins. Then he was slipping, wraithlike, between the trees, creeping toward the camp. Indy wanted to call out to him, tell him it wasn't safe. She had a bad feeling about this and wished they'd waited for Nash and his backup to arrive.

Mack dismounted and motioned for Indy to do the same. "I'm going in," he whispered. "I want you to stay here and guard the horses."

She shook her head emphatically. If they could go in, then so could she. But it seemed the horses could feel the unwholesome aura that hung over this camp, and Gypsy whickered nervously. She lay a hand on her horse's neck to calm her.

"I need you to keep the horses quiet and calm until we know what's going on," Mack said quietly, looking her straight in the eye. Indy wasn't happy about being left alone, but she nodded once, then watched Mack step stealthily through the bushes, heading in a different direction than the one Finn had taken.

Surrounded by the horses, Indy spent the next excruciating minutes listening and watching for any sign of movement. She spoke quietly to Picasso when he shifted nervously from foot to foot, and Sahara, whose ears flickered back and forward anxiously. What the hell was going on? Why was it taking so long?

She'd just determined that she was going to tie the horses to the nearest tree and go and find out what was going on, when Finn appeared from behind an acacia tree.

"Shit, Finn, you scared the daylights out of me." Her hand had gone to cover her heart in an unconscious move. "What did you find? Is anyone there?"

Finn's face was grim. He walked right up to her and lay a hand on her arm. "Yeah. We found out what was attracting the crows." He made a grimace of distaste. "But it's not pretty. You probably don't want to see this. There's been another murder." His fingers squeezed her arm, conveying his discomposure more than his facial expressions ever could. He was trying to protect her from whatever it was they'd found. Touching as it was, his concern was unwarranted. After seeing Wombat's mutilated body, she thought she was immune to just about anything.

"Thanks for trying to spare me the details, Finn, but I'm not staying out here." Whatever was in that camp might be bad, but the not knowing was worse. Besides, she was too freaked out to stay here by herself any longer.

"Come on in, then," he said with a sigh. "But don't say I

didn't warn you." Finn took Sahara's reins and Indy followed him to the perimeter of the primitive campsite with the other two horses. They tied their animals to a low branch and Finn took Indy by the hand to lead her around the edge of the camp, to where Mack was talking quietly into the sat phone. She heard him give their coordinates; he must be relaying what they'd found to Dale. It took her a moment to understand that Finn had taken her hand as much to keep her out of the crime scene, as to offer her comfort.

That's when she saw him. The dead guy. She put her hand to her nose. The smell was indescribable.

Oh, God. Finn had been right. If anything, this was worse than seeing Wombat's butchered body.

This man had clearly been dead for days, and the crows and other wildlife had gone to town on him, feasting on his body as if it were indeed any other bit of carrion.

His face was almost unrecognizable. Her stomach heaved, and she had to fight down the urge to be sick.

"Oh, that's..." She turned her face into Finn's shoulder, trying to block out the sight. "How are they even going to identify...him?" she asked, voice muffled slightly by Finn's shirt.

"Dental records, probably," he answered matter-of-factly, never taking his eyes from the scene in front of them.

Indy steeled herself and turned her face to survey the remains of the campsite. It looked as if there'd been a fight, the single table had been turned over, scattering pots and pans and items of food on the ground. Two folding chairs were also tipped on edge. There was no campfire; they'd obviously used a gas cooker.

"Do you think this is related to Wombat's murder?" she asked the obvious question.

"It's a definite possibility," Finn conceded. "The camp was set up to stay hidden. No campfire. They obviously didn't want to alert anyone to their presence by smoke. I haven't been near the shelter, but from here it looks like there was room for more than one. Add that to the pair of chairs, mugs, and crockery and it looks like two people were camping here for some days before…" Finn pointed to the body.

"So where is the other guy?" she asked, casting her gaze warily around the camp. Was the guy who'd killed this man the same one who killed Wombat? And was he still lurking around, waiting for his next victim?

"That's the million-dollar question," he replied. "We need to stay alert, just in case."

Yeah, she'd already figured that one out on her own. Indy moved closer to Finn's reassuring presence.

CHAPTER NINE

Finn gritted his teeth and tried not to yell at the young Constable Willow. The guy wasn't being nearly as careful as Finn would've liked as he stood guard inside the camp. He was supposed to be preserving the scene, stopping other people from entering, but every footprint he left behind, everything he touched, had potentially contaminated the site. This wasn't Finn's crime scene, however, and he couldn't say anything in front of all these people.

It was nearly the middle of the night, but the place was lit up like Grand Central Station. Portable floodlights had been stationed in all four corners overlooking the camp, the loud hum of their generators making it hard to talk in a normal tone. The site was inundated by police from all divisions and units. The same team from forensics was back, as well as the homicide boys, and some big brass Sergeant from the Cairns station, along with no less than two junior cops, who were getting their first look at a proper full-on murder scene, plus the other two who'd carried out the warrant to search the other night. Detective Sampson had returned, this time flanked by another, slightly older female detective sergeant named Coldwater. Looked like the top brass no longer trusted Sampson to handle this on his own. They were talking to Mack and Dale over on the opposite side of the camp. Finn idly wondered how many cops it took to process one crime scene.

His gaze searched for Indy until he found her, standing, pale and drawn, next to the horses. It'd been a long night. It was time to take her home. Wait. He stopped that overprotective thought in its tracks. Indy was a strong, independent woman. Just because he was getting close to her, because she was getting under his skin, didn't mean she was his to protect. He readjusted his thoughts. It was time for them *all* to head back to the stock camp. All three of them had spent the night telling the same story to what felt like ten different cops about how the crows had led them to come looking for the camp. At least Nash and his offsider, Willow, had been the first to arrive, and Finn hurriedly filled him in with everything he suspected about this illicit camp. He trusted Nash not to tell anyone who wasn't already in the know about Finn's true role here.

He still needed to update the sarge, and his sat phone was back in his tent. Undoubtedly, his boss would've heard rumors of what was going on out here through the grapevine already, but he needed to give him the finer details, so Mike could negotiate *again*, to keep Finn's undercover persona a secret, as well as work with the team to find out what they knew. And he needed to decide whether to tell Mike what he'd found inside the shelter. It was incriminating evidence, but he might be the only person who understood its relevance.

"Senior Constable," Finn said, beckoning Nash away from where he was staring intently down at one of the forensics team, who was carefully peeling back a section of the corpse's clothing to reveal the bloated, blotchy skin on his chest.

Nash stepped gingerly over to where Finn was standing. "Are we free to leave, sir?" he asked, deferring to Nash, just in case anyone was watching.

"Yes. As far as I'm concerned, I've got everything I need," he said, blue eyes meeting Finn's with a steady gaze. "You'll have to check with Sampson, though. He's running the show. At the moment," Nash added. They both understood that Detective Sergeant Coldwater was hovering over Sampson, watching his every move, ready to swoop in and take the investigation away from him at the slightest wrong step. Finn felt sorry for Sampson, but decided he couldn't really blame his superior. A single murder investigation had blown up into a complicated case, with multiple victims and a possible link to an international drug syndicate, and perhaps it was above the level of what Sampson was capable of handling.

"I still can't believe a crow tipped you off," Nash said with a quiet laugh. "And if a country cop like me is finding that hard to swallow, you can bet those city boys are downright disbelieving."

Finn shrugged and gave a wry smile. "We've got plenty of witnesses that'll tell them the same story," Finn replied, referring to the rest of the muster crew who'd seen the eyeball lying in the dust. "Things happen a little different in the outback," he joked.

"I'm sure I'll be seeing more of you over the next few days," Nash said. Then he narrowed his eyes slightly and lowered his voice. "This thing gets more interesting by the day. I wouldn't mind a quiet chat sometime. Off the record."

Finn raised his eyebrows, but said nothing more. He wondered if Nash knew something he wasn't letting on to the rest of his peers. Either that, or he had questions that only Finn could answer.

Five minutes later, after checking with Sampson that they were free to leave, he and Indy mounted up. Indy would lead Mack's horse Picasso back to camp, and Mack would catch a ride home with Dale. When they might make it home was anyone's guess. Now that the police had finished questioning them, Finn thought Dale might be staying on as much to find out anything more he could about the case, as to appear helpful. Sampson and the other cops were trained to remain tight-lipped, but just by hanging around the camp and listening in to the forensics guy's comments, telling Sampson or homicide what they'd found on the body so far would give away hints. On how this guy died. And who killed him.

"Are they any closer to identifying the body?" Indy asked, once they'd moved away from the floodlit river bed. Darkness engulfed them as soon as they left the bubble of light, and he lifted his head to get his bearings. There was the outline of what he'd nicknamed Repeater Hill directly in front, and there was the low saddle they'd crossed through earlier. A full moon was slowly rising in the dark sky, and while the bush looked different at night, he didn't think they'd have any problem finding their way home.

Finn shook his head by way of an answer to Indy's question. Like he'd said before, they'd probably need dental records to confirm absolutely who this guy was. They sure as hell wouldn't be relying on any facial recognition; the man's face was practically eaten off. Finn shuddered, as he remembered and then tried to rid himself of the image. When he'd first arrived on the scene, it was clear the man was dead; had been dead for at least a couple of days. But protocol dictated he check for signs of life. So, he'd leaned in to try and find a pulse. He'd gone for the wrist instead of the carotid artery, as it seemed some large carnivore, perhaps a dingo, had lunched on the man's neck.

"There was no ID on the guy. I checked his pockets before Nash got here," he revealed. Finn had even gone so far as gingerly rolling the corpse over using a stick to see if there was anything in the back pocket of his jeans. He knew he was contaminating the crime scene by doing so, but he needed any information about this man he could get. Just in case homicide was slow to pass on any clues. He needed to be on top of every small detail. If this man was linked to Wombat's murder, and to the drug shipments—as Finn suspected that he was—and they worked out his identity, it might lead them to someone farther up the chain of command.

"Even if they did know who he was, they need to alert the next of kin first. It'll be days until we find out a name," he replied with a sigh.

"Yeah, that might be true for normal people," she countered. "But, surely, with your connections...?" She let the question hang in the air.

"We're certainly doing the best we can to find out," he told her. "But I'm more worried about who the other guy in that camp was," he mused. "And where he might've gone."

"You mean whoever murdered the guy on the ground?"

Shit, he hadn't really meant to say all that out loud. He didn't want Indy to worry unnecessarily. "We can't jump to conclusions," he said hurriedly. "Just because we think there was someone else there, they could've been an innocent bystander. Or they could've been attacked themselves and fled, leaving the other guy to take the brunt of the assault."

"Oh, right. I didn't think of it that way," she mused, her voice the only sound beside their horse's soft hoofbeats in the dark night. "But if the missing man *is* the killer, surely he's long gone by now? It's been days since that guy was murdered."

That was the assumption all the other cops were under. But Finn wasn't quite so sure.

Indy watched his face, and as if she caught his sudden hesitation, she said, "Are we safe out here? That missing man isn't still around, is he?" She suddenly sat up straighter in her saddle, casting an uneasy glance at the surrounding bush, pushing Gypsy a little closer to his horse.

"You're with me," he said, puffing out his chest, and thumping it, Tarzan style, in an attempt to make light of the situation. "Of course, you're safe." He reached across and grabbed her hand, squeezing it gently.

Her nervous expression morphed into one of cynical amusement. "Yeah, right, you're my hero," she said, but squeezed his hand back for a second before letting it go. The touch was fleeting, but her warm hand left an impression on him long after it was gone. Her eyes flashed in the moonlight and for some strange reason, he suddenly wished he really could be her hero. He wanted to reassure her. Tell her he'd protect her no matter what. The stupid thing was, there was a deep, kind of growly voice he'd never heard before in his head, telling him to get her out of here. Get her away from this camp and whatever kind of danger lurked behind every tree. He had no right to tell her what to do. And his gut had no right to demand he shield her, because she wasn't his to safeguard, no matter how much that voice kept telling him she was. There was no way she'd want to hear any of the macho bullshit that was circling around in his gut at the moment, and so he clamped his mouth shut.

But she may well be correct to be worried. Finn glanced down at the small leather pouch he'd attached to the back of his saddle. Everyone assumed it contained a water bottle, when, in fact, he'd stashed his handgun in there. There was no way he was going out into the bush to investigate the source of a human eyeball without some kind of insurance. At least he was confident he could keep Indy safe, if anything…untoward happened.

"Maybe I should've brought the dogs, after all," she murmured.

"No, you made the right decision not to bring them," he replied, shuddering at the thought that Digger might've found the body first and run around the camp willy nilly, destroying footprints and other evidence, perhaps even snacking on the corpse.

"Are the two murders connected? I mean, was it the same person who killed Wombat and this guy?"

"Not sure about either of those questions. Once the coroner comes back with a definitive time of death, that'll help us figure out if he was killed on the same night as Wombat." Which would make the coincidence too big to ignore.

"It sure looked like he'd been there a while. At least two or three days, which would be the right timeframe," she said, not wanting to drop the subject.

"Yep," Finn agreed, but he wasn't going to speculate any further. There were too many variables. Too many inconsistencies. The dead guy in the camp looked like he'd been beaten to death. Or perhaps strangled, but it was hard to tell with all the post-mortem wounds, and that was up to the coroner to determine. One thing was for sure, he hadn't been hacked to death by a machete or some other type of long knife, like Wombat. Now, if the murder weapon used on Wombat turned up in that clandestine camp, then that may be another thing altogether. But in Finn's hasty assessment of the camp, nothing had shown up.

Then there were the tire tracks a little farther down the dry creek bed. To Finn's assessing gaze, they looked to belong to some kind of long-wheel-based, four-wheel-drive. The fact it was no longer there also pointed to the fact the other man had fled. But if he had been the murderer, why had he not tried to cover his tracks? Left the body and everything exactly as it was, almost as if they wanted it to be found. Was this another warning? And if it was, who was it meant for?

They rode the rest of the way in relative silence, both brooding in their own little worlds. When they arrived back at camp, they worked side by side to bed down the horses, and then walked toward the silent camp. Everyone else had turned in for the night, tired of waiting for them to return. He walked Indy to her tent.

"I'm fine now," she protested quietly. But he shrugged and gave her a smile. Call him old-fashioned, but he wanted to make sure she made it safely to her home.

"Shh," she shushed her excited dogs, who were leaping at the ends of their ropes in greeting. Finn waited while she patted each dog in turn and made sure their water bowls were full. Then ghosted in her wake as she crossed to stand in front of her lodgings. It wasn't large, an old canvas-style tent probably dug out of the Stormcloud storage for this yearly event. It was big enough for her to stand up in, and as she swung open the flap and turned on a small light inside, he glimpsed a camp bed in one corner, with a folding table beside it, and a large duffle bag at the end, all neat and squared away, the same as the night he'd watched with her as the police had carried out their search warrant. Not as big as the marquee he shared with Dave and Carrot, and somehow more homey than their all-male territory.

"Thanks," she whispered, removing her hat and turning around to face him. "I'm safe now, you can go." She gave him a smile and then tipped her head toward the sky to look at the stars. Her skin glowed in the moonlight, high cheekbones and aquiline nose silhouetted against the heavens. His heart jolted in his chest, and his cock stirred. She was the most beautiful thing he'd seen all day. All week. All year. She was so close, he could almost breathe in her scent.

He wanted to reach out and take her in his arms, just like he'd done up on the hill the other evening. But he had no excuse this time.

"Indy, I..." He what? What could he say to this woman who captivated him like no other? He had a job to do here, and it didn't involve getting attached to this woman, whom he hardly knew. The lines between his job and his reality were blurring. The lines between him and Indy were blurring. He reached out and cupped the curve of her cheek with his hand. A feather-soft touch. After a second's hesitation, she leaned into his palm, closing her eyes momentarily, as if she enjoyed the feeling. When she opened her eyes, their gazes locked, time standing still for those precious seconds.

The unspoken words lay between them, like a veil.

She searched his eyes for an answer. Even though he'd started this, he knew he needed to be the one to stop it, before it went any farther. With a great effort of will, he removed his hand from her face. His work wasn't finished tonight. He still needed to report to Mike. Needed to get his weapon safely back into its hiding spot. He needed to figure out who this goddamned killer was.

He said the only thing he could decently say to her, that wouldn't lead him to take her lips with his; that wouldn't lead him into her tent. "I need to know you're okay before I go. Tonight was..." Shocking, harrowing, all those other adjectives. But Indy seemed to have come out of it relatively unscathed. He wanted her to know that he was there for her. "If you want to talk about it, don't hesitate to come to me." He wanted to add that he'd be happy to sleep in her tent, if she needed it. To keep the nightmares at bay, if they came. And to give himself peace of mind. But that would lead to temptation he wasn't sure he was strong enough to withstand.

The glow in her eyes cooled, and she took a step back. "Thanks, Finn. I'm sure I'll have lots of questions tomorrow. But I can see you have things you need to do." She was withdrawing, exactly as he wanted, but his gut twisted in reaction. Her gravitational pull was so strong, he nearly reached out for her again.

"I just want you to know you can talk to me about

anything. Okay?" he said softly instead.

"Okay. Goodnight, Finn." She stepped back and let the flap fall, blocking her from view.

Shit. He hadn't handled that well. Standing outside Indy's tent, he debated what to do. His heart told him to walk straight in there and kiss her, wash away the uncertainty and fear in her eyes. Replace it with the inevitability that they should be together. At least for tonight. But his head was clamoring with all the practical things he needed to do tonight.

Finally, he stepped away from her tent and stalked into the darkness.

It took him only a few minutes to sneak into his shared tent to replace his weapon in its hidey-hole and retrieve his sat phone. Dave snored away, oblivious; that man would sleep through an earthquake. Carrot turned over and muttered something, making Finn freeze in place for a few seconds, until the man's breathing became deep and sedate once more.

As he made his way out into the bush, weaving his way through the ghostly tree-trunks, he was surprised to find the night was full of animal noises and movement. Insects buzzed, frogs sang from the billabong, an owl called as it flew overhead, his wings soft and deadly in the dark. Something jumped away through the long grass off to his left—Finn assumed it was a roo. There were more beasts out here than during the day, it seemed.

When he was far enough away from camp not to be overheard, he fired up the sat phone and waited. He had no doubt that Mike would be awake and waiting impatiently for his call.

"Griff, what the hell is going on out there?" His boss answered on the first ring.

Finn got down to business, relating his evening's expedition, laying everything out in chronological order so

Mike could follow along.

They talked for nearly twenty minutes, going over all possible scenarios, but in the end, they were no closer to an answer than Finn had been when he found the body.

Finn was just about to say his goodbyes and hang up—he needed to get some sleep—when Mike said, "Wait, Griff. A man matching Garrett's description was seen driving one of those cattle trucks into Townsville yesterday. It looks like he might've taken over Wombat's role."

"Are you sure?" Finn screwed up his mouth in a grimace. Shit. If this were true, it put Garrett in the vicinity. And it made the clue he'd found in the murdered man's campsite even more incriminating.

"Yes, I'm sure. The information came from Joe."

"Shit." This time Finn swore out loud. "Sorry, boss," he apologized. Joe was one of the other undercover agents from his team. He'd infiltrated the dockworkers crew in Townsville, where most of the cattle were shipped from all the northern stations and loaded onto large ships to be sent to Indonesia, or the Middle East. There was a dock in Cairns, too, but that was more of a cargo hub, supplying a lot of the mining sites around the top end.

Should he tell Mike what he'd found in that camp tonight? Finn took the cigarette lighter out of his pocket and turned it over in his hands. He'd found it lying in the dust a few feet outside the main shelter, and recognized it instantly. A vintage lighter, made from sterling silver, embossed with filigree leaves. It was an unusual lighter, but with no identifying marks, it might've been hard to trace back to its true owner. But Finn knew it was eerily similar to the one Garrett had played with when he'd paid them a visit after Kayleigh's birth, flicking the lid continuously, making a small, annoying *snap* sound. Almost as if it were a set of worry beads, or a fidget toy; he seemed to be unaware of his annoying habit. Finn had taken a good look at the thing because it was so unusual. This lighter could belong to anyone, but something in his gut that told him, without reservation, that the lighter belonged to Garrett.

"This is fast getting out of hand, Griff," Mike said, breaking into his thoughts. "I was already considering pulling you out. It may be too dangerous to leave you where you are. And now with Garrett in the area, joining the team of drivers..." Mike left his unsaid words hang in the air like daggers waiting to fall. But Finn got the gist. His boss was getting antsy. He needed reassurance things were still going according to plan. At least it made his decision to not tell Mike about the lighter easier. He'd keep that little tidbit to himself. No point in giving Mike the ammunition he needed to pull Finn out.

"I don't believe I'm in any danger personally," Finn said smoothly. "This is a tight-knit team, and I trust them. They'll have my back if anything goes wrong."

"You don't know that. We've already discussed this. The killer could be one of your muster team, hiding in plain sight," Mike retorted.

Which was true, and something Finn had turned over and over in his head. But on the flip side of that coin, if it turned out there was a bad influence in the camp, Finn needed to stay right where he was to make sure Indy was protected. Now that she knew his true identity, she might be at risk. If anyone from the drug ring found out she could dish the dirt on him, they might decide she was an interesting target. She was fast becoming his Achilles heel. If they found out how much he was coming to care about Indy, they could use that against him.

"I need to stay, Mike." He wasn't going to plead, and he didn't tell his boss that if he ordered him to leave, he might well disobey that order. "We've got two more trucks arriving early tomorrow morning to take out another load of cattle. Now that we know what to look for, if they're transporting the ice, I'll find it. I'll phone it in, and you can nab the drivers on their way up to Townsville." He was dangling a carrot, and he hoped his boss would bite.

After many moments of silence, Mike finally let out a heavy sigh. "Right. I don't like this, but let's play it day by day from now on. See what you can uncover tomorrow morning, and we'll take it from there."

"Thanks, Sarge." Finn released a breath. He'd been given a reprieve. Now all he had to do was find a way to get underneath those trucks tomorrow morning without being spotted.

He stifled a yawn. Jesus, it was late. As it was, he'd only get a couple of hours' sleep before it was time to get up and load the cattle.

Heading back to the camp, Finn silently crossed his fingers that Garrett wasn't one of the drivers of the trucks arriving tomorrow. That could put him in all manner of awkward situations.

At least Joe spotting Garrett in Townsville yesterday meant that his brother wasn't hiding in the outback somewhere, perhaps sneaking around in this very stock camp. If his brother had been involved in the murder of that man in the other camp—and Finn was appalled at the mere idea, but experience told him that nothing could be discounted in this dark underworld his brother lived in—then he'd left soon afterwards. Which took a weight off Finn's mind. Because even when he'd been assuring Indy that they were safe riding back to the camp in the dark, a small part of him had been unsure.

The most interesting question, however, was, did his brother know that Finn was out here? Working undercover?

CHAPTER TEN

Indy stifled a yawn. It was only nine in the morning, and it was already hot, dry, and dusty. And she was coasting along on only a few hours' sleep. Which wasn't good. You needed to have your wits about you when you were dealing with feisty bush cattle.

At least Dale had called off the muster today, in light of last night's events. But just like the last time muster had been delayed, that didn't mean there wasn't still a lot to be done. Steve and Daniella had arrived with Aaron in the red helicopter again this morning. It was becoming a familiar routine for the poor owners, and Indy felt for them. Not one dead body, but now two had interrupted this muster. Steve had talked to all the crew and staff individually over the morning, making his rounds as everyone went about their business. Unobtrusive, but also making sure everyone was all right, and that they knew he cared and was on their side.

Indy shook herself and focussed on the cattle milling in the loading yard below. She stood on the middle metal railing of the fence, waving a long stick, ready to prod any reluctant weaner who balked at the loading ramp in front. Mack stood on the other side of the ramp, encouraging the cattle from his side. Shouts and loud mooing filled the air. Dale liked to keep the cattle as calm as possible, but loading was always going to be a stressful experience, no matter how hard they tried.

The first truck, hauling its double trailers, was already loaded and wheezing its dusty way up the road, cattle packed in like sardines. There'd been a hitch with that one, when the truckie suddenly discovered one of his tires was flat just as he was maneuvering it into place, and they'd had to wait while he fixed it.

They were loading the first trailer on this truck, which was nearly finished, then they could move onto the final one. All Indy could think about was the hot cuppa and fresh scones Bindi would have ready for morning smoko once they finished here. Her appetite seemed to have deserted her at breakfast, when everyone crowded around, wanting to know what the hell had happened in the night. She let Finn and Mack tell most of the story, standing in the background, flapping her hat against her thigh and trying not to grimace as they recounted the state of the body when they'd found it. Really, her only role in the whole thing had been the eyeball that'd conveniently dropped at her feet. Vaguely, she wondered if they would've ever found that dead man without the crows. Dale warned them that the cops would most likely be back today with more questions, but the rest of the crew would have nothing to offer, as they'd all stayed behind. Indy suddenly wished she hadn't demanded to go with Finn and Mack. If she'd just stayed at camp like everyone else, her stomach wouldn't be roiling with abhorrence as the images from yesterday evening kept replaying in her mind.

Indy waved her arms and shouted at a young bull, who was showing the whites of his eyes, refusing to go up the ramp. "Digger, in," she commanded, and her brave little dog slipped through the metal bars and barked at the cow's heels, sending the animal up the ramp with a bellow of frustration.

"Digger, out," she said, and the kelpie was back at her feet in a flash, tongue lolling in a happy smile. He loved to work cattle, more so than Barbie. He had a fearlessness—or perhaps it was more of a reckless streak—where Barbie was a little more circumspect. Both different personalities, but both good at their jobs.

A flash of blue caught Indy's eye. She turned just in time to see Finn wriggle beneath the truck's chassis.

What the hell…?

Indy realized with shock that he was probably looking for evidence of the drugs he kept talking about. He'd told her they suspected some truckies were being paid to haul them across Queensland. God, she hoped no one spotted him. He was taking a risk. This trailer was nearly full. What if he was still under there when the driver moved the second trailer into position? He'd be crushed. At least she seemed to be the only one who'd seen him go under. Perhaps he'd chosen his timing and this spot for that exact reason. Because he knew she'd keep his secret.

"Hey, Indy." Mack's shout brought her attention back to the cattle, which had bunched up at the neck of the ramp, one refusing to climb in. Shit. She slapped the recalcitrant weaner on the rump a few times, shouting, "Ha! Ha!"

But her gaze kept darting back to the spot where Finn had disappeared beneath the truck, willing him to come out.

Suddenly, the driver appeared next to Mack. "How's it going?" he drawled. Some drivers were hands-on when it came to loading cattle onto their trucks. They were often very specific as to how the animals were spaced, checking on their welfare, that kind of thing. Not this guy. He'd wandered off to the mess tent to snaffle one of Bindi's hot scones, leaving the hard work to Dale and his team. Judging by the man's bulging belly, he liked to snaffle more than one scone whenever he could.

"Nearly there," Mack replied.

To Indy's horror, when she looked back at the few remaining cattle, she could see he was right. Only a minute or so and they'd be finished. She shot another glance down the side of the truck. *Come on, Finn. Where are you?* But he still hadn't emerged. She'd been keeping one eye out the whole time.

"I'll go start the truck, then. Yell out when you're ready for the next trailer."

Oh, shit. The man began to amble toward the front of his truck. The driver would either see Finn as he scrambled out from underneath, or Finn would be crushed when the driver moved the vehicle.

"Oh, ah, excuse me, sir," she yelled as loudly as she could.

The truck driver stopped and raised an eyebrow. "Yeah, luv. What you want?"

Hell, what did she want? She needed to warn Finn, but how?

"You… Ah, you can't move the truck yet. We're not finished loading."

"I can see that, *luv.*" He laid a thick emphasis on the word luv, and she wanted to curl her lip at him. "I won't move it until you tell me to. Okay?"

"Right. So, you're going to move the truck soon?" She was shouting at the top of her voice now, and Mack gave her a curious look. She knew she was acting foolish, but all she could hope was that Finn overheard her conversation.

"Yes. But not until this here bloke tells me it's okay." The truckie shook his head as he walked away, as if he were talking to an imbecile. And she didn't blame him, because that's exactly how she felt.

The driver disappeared as he walked the length of his truck toward the cab, and Indy let out a groan of dismay. She'd tried to help Finn, but she'd clearly failed, because—

Finn rolled out from beneath the truck in a flurry of dust a few meters away. Got to his feet in one quick movement and was headed toward a nearby stand of trees before Indy could properly close her mouth.

Why, that bloody…!

She was going to have some choice words to say to him at smoko.

At the last second, Finn glanced over his shoulder and gave her a cheeky smile and a thumbs up.

Great.

"What was all that about?" Mack asked from beneath the brim of his black hat.

Indy sighed. What, exactly? Now she was going to look like the camp fool. And all for what?

* * *

Indy walked up behind Finn, resisting the urge to slap him. He was leaning against a tree trunk on the outskirts of the cleared area around the mess tent, waiting for the queue for scones and coffee to reduce. She couldn't help the way her gaze traced up his legs to his backside, snug inside his well-worn jeans, then followed the contours of his straight back up to where his impressive shoulders filled out his blue chambray shirt. Why was a man in a pair of jeans and cowboy boots such a turn-on? His hat dangled in his hand, his hair curly and dark on top.

"Hey, you," she said, coming around and planting herself directly in front of him. "I have a bone to pick with you." She kept her voice low, so no one overheard.

He flashed her a grin that was half cheeky little boy, half sheepish. "Hi, yourself," he replied.

A streak of dirt—probably from where he'd climbed under the truck—covered his left cheek. Before she knew what she was doing, she reached up and brushed the offending smudge away. Finn stilled at her touch, his eyes locking on hers.

"You had some dust..." she trailed off as his gaze remained fixed on her, pupils darkening. How could a single contact set off such a reaction in her? Shit, she needed to remember not to touch him like that. Not in broad daylight, where everyone could see, anyway.

"Thanks," he growled, then cleared his throat. And she had a stupid sense of triumph. He was just as affected by her touch as she was. And she liked that.

She leaned nonchalantly against the other side of the tree, pretending nothing major had just passed between them.

"And thanks also for your help this morning," he continued.

"I looked like a complete idiot," she grumbled.

"Yes, but you may well have saved a police officer's life. Small recompense, I say," he replied lightly, giving her a wink.

Now that the sexual tension between them had eased, she could feel an aura of excitement around him.

"You found something, didn't you?"

"Is it that obvious?" he asked with a scowl. Even frowning at her, Indy was struck by his handsome features. Piercing blue eyes and rugged jawline, firm lips drawn into a thin line of concentration. Be still her fluttering heart.

"Yeah, you need to work on your resting cop face some more," she quipped. But perhaps it was just her. Perhaps she was more attuned to his moods and slight facial expressions than most.

He gave her a look that said he was torn.

"Go on," she prompted. "You know I won't tell a soul."

He gave an exasperated sigh, but couldn't seem to help bouncing lightly on his toes. "Yeah. I found something. A hidden compartment, stuffed with bags of crystal meth. I had to bust the lock open, but it was worth it."

"Oh, wow." Indy covered her mouth.

"It's one of the breakthroughs we've been waiting for," Finn continued. "Now we've confirmed how they're transporting the drugs, we can start to lean on the drivers to get information about who's controlling them."

"That's great news." She lowered her hand and stared contemplatively at him. But perhaps not such great news for her. If Finn broke this case, then perhaps he'd leave soon, his undercover job over in the blink of an eye. Leaving her alone again. She took off her Akubra and slapped it against her leg, staring off into the distant floodplains.

"Anything more on the second murdered man?" she asked. More to keep the conversation going, then to get answers. She was suddenly over this whole goddamned thing. All she wanted was to go back to her simple life working at Stormcloud, where no one died, and no one was a suspect in a murder. Back to a time before she'd met Finn.

"No, not yet." He touched her arm lightly. "You okay?" He leaned around the tree trunk so that he could look at her.

"Hmm?" She looked up to meet his gaze. Which was a mistake, because the confused concern hovering in their depths only made her want to reach out to him once more. "Oh, yeah, I'm fine," she replied. "I was a bit on edge about the whole secret camp with a dead guy in it last night, but I'm okay this morning. He obviously wasn't a good man, and perhaps he even deserved what he got." Not that anyone really deserved to be killed in cold blood and left to rot in the bush. But that wasn't the point.

"No, that's not what I meant." He pursed his lips. "There's something else going on in that clever head of yours, I can tell."

She narrowed her eyes at him. "Nope, nothing else is going on," she denied. There was no way in hell she was going to ask him how much longer he was going to be working here.

No way in hell she was going to let him see how much she wanted him to stay. She wasn't even clear inside her own head with what she wanted from Finn. There was no logical reason that she should ever have a relationship with him. He was still technically married, even if he hadn't lived with his wife for three years. His life was in the city. Hers was… Well, it was out here, for now. Just because there was this fizzing attraction between them. Just because he was the most beautiful man she'd ever come across. Just because she found him easy to talk to, easy to be around, like she was wearing her favorite fuzzy slippers, didn't mean anything. Short-term attraction, that was all it was. In the long term, that'd all fade, and she'd forget him soon enough once he left.

"Why don't I believe you?" he queried, lips still pursed.

She shrugged and pushed away from the tree. Time to join the crowd and get away from his tricky questions. Finn was right on her heels, she didn't even have to turn her head, she could feel his presence, like tiny prickles of awareness all over her back, as if he were the sun, shining out his warmth onto her back.

Just as she joined the end of the queue, however, the low drone of an arriving vehicle made her stop and stare at the road. All heads in the line also swiveled toward the sound. It was Nash, in his police Land Cruiser. Indy could feel the tension in the air ramp up as Nash exited the car, placing his dark-blue police cap on his head as he came, indicating he was here on official police business.

Dale strode out to meet him, and the two men disappeared inside the mess tent, heading to a small table set up at the back for privacy. Steve and Daniella came in a few minutes later to join them. Indy wished she could be a fly on the wall and hear what Nash had to say. Finn was practically quivering behind her, and she understood he probably wished exactly the same thing. But they'd have to trust Dale to tell the rest of them what he knew after Nash left.

Everyone took their time eating, probably not wanting to leave, in case there was news. Dave and Carrot both went back for seconds, and then thirds. They *were* Bindi's special scones, but even Dave patted his stomach after the third one and admitted defeat.

Indy had taken a seat next to Beth Scanlon and resumed their conversation about the best online sites to order clothes, doing her best to ignore Finn sitting on the opposite side of the circle. Indy knew she and Beth were only filling in time until Nash left, but it was good to talk about something mundane and simple. There'd already been unending discussions, people expounding their own theories and supposition about what the hell was going on in this neck of the outback. She and Beth talked about the website where Indy had bought the pink-checked shirt she was wearing today. And they both agreed that just because they lived and worked alongside the men, getting just as dirty and weatherbeaten as the male folk, there was no reason they couldn't look like women while they did it. Perhaps even add a touch of glamor to this unglamorous life.

Beth and Maddie finally went off to help Scanner mend a broken door on the rear of their truck. It was a job that'd been put off for a rainy day, and today looked like it.

Then Mack drew her into the conversation he and Aaron were having about the upcoming rodeo season. Mack had been a bloody good bull rider, by all accounts, and he was hoping to get back in the ring this season, much to Bindi's secret annoyance. Bindi didn't think his ankle was properly healed yet from where he'd ended up down a mineshaft last year. Indy wasn't about to be dragged into that argument. But Mack asked whether she'd ever competed in any of the events, and she told him she'd done quite well in calf-roping a few years back. But everyone kept at least one eye fixed on the mess tent, all waiting to hear what Nash had to say.

Indy was just about to excuse herself from the rodeo discussion, and head over to let her dogs off their chains, and give them the tidbits of scones she'd saved from her plate, when she heard voices, and the group emerged from the back of the large marquee. Nash shook the trio's hands and headed back to his Land Cruiser. Conversation died around the camp, as people looked expectantly at the owners.

Steve and Daniella stood at the entrance to the mess tent, allowing Dale to take the lead. This was supposed to be his muster, after all. Not for the first time, Indy felt sorry for Dale. How was he ever going to prove to his mother and stepdad that he was ready for this role when all this shit he had no control over kept happening? She guessed it was perhaps in the way Dale dealt with the shit that mattered, in the long run. Indy wondered if Steve was itching to step in and take over? If he was, he was doing a good job of staying calm and letting Dale do his thing.

Dale called for quiet, and everyone stopped talking, the rattle of tin plates settling down. Bindi came out from where she was cutting sandwiches to stand around the campfire to hear what he had to say.

"I know we're all looking for answers, and I want to put your minds at ease. I know some of you are thinking about moving on," Dale flicked a quick glance in Brian and Rosie's direction, "And I won't blame you, if you do. But I'm here to ask you to stay. I know the muster has been disrupted, and I know that these deaths are putting everyone on edge. Nash has said he can't see any reason why we shouldn't finish the muster, and that's what I'd like to do."

There were sighs of relief from some, Indy among them. It took time and money to organize a muster, which was planned months in advance. The contract musterers all had other jobs to move on to in a week or so. If they had to postpone this one, who knew when they'd next get back out here to continue.

"I'm not privy to all the information the police have," Dale continued. "But Nash has told me that while they believe Wombat's murder and the dead man found out in the bush may be connected, he doesn't think the rest of us are at any risk. Whatever Wombat and this other guy were mixed up in has nothing to do with us, or the cattle."

"So, we don't need to be worried that we'll be the next one murdered in our sleep?" Dave quipped with a laconic grin. But there was a smidge of apprehension in his words. Indy didn't blame him; she'd been wondering the same thing herself. But at least she was privy to Finn's insights on the case, and he'd allayed the worst of her fears. He said the murders were all centered around the drug ring, and nothing to do with the innocent people in the stock camp. As long as they *were* all innocent. Finn was supposed to be looking at how the drugs were transported from hub to hub, and that was all. But Indy worried the links might go deeper than that. What if they were also using others in the mustering community as couriers?

Nash wouldn't have divulged the drug link to Dale, as Finn's boss wanted it kept on the down-low until they could break the links and bust the kingpins of the operation. Without that key information, to Dale and the rest of the crew, these murders might seem completely random. Indy fidgeted from one foot to the other. She didn't like having clandestine information and not being able to pass it on to her employers. It felt like she was betraying them, somehow. She didn't understand how Finn could do this sort of thing every day. Keep secrets and tell lies. How did he manage to keep everything straight in his head?

She glanced up to find him watching her with those serious, blue eyes.

"No, there is no risk of that," Dale replied. "But like I said earlier, if you feel like you're in any kind of danger, you're more than free to leave."

Indy watched Brian and Rosie out of the corner of her eye. It was as if they were pretending to ignore each other, but Rosie was jiggling her foot agitatedly. The pair had kept their own counsel ever since Wombat's body had been discovered, but Indy could tell Rosie wasn't happy with the situation. Perhaps she was the one who wanted to leave, but couldn't convince Brian to go. The pair had told Indy on the first night around the campfire that they were saving to buy a property down south. They were so close to their goal, Brian had said candidly. This season should be their last. But if they pulled out now, they'd lose a couple of weeks' worth of pay, and maybe Brian was pressuring Rosie to stay for that fact alone. Money was always a big motivator.

"We're staying," Scanner said from the rear of the crowd. He and his daughters had rejoined the crew at some stage during Dale's speech. "As long as what that cop said is true and we really can get right back to work."

"Yes, it's true," Dale replied. He shifted his gaze to take in Dave, Carrot and Finn.

"Yeah, yeah. Of course, we're staying." Dave slapped Carrot on the back and the red-headed man gave a cocky wink.

"We're not scared of no boogeyman," Carrot echoed. "Ain't that right, mate?" His gaze travelled to Finn, seated on Dave's other side.

She looked at Finn, as did quite a few other pairs of eyes. She already knew his answer. Or she thought she did. He'd stay as long as there was still a case to be solved.

"Right as rain, mate," Finn replied, blue eyes landing on hers. "Let's get this muster back on track."

CHAPTER ELEVEN

Finn puttered along on his motorcycle, one eye on the cattle walking along beside him, the other on the ground in front, looking for potholes or logs, anything that might unseat him. The cattle were compliant now, after gathering the feisty mob this morning, the long walk back to the yards had cured most of them of the notion of escape. Another long day in the desert heat was nearly over. Things had pretty much gone back to normal now, three days after he and Indy had discovered the dead body in the bush.

Finn found himself slotting back into his undercover role easily once more. Almost as if he were made for working the country. Sometimes he had to remind himself he was actually here to bring down an illegal drug gang, not to get sucked in by the camaraderie and friendship built around a day's hard work and good food eaten next to a campfire. There'd been no more disruptions, no more murders, and the stock camp was ticking along just like it should. He'd had no further opportunity to examine any more cattle trucks before they were loaded up, as he was out droving the floodplains to gather another mob by the time the sun rose in the sky. Dale and Mack loaded the cattle gathered from the day before and then joined the crew later in the morning.

Without conscious thought, Finn's gaze slid to where Indy sat atop Gypsy on the opposite flank of the mob. While everything else in this stock camp came to him easy, made sense to him now, she was the one thorn in his side. He tried to ignore the way his body reacted to her every time she came within five feet. Tried to treat her the same as the rest of his co-workers, with friendly affability. If only she wouldn't watch him with those dark eyes. He could feel her gaze on him as he moved around the camp. He knew what she wanted. Because he wanted it, too. And time was running out. He'd be pulled out of this job soon, or the muster would finish at the end of the week. Either way, they'd go their separate ways. And he'd never see her again. The idea made his chest ache.

They danced around each other all day, both fighting their feelings, trying to ignore them. He'd thought that if only he could keep her at arm's length for the next few days, then it'd be easier to leave when the time came. Problem was, it was practically impossible to escape her; they all worked together closely, and then spent every evening together around the campfire.

He knew he was falling for Indy. She was everything he hadn't even known he was looking for in a woman until he met her. Fiercely independent. Unafraid of hard work, dust, and long hours. Compassionate. Perceptive. Insightful; she certainly could read him like a book, and seemed to have an uncanny ability to understand what made other people tick. Was passionate about her animals; loved them like they were part of her family. And when she was going in a flat-out-gallop on Gypsy's back, chasing a run-away heifer, well, there was nothing more courageous and beautiful in this whole world.

Vaguely, he wondered if she'd replied to that dick of an ex-boss yet. He didn't want to look like he was prying into her love life, but he'd give anything to spend five minutes alone with that guy. How dare he treat her like she was nothing, use her, and then throw her away, only to realize his mistake and think she'd come running back as soon as he crooked his little finger. Because if Finn were given the chance to make Indy his—if things were somehow different—he'd hold on to her so tight, make her feel like the most special woman in the world. Besides, Indy had more integrity in her little toe than that man had in his whole body. Finn just hoped that Indy used some of that integrity to decide to tell him to fuck off once and for all.

He'd found himself hanging around her tent late at night. Not in a creeper type of way, but just to make sure she was okay. It was in those late-night hours that he finally gave into the need to be near her. Just knowing she was sleeping peacefully a few feet away made his heart finally rest easy in his chest. So, after he'd checked in with Mike, he'd wander to the edge of camp, and stand staring at the canvas barrier. Her dogs knew him well enough to merely give a whine in greeting, and he'd go over and offer them both a pat between their silky ears. They seemed to understand his mystifying need to be near Indy, perhaps better than he did.

But there was also this vague uneasiness that wouldn't leave him. He couldn't put his finger on the feeling, but it made him want to prowl around Indy's tent all night like some sort of human guard dog. The sarge hadn't mentioned Garrett again over the past few days, but perhaps Finn should make a point to ask if his brother had been spotted since that one time in Townsville. Something about Garret's involvement was making Finn's skin prickle, but he had no idea why.

Thinking about talking to his boss tonight had his mind back on the topic of bringing down the drug ring.

He'd struck gold when he'd found the meth hidden in the

truck three days ago. It was partly thanks to Indy that he managed to slip in and out unseen. He'd passed the info on to Mike and then waited impatiently until that night to hear back from his boss. They'd managed to detain the truck driver on an isolated stretch of road twenty kilometers out of Townsville. Swapping the driver out for one of their operatives, they'd put a tiny tracker in with the drugs to see if it would lead them to a dealer, or even better, one of the major players. The driver hadn't been of much help, merely saying he'd been contacted by phone whenever there was a shipment needed hauling, never met anyone face-to-face. He wouldn't reveal where or how he collected the drugs, or what happened to them when he arrived in Townsville. Mike's team were still tracking the drugs, which had stayed stationary once they reached the docks, and were sitting in an old shipping container, perhaps waiting to be collected and distributed.

"Hey, Finn, you there?" Dave's voice crackled over the two-way.

"Yeah, man, what you want?"

"We need your magic hands over here for a second. Beth's ATV just died."

Finn glanced over his shoulder toward the rear of the mob. Dave was astride Amigo, waving to him and pointing toward Beth's ATV, which was being left behind in a wave of dust as the cattle moved on without her.

"On my way." Finn gave the thumbs up and turned his bike around. "Can you take my place on the flank?" he asked Dave, as he trundled back the way he'd come. Dave gave him the thumbs-up in return and trotted up to replace him. Finn had become the unofficial mechanic around camp. For some reason, because he rode a bike and seemed to know a little about engines, he was the one everyone called if anything went wrong.

* * *

Two hours later, he'd fixed Beth's ATV, and they were back in camp for the night. Finn was on his way to have a shower. There was no official roster for who showered when, but Finn had decided early on to get to the outdoor ablutions sooner, rather than later after they got in from the day's ride. Twelve people were a lot to cycle through one measly shower, but it seemed to work. Most of the women chose to wash after dinner when they could take their time. Which left the men to fight it out before the meal. The shower was your basic outdoor variety. Because this was a permanent stock camp, Steve had recently replaced the hessian walls with sturdy wooden walls and a concrete floor. The run-off was directed into a deep ditch, so it wasn't left to turn the whole area into red mud. It was Bindi's job to start an old generator right before everyone returned to camp to heat a large tank full of water and provide the pressure. The rules for use were simple. Keep it short, and if there was a queue, then you waited your turn. For a makeshift shower, it wasn't bad, and Finn was looking forward to washing off the dust from his long day.

Carrying clean clothes and toiletries in his arms, he wasn't watching where he was going as he rounded the side of the water tank, and so nearly collided head-on with Indy coming the other way.

"Oh, sorry," he exclaimed, grabbing her arm to steady her as she stumbled.

Her wet hair was slicked back from her face, and she was wearing only a skimpy pair of shorts, a tank top—no bra—and flip-flops; obviously on her way back to her tent to get changed. His palm burned where it was still connected with her warm, freshly washed skin.

She smelled fantastic. Something sweet and citrusy, like a ripe mandarin. Was it her shampoo? He couldn't help himself, he had to draw that scent deep into his lungs. "You smell good." All that fresh, clean skin was going to be his undoing. He wanted to dip his head and taste her. Run his tongue down the soft expanse of her throat. This was the first time he'd seen Indy without jeans and a long-sleeved shirt, and it was doing strange things to his insides. Her legs were trim and firm, just as he'd expected, although pale from lack of sunlight. Her collarbone stood out in the curve of her shoulders, and he was surprised at how delicate she looked without her bulky work clothes on.

"Yeah, well, you don't," she quipped, then looked up into his eyes, the smile dying on her lips as she saw the hunger he couldn't hide. The air between them became charged, almost alive, and they stood, immobilized by this sudden, unexpected contact.

"Does that bother you?" he asked, voice strangely husky.

She licked her lips, then shook her head slightly.

Without thinking, he shifted his hand from her arm and feathered his fingers up her shoulder to the nape of her neck, feeling her damp hair against his skin. His thumb rubbed along the curve of her jaw, relishing the way her skin felt beneath his hand. She sucked in a sharp breath, but didn't move away.

Finn lowered his head, resting his cheek alongside hers, their mouths so close... But he needed to let her come the last little way. Needed her to want this, too.

For a second, she hesitated, then with a soft groan, she turned her mouth and met his. Their lips clashed, hungry and demanding, his hand behind her neck pulling her in closer. Their bodies melded, clothes and toiletries crushed between them. He couldn't get enough of her, as if he wanted to devour her like he was a hungry beast. If he could, he'd draw her soul out, to mingle with his. Backing her up until she was against the corrugated iron of the water tank, he pushed his knee between her legs, dropping his hand to run it down her thigh until he found the hem of her shorts, then swept his finger up, under the fabric, finding the edge of her lacy panties. She melted into him as if she suddenly become boneless, and he was the only thing holding her up. Making a small noise at the back of her throat, one of her hands began tugging at his shirt, then her palm was skimming over the skin on his waist, fingernails digging into the muscles of his lower back. She tilted her head, angling it so she could kiss him deeper, hotter. Her small, pert breasts pushed into his chest, and he—

The sound of approaching voices broke them apart in an instant. Dave and Carrot were coming up the path, bickering about who got first dibs on the shower. They'd be here any second. Indy fled without a word, leaving Finn dragging in ragged breath after ragged breath. Some inner instinct made his feet move, even as his mind struggled to catch up, before Dave and Carrot came around the tank and spotted him. God, what might've happened if they hadn't been interrupted?

This thing with Indy was going to kill him if he didn't do something about it soon. It was going to be a cold shower for him tonight.

* * *

"They found the murder weapon used to kill Wombat." Mike's voice resounded over the sat phone, and it took a few seconds for Finn to process the words.

"What?" He straightened. This was good news. "Where?" This was exactly what he needed to hear. Something to get his head back into his job and off Indy and the scorching kiss they'd shared earlier this evening.

"Buried in a shallow hole at the bottom of the dry creek bed near the campsite where you found the dead guy."

Better and better. The incriminating evidence had been

found at the other crime scene. Which made it less and less likely someone from this muster camp was involved.

"That's good news," Finn replied, leaning his hip against a tree trunk and tipping his head back to study the stars through the leaves. He came to a different spot every night to talk to his boss. Never be predictable. It made it harder for anyone to track him. The full moon from a few nights ago was now waning, but there was enough light for him to make his way cautiously thorough the bush, until he found a place that looked good. Somewhere with clear space around it. He'd learned his lesson that first night when Indy had snuck up on him.

"Yes. And they're analyzing the blood found on the blade, see if they can get any hits."

"Good. Good," Finn said distractedly. Mike had already filled him in on all the other pertinent details. They had a name for the victim. Ronaldo Dimitri. He was well known to the police. Had a long record of petty crimes—theft, drug possession, illegal firearms. The man had been a bouncer and bodyguard for an Italian *"businessman"* who ran a series of nightclubs and strip joints down in Sydney for a while. Then he'd disappeared off the police radar around two years ago. Until he'd turned up dead in the middle of the outback. Mike's team was scrambling to find out more about his dealings for those past two years. If he was now perhaps working for one of the bigwigs in this drug ring, it might be another clue they needed to get this gang.

"I'll let you know if any more of the puzzle pieces drop in once we have the results from the DNA," Mike went on. "Anything else you want to report? Any more questions?" His boss was clearly itching to go, probably wanted to get to bed, much like Finn. These late-night debriefs, while essential, were also taking time away from much-needed sleep. And Finn needed to stay sharp. Not become complacent.

But there was one small detail Finn desperately wanted to know. He drew in a breath and screwed up his nose. "Have there been any more sightings of Garrett lately?" he asked, going for feigned nonchalance.

"No. Why?" Mike cut back sharply. Clearly, his casual tone hadn't fooled Mike Rogers. Probably one of the many reasons he was a detective sergeant. Nothing got past him.

"No reason. I was just wondering if he'd turned up again, that's all."

"You haven't seen him, or heard from him? Have you?" Mike asked.

Finn nearly laughed out loud. Heard from his bother? Who was Mike kidding? Garrett was the last person to contact him. He knew better than that.

"No, I haven't," Finn promised.

"Good. If that's all, I'll talk to you tomorrow."

"Goodnight, Sarge." Finn rang off, and placed the phone in his pocket. Wending his way back through the trees, he knew he wasn't quite ready for sleep yet. The same as he'd done over the past three nights, he headed toward Indy's tent. He'd check on her once, just to be sure. The tent was dark and quiet. She must be asleep, like the rest of the muster crew. Digger whined a welcome, and Finn shushed him, going over and patting the dog's head. Stalking around the back of her tent, he made sure the area was secure. Everything was quiet, nothing was amiss. He should go to bed now and try to catch some sleep.

As he turned on his heel, ready to head back to his own tent, a wraithlike figure appeared in front of him.

"Holy shit," he whispered, jumping back in surprise. "What the hell are you doing out here?"

"I could ask you the same question," Indy said, crossing her arms and tipping her head on the side. Even in the dark,

Finn could tell she was glowering at him.

"Ah… I was just on my way to bed. I've been—"

"Cut the crap, Finn. I know you've been hanging around my tent at night. What are you up to?" Her voice lost some of the sharpness from before.

"I want to make sure you're safe." He knew enough about Indy to understand the truth was his best course of action. But then, perhaps he shouldn't make it seem like he was singling her out. "It's my job to make sure the whole camp is safe," he added blandly.

"Maybe. But I don't see you creeping around anyone else's tent at night." Her voice was smooth, almost a purr, and she stepped closer.

Hell, she had him on that one. How did she know about his nocturnal missions? Perhaps she'd been watching him all along, when he thought she'd been sleeping soundly. Some kind of detective he was, if he couldn't even perceive whether a target was awake or asleep. But Indy had that effect on him. She addled his brain, turned his normally-razor-sharp instincts to mush. Especially, when she stood that close, wearing…the same attire she'd had on when he caught her coming out of the shower.

Oh, no. She had no bra on for the second time tonight. His mind went back to the feel of her breasts, nipples taut and pebbled against his chest. His cock ached at the memory.

He scrubbed a hand through his hair, but it didn't help ease the tension in his groin.

She took one final step until she was pressed up against him. Unfolding her arms, she wrapped them around his waist instead and stared up at his face.

"I can't stop thinking about you. That kiss tonight…"

Finn groaned and did the only thing possible; he slung his hands about her tiny waist, leaning into her petite body. So close he could feel the flutter of her heart beneath her ribcage.

His heart was beating a million miles an hour, too.

"What are we going to do?" he moaned. This was impossible. The two of them were impossible. Why, then, did she feel so right in his arms? Again, he caught that trace of sweet citrus, and it set his senses alight.

"I don't know about tomorrow, but I do know I want to continue that kiss tonight. Even though it's wrong, and even though you're still technically married." She stood on tiptoe and licked his neck, setting off small explosions in his gut and farther down; his cock standing to attention. Gathering her up, he lifted her feet off the ground so he could reach her mouth and give into temptation.

She wrapped her legs around his waist, and her arms around his neck, kissing him with abandon. He supported her weight with a hand under each buttock, enjoying the feel of her firm, muscular backside in his palms. His tongue delved between her lips, their mouths moving in perfect harmony. He tried to hold back, tasting her skin with his tongue, but she groaned and pulled his mouth back to hers. He'd been waiting so long for this; it felt like they were one entity now, as if he were a part of her.

"I'm getting a divorce," he told her between kisses. "I promise, there's nothing left between me and Chloe."

She broke the kiss and studied him for a moment. "Put me down, Finn," she demanded, her breathing uneven.

He didn't want this to end, but she was right, they needed to stop this before it got out of hand, and of course he obeyed, even as disappointment flooded his veins.

But when her feet hit the ground, she snagged his hand in hers, and tugged him toward her tent. Lifting the flap, she invited him in with a secret smile.

CHAPTER TWELVE

Indy had no strength to fight this anymore. When she was around Finn, she felt warmth and joy, and she didn't want to lose that. Not tonight. She wanted to drown in a sea of carnal pleasure and forget the images that still haunted her of mutilated bodies; replace them with Finn and his perfect body.

He reached up and tenderly brushed his thumb against her lips. "Are you sure about this?"

Was she sure?

It would be the first time she'd had sex since... Since she lost the baby. Wow, that thought almost made her pause for a second. And probably seven months since she'd last slept with Patrick. There'd been no one else in the ensuing months. Indy hadn't been interested. Sex was the furthest thing from her mind.

Until she'd met Finn, and every nerve in her body seemed to have been switched back on.

Losing the baby had left a hole in her heart, taken a little piece of her that would never be replaced. And for a while afterwards, she'd felt numb and hollow. But when she'd taken up her position at Stormcloud, away from Patrick and all the reminders of what she'd lost, and her mind was occupied with work and new friends, she'd slowly come back to herself. A part of her would never get over her miscarriage. She'd been a mother, if even for only a few weeks, and the hurt of losing that would never go away. But she was also a woman with needs and wants. A sensual being who enjoyed sex and orgasms. Her body was craving what Finn could give her. He was the one who could turn on all the switches inside she'd turned off, and ignite the passion once more; make her whole again.

"Absolutely." She'd never been surer of anything in her life. Small tremors of anticipation ran through her. *This* was what she needed.

Stepping toward her, Finn's mouth landed on her neck, the warmth of his breath causing her stomach to clench. He moved up her throat, nipping at her ear, sending more shivers down to her belly. Running a hand through her hair, he inhaled deeply.

"Your hair is nice loose," he said huskily. Even though it was only shoulder length, she always kept it tied back in a ponytail. His fingers tangled in the strands and tugged gently, so she had no choice but to tip her head back until her mouth was at his disposal. And his lips descended to take her in a hot, heavy kiss.

Her tent wasn't huge, but it was big enough for them both to stand up. Her camp bed took up one side of the space, her bags and a small table took up another. Which left them some room in the middle to…maneuver. Her eyes were more than accustomed to the dark by now, and the soft moonlight cast enough of a glow to seep through the thin fabric of the tent so that she could almost see him clearly in the dim light.

"Let me…" She pushed gently at his chest, making room between them so she could undo his shirt buttons. Quickly, as if he might suddenly change his mind, she flicked each button and then let the shirt glide over his shoulders and fall onto the floor of the tent. A sigh escaped her lips as she let her fingers trail over his chest and abs, learning the muscles and ridges of his body. His skin jumped at her touch, and he let out a low moan.

Next, she reached for his zipper, slowly drawing it down, her eyes fixed on his. "I want you," she murmured. "I want this," she reaffirmed.

Finn kicked off his boots and then helped Indy guide his jeans and boxers down over his hips and off.

She walked backward and took the time to admire him. Tall, long-limbed, slim, but still muscular where it counted. He stood there, a man confident in his own skin, letting her look her fill, not hiding how his manhood stood out proud and vigorous. It was the most sexy, the most sinful thing she'd ever seen. She drank in the sight of him.

The urge to feel his hands on her skin drove her back into his arms. He grasped her face in both his hands and kissed her long and slow and deep, his actions modeling her intentions for the night; he was going to take his time, savor her. If he were as good a lover as his kisses implied, she was going to enjoy this. They were going to enjoy this. Indy returned his kiss, running her lips down his neck, down to his shoulder, roaming over every inch of his chest, exploring all that musky skin, sprinkled with curls between his pecs and trailing down toward his waist. Down, down, down she went, her lips trailing past his bellybutton almost to the thatch of dark hair. Her tongue reached out to touch the silken skin on the tip of his—

With a noise somewhere between a strangled cat and a grunt, Finn tilted her chin and brought her face back up to his.

"If you keep that up, this night is going to be over before it even starts," he said in a voice deep with desire. "Besides, you have way too many clothes on."

"Yes, I do," she agreed. Taking a deliberate step backward, she raised her hands above her head and challenged him with her eyes. She was his for the unveiling, if he were brave enough to come and get her.

Her courageous detective accepted the challenge with a wicked grin. Taking the hem of her tank top, he drew it slowly, ever so slowly, upward, baring her stomach, then breasts, then sliding it up her arms until he had her by the wrists, her top dangling, forgotten. Still holding her wrists trapped above her head, he moved in with the grace of a lion about to taste its kill, then his mouth was on hers and he kissed her, hard. Not letting go of her wrists, his tongue travelled down her body, lavishing each breast in turn, and turning Indy's blood to fire in her veins. She made a noise that seemed to come from someone else. A whimpering, almost pathetic sound. That was what he did to her; turned her into a pile of incoherent jelly.

Finn finally released her arms and hooked his thumbs into the top of her sleep shorts, sliding them gently all the way down, letting her step out of them before throwing them to the corner of the tent.

And she was now completely bare to Finn. Perhaps in more ways than just her skin. She felt as if he'd stripped away all her emotions, could see right through to the core of who she was.

"You are stunning," he whispered into her ear, wrapping his arms around her once more and pulling her close.

Tilting her head forward so her brow rested on his chest, she breathed in the scent of him.

The sounds of the outback night just outside the tent walls were familiar and peaceful, the smell of the country air like a balm to her soul.

Finn tilted her chin up so he could stare into her eyes. "I meant it," he said. "You are a stunning woman. And I'm one lucky man." He kissed her, mouth melding with hers, becoming more demanding as their thighs entwined, and her wandering hands smoothed down his strong back and over his muscular buttocks.

They needed somewhere to get comfy, and her camp bed just wouldn't cut it, it wasn't nearly big enough for what she had planned. But the blanket from her camp bed *was* just what they needed. Breaking their kiss, she ripped it off the bed and lay it on the tent floor, getting down onto her knees and dragging him with her.

Needing no further encouragement, he lay her gently on her back and then his body covered hers. The heavy weight of him setting her heart pounding. Her lips found his, and this time he didn't hold back, his hands were all over her body, squeezing her breasts, rolling her nipples between his thumb and forefinger. She couldn't get enough of his warm skin beneath her palms. Her belly began to quake and a growing heat crept lower down her thighs. Her hand crept between their bodies, to find the velvet steel of his cock pressing into her stomach. She stroked it and delighted in the way he sucked in a sharp breath at her touch. Which reminded her...

Without telling him what she was doing, she crawled over to her bag on the floor and rifled through it until she came up with her prize. Then she crawled back and pressed the silver package into his palm. Protection was important to her; she needed to know she wasn't going to get pregnant. Not after what happened with Patrick. Safety was a priority, now. She had a whole packet of them back at the lodge, but this one would have to do for tonight.

"Oh, good," he said, giving her a sheepish smile. "I hate to say it, but I didn't come prepared. I never thought..."

She covered his mouth with her own to stop his words. It was a sign of his decency that he'd never even considered having sex with someone while he was undercover. It was a sign that this thing between them had come as much of a shock to him as it had to her. A sign that perhaps he hadn't slept with anyone since his wife had left him. But she didn't want to think about any of that right now.

Instead, she rocked back on her heels and watched, unabashed, as he sheathed himself. She only had one condom, so they'd better make this good. But somehow, she knew already this was going to be better than good.

Slowly, tantalizingly, she lay back on the blanket, drawing him with her. Staring deep into his eyes, as he hovered above her, she wanted to tell him to hurry up. She wanted him inside her, could feel his cock resting at the entrance to her core.

"Finn, I need you," she whispered.

It was all the encouragement he required as he slipped inside her and Indy drowned in the sweet feeling of having a man making love to her. Oh, so good. The world seemed to blur around the edges, and there were only her and Finn, together. Nothing else mattered. No one else mattered. They moved to a rhythm immemorial, his thrusts becoming harder and deeper as she rose to meet him. It didn't take long for Indy's blood to sing through her veins.

"I'm close," he said, as they rocked back and forth, hips grinding, the sweet ecstasy building inside her. "But I need you to come with me."

Oh, yes, she was so close, too. She moved with him, accepted him even deeper, and then suddenly the wave built until it could no longer be contained. She couldn't help it, she cried out as her nails raked down his back. He called her name a split second later, as they both finally let go.

He lay on top of her, panting for many minutes, until his breathing returned to almost normal. Without letting go of her, he rolled to the side, and rid himself of the condom, then gathered her back into his arms. They lay together; him spooning her from behind, his warm breath on her neck, arms enfolding her in a cocoon of pure bliss. There was no need to speak. His touch said it all. The slow rhythmic beating of his heart against her back.

She couldn't remember the last time she'd felt so... cherished. As if Finn had branded her as his own with every single kiss. Certainly not with Patrick. And not with any of her previous boyfriends, either. Finn was different. Special. When she was with him, she felt like the only one who truly mattered to him.

"I want to stay here with you," he muttered dreamily, breaking their cloak of delicious silence. "But I need to get back to my tent."

Indy wanted him to stay, as well. To lie, legs entangled, enveloped in his arms until the morning light edged the sky. But that wasn't how this worked, and she knew it as well as he did.

So, instead of asking him to stay, she let him go. Got up and piled her blanket back on her camp bed, then watched him as he dressed. They kissed goodnight, long and deep, and she stood naked and alone as he walked in the bush through the dark night.

CHAPTER THIRTEEN

Finn hid a yawn behind the back of his hand as he waited his turn to fill his plate with breakfast. There was a nip in the air this morning and he returned his hand back into the pocket of his sheepskin coat. But no matter how tired he was this morning, it'd all been worth it. He turned to stare at the skyline, where the sun was turning the indigo sky to the palest pink. Those few minutes before the sun rose over the horizon were always the most beautiful, to Finn's mind. If only he could've still been lying in Indy's arms, watching the sunrise through the open zipper of her tent, it would've been the most perfect morning ever.

Indy hadn't joined the queue yet, and he wondered if she'd struggled to get out of bed as much as he had this morning. He could still hardly believe he and Indy had made love. He'd never really believed that it would happen, even though he'd been fantasizing about it constantly over the past week. Even though the air between them had buzzed with unrequited sexual tension. Even though he dreamed about her every night, and could hardly think of anything else during the day. It still came as a shock to his system. A good shock, but one that he wasn't sure what to do about now in the cold light of day. Had it been a one-night thing? Their craving for each other too hard to ignore, gratified by one magical night, and then pushed aside because reality kicked in?

Part of him truly hoped for more. Was desperate to be with Indy again. The way she set his body and soul on fire was hard to ignore. The way her fierce independence, and at the same time her soft vulnerability, called out to the man inside him. Even the smallest things, like the way she tilted her head ever so slightly to the side when something confused her, the way her dark eyes reflected the starlight late at night, as if the stars lived in her very soul, or the way electricity buzzed over his skin when she touched him.

A nagging voice kept asking if he was ready for anything more than one night? He would never tell Indy this, but a small part of him somehow felt like he was betraying his marriage to Chloe. Betraying his connection with his daughter by sleeping with another woman. For so long, his perception of himself as a man had been tied to the fact that he was a husband and a father. Of course, he knew he was lots of other things, as well. A police detective, a brother, a son, a friend, and a bloody good squash player—when he had the time. But once you had a child, they were tied to your heart forever; no matter if you never saw them again, they always lived inside you.

Was he really ready to finally move on? To sign those divorce papers? He would always be Kayleigh's father, but if he let another woman into his life, how would Kayleigh accept that? Would she reject him? See him as her father no longer? Finn huffed. It was more complicated than he'd first imagined.

Indy suddenly appeared around the edge of the mess tent and he couldn't help the warm flash of recognition that surged through his chest. She caught his eye and ducked her head. But the soft smile she tried to hide at the sight of him warmed his heart. She was dressed in a warm overcoat, jeans, and boots, hiding all those glorious curves. But he knew they were there, and his cock hardened at the mere thought. Even with all these confusing thoughts going around in his head, he still wanted her. *Down, boy.* Think about something else; anything else. The last thing he wanted was to scare everyone away from their breakfast with his raging boner. It'd also be a dead giveaway that something was going on between him and Indy. And he needed to keep that quiet. For now. Even though he wanted to shout it to the world, that Indy made him incredibly happy, made him feel like he was invincible. Apart from the fact he was working an undercover case, and he couldn't risk revealing himself to anyone else but Indy, he also wasn't ready to do that. He had a lot of shit to sort through, first.

Dale sauntered up to stand beside Bindi, who was behind the table, piling more toast onto a platter and making sure Dave left some of the bacon for the rest of them.

"I need someone to stay back at camp with me today," Dale said. "One of the bore pumps has broken down over at the north paddock, and I'm sending Mack to fix it. But that means I need another hand to help load the cattle onto the trucks this morning."

There was silence as people digested Dale's words, then feet began to shuffle in the dust. No one really wanted to stay back. They would if they had to, but everyone was waiting for someone else to offer first.

"I'll do it," Finn said. He almost put his hand up like a small child at school, but didn't want to reveal his eagerness.

This could be the break he was looking for. A chance to snoop around the camp while everyone else was away for the day. If he could get away from Dale for even fifteen minutes, it would help.

Indy cast him a strange look, perhaps guessing what he

was up to. Hopefully, no one else suspected his motives.

Even though it was part of the reason Mike had put him in this undercover position, he'd had very little chance of much investigation so far. There was always someone around, making it nearly impossible to sneak into people's tents or take a look through their vehicles. Finn had scored a major coup, by confirming how the drugs were being shipped, and now Mike's team was watching each and every truck that came in and out of this stock camp, as well as other camps in the area like a hawk. Some people might think that Finn had achieved the job he'd been sent to do. And some of the younger, less knowledgeable detectives might agree and perhaps even want to pull him out. But Mike still suspected there was another link that they were missing with this drug ring. And Finn agreed with him. There must be some reason the syndicate had decided to use this transport option. Apart from the fact that the cattle trucks used the back roads and byways and were less likely to be stopped and searched on their way to the docks. Some important link they were missing. And of course, now they were dealing with two murders, it wasn't merely drug shipments they were worried about. Finn remained on the lookout for signs of any other illegal activities.

In their last stock camp before they'd come to Stormcloud, he'd uncovered a small-time drug dealer, when the station manager had hinted that he might have access to *something to help Finn get through the long days*. After cautiously talking to a couple of the station stock hands, and witnessing one guy's erratic mood swings and behaviors, as well as noticing more traffic going to and from the farmhouse than was normally warranted, Finn decided the rumors of cocaine usage in the camp might well be true. He passed on the details to the sarge and after he and Dave and Carrot moved on, the local cops raided the station homestead and found large amounts of cocaine and money. The manager had been arrested and charged and was waiting for a trial date, and so far, Mike had gained very little info from him. It seemed the manager had been using his position of trust to become the local drug lord in the area. But this man was small fry compared to what Mike's team was looking for. Cocaine users and meth users rarely mixed, but they couldn't completely discount the fact they may be connected, somehow. It wouldn't be the first time a gang was extending their reach and dealing in more than one illicit drug. Not putting all their eggs in one basket, so to speak.

"Great, we'll join the muster later on this morning." Dale nodded in Finn's direction. "Come and find me once the rest of the crew has gone out. The trucks are due to arrive in the next half an hour."

Ever since word had got out that a truckie had turned up dead after spending the night in the camp, most of the other drivers were opting to overnight in their trucks in the small township of Dimbulah, or leave Townsville extra early in the morning to make it here on time. Finn didn't really blame them. Truckies were a tough breed, but they could also be a superstitious bunch.

"Will do," Finn replied.

Finn sat across the fire from Indy to eat his breakfast. He didn't trust himself not to reach out and touch her if he sat next to her. So, he put himself out of temptation's way. But he couldn't help the way his eyes were drawn to her, like a moth to a flame. She'd tied her hair back into her customary neat ponytail, sleek and put-together once more. The image of that dark hair fanned around her face as he thrust into her last night startled him with its intensity, and he nearly dropped his plate. Wow, he needed to get himself under control.

"You drew the short straw today," Carrot said, taking the chair beside him, already shoving a forkful of beans into his mouth before his bum had even hit the seat.

"Nah, mate." Finn tore his gaze away from Indy to concentrate on the other man. "Someone had to do it, and I don't mind giving the boss a hand."

Carrot screwed up his nose. Given the chance, they'd all rather be out there chasing cattle through the bush, enjoying the adrenaline rush and the freedom, than back here in the hot, dusty cattle yards.

"Whatever." Carrot waved away his arguments. "We've probably only got another three days out here, then the job will be finished. Dave's already lined us up another gig farther west, at a station called Muglibimby. Personally, I'm looking forward to getting outta here. This place is cursed." Carrot lowered his voice as he said this and glanced around to see if anyone else was listening.

No one would say it to any of the Stormcloud staff's faces, but it was what all the contract musterers were thinking. Which was sad, and Finn felt for Dale, because he must be able to feel this undercurrent of unease running through the group. But he had to hand it to all of them; they'd stayed on to finish the job, even under these strange circumstances. Country folk weren't easily scared, but a lot of them had a strong skeptical streak. Finn wondered if Steve and Dale might struggle to get contract musterers next year, once word got around.

Finn knew this job would be coming to an end soon, but he hadn't realized it'd be that soon. Would Mike want him to stay with this team? Want him to keep turning over every rock until they cracked this drug syndicate? Or would he decide they had enough info now and pull him back to help the team follow up with the great information they had? Finn wasn't looking forward to the conversation between himself, Dave, and Carrot if Mike recalled him. It would mean he'd be leaving their team of three one man short, and he didn't like the idea of not following through with a job. Be it a fake, undercover job, or not. He'd signed on with Dave for the next three months, minimum. What would they do if he left them in the lurch half-way through the season? Would they be able to find someone else to replace him?

Finn's gaze rested on Indy across the fire. Whatever happened next, he'd be leaving Stormcloud soon. Would never see Indy again. His chest constricted at the thought.

After breakfast, Finn couldn't help himself, he followed Indy back to her tent, making sure he wasn't seen. Everyone was too busy preparing for their day to notice much else going on, anyway. He caught her elbow right before ducking through the flap into her tent.

"Indy, wait. I just needed to make sure you're okay this morning."

She gave a small squeak of alarm before she turned and saw who it was. "Jesus, Finn. You have to stop sneaking up on me."

"Sorry," he apologized. But he wasn't, really. He was close enough to draw in the distinct smell that was Indy, feel the presence of her body so close to his. "Are you? Okay?"

Her pinched face softened, and her eyes crinkled as she held back a smile. "Yes, Finn, I'm fine." She studied him for a few seconds. "More than fine," she admitted, tipping her chin up. "And I don't regret a minute of last night, if that's what you're asking."

"Me, either." He had no control over the wide grin that overtook his face. The urge to lean in and take her mouth with his was so strong, he was almost overwhelmed.

Her dogs began to yip with excitement; they knew they were about to be let off to go on the muster. She turned her head and shushed them. "I have to go."

"I know," he replied, the cheeky grin refusing to leave his lips. "I'll see you later?" The question hung between them, unanswered. They both knew he wasn't referring to seeing her out on the muster later this morning. He was asking if he should come back to her tent tonight. If she said yes, he would come. All his complications be damned.

She gave a quick nod, and his heart jumped into his throat. He wanted to fist-pump the sky. Instead, he raised a seductive eyebrow and quirked his lips as he nodded his own reply.

Then he watched her slip into her tent, and he sauntered back to the mess tent to get his orders from Dale.

"One of the truck drivers just radioed in. He's blown a tire. They're only just down the road. The other driver has stopped to help him. But they'll be twenty minutes late."

"That's not good." Finn grimaced, but inside he was doing a cautious, happy dance.

"Not ideal, no." Dale removed his hat and scraped a hand through his hair. "I'm gonna see the crew off. Looks like you got twenty minutes to yourself. I'll come get you when they're on the way."

"Thanks, boss." This morning was just getting better and better. The cards seemed to be falling Finn's way.

Where to start his search? The police had already searched the campsite the day after they'd found Wombat's body. So, if he was going to find anything, it'd most likely be extra-well hidden, or in a place they hadn't looked already. The police were usually pretty thorough in their searches, but it didn't mean they were infallible. They'd turned up a handgun hidden beneath the driver's seat of Brian and Rosie's truck. And while the weapon had been concealed, they hadn't gone to any great lengths to hide it. Not like the purpose-built secret lockboxes he'd found beneath the cattle trucks.

Finn stopped in his tracks and tapped his finger to his lips. Come to think of it, the cops carrying out the warrant had done a cursory search of all the vehicles in the camp, but had they done a methodical, inch-by-inch search beneath the chassis of each one, looking for say, an extra muffler, or a secret metal door that might not stand out to a non-mechanically minded officer? He didn't think so. Finn decided he may well have found his first port of call for his search.

Brian and Rosie's truck was by far the biggest, an articulated, eighteen-wheeler which they'd converted into both living and storage quarters. They had a large, canopied area set up so that it extended from the top of the trailer and ran half the length on the outside facing away from the main camp, giving them a covered area where they could sit, and also store boxes of equipment. Finn glanced quickly over his shoulder. No one was around. A cloud of dust marked the spot over near the stabling yards, where everyone was gathering to set out on muster.

Finn sidled around the back corner of their truck. Boxes and other equipment were set up neatly beneath the annex. He tried the door, but it was locked. Unusual. People didn't tend to lock things out here. There was no point. So why had Brian locked his truck? Finn shouldn't read too much into it, perhaps Brian was just being ultra-cautious. This might be his only chance to get inside, however, so Finn pulled out his army knife and took out two small pieces of wire. Picking the lock was easy, and the door clicked open after only thirty seconds. Taking one more quick look around, he climbed the step and closed the door behind him. Inside, it was just as neat as the outside. Probably Rosie's influence, he decided. There was a small galley kitchen, a small table and a bench to sit at, and a double bed at one end that took up half of the space. The rest of the space had been converted to storage, with all sorts of things jammed in behind cupboard doors. Finn opened and closed a couple, finding tinned food and staples in one, plastic containers, cups and plates in another, and a drawer full of different sized screws and other odds and ends. Leather working tools, mechanical tools, spare tire tubes for the ATVs. You name it; it was probably in there somewhere. He pulled out a drawer beneath the small table. It was filled with receipts, paperwork, pens and other stationery. A quick riffle through it all turned up nothing of interest.

Finn wondered how well the police had searched this place. If they'd done it properly, it would've taken hours. But they'd done the whole camp in one night, so it seemed unlikely they'd been particularly thorough. And Finn certainly didn't have that much time. He thumped the wall with frustration. How was he ever supposed to find anything in here?

Abandoning the interior, he opened the door a crack and checked outside to make sure no one was around, then relocked and closed the door. Staring at the piles of boxes, Finn wondered if he had time to tackle those. Brian and Rosie would be stupid to keep anything incriminating out here, wouldn't they? But it wouldn't be the first time things had been hidden in plain sight. Finn lifted the lid of a large plastic storage box. It contained kitchen items such as a roll of aluminum foil, some plastic wrap, paper towels, small Tupperware.

Nope, nothing in there. But as he replaced the lid, something fluttered to the ground. Leaning over to pick it up, he inspected the small, square Ziplock bag. So small. So insignificant. He recognized it immediately. It was the same type of bag that drug dealers used to distribute a single hit of meth. A chill ran over Finn's neck. And a heavy feeling of surety settled in his gut. Was this the clue he been looking for?

He stuffed it in his back pocket and made a decision. He needed to get a look underneath the truck.

Lying on his back, he shuffled beneath the chassis, right next to the rear wheel. Remembering where he'd found the secret metal box beneath the cattle truck the other day, he went straight to where the cavity should be beside the rear wheel. And something wasn't right. Bingo. A large, metal box had been welded into the spot. If you didn't know what you were looking for, it may well blend in with the rest of the chassis. It was caked in dried mud, and starting to rust, and at a quick glance, it looked like it belonged there. Shuffling over to the other side, Finn found an identical box beside the other wheel. Brian, or whoever had these installed, had evened it up, so they look symmetrical. Another trick to make it meld with the rest of the undercarriage.

Both boxes were locked, and no amount of pulling would budge them.

Bugger.

Finn decided to go and look for an extra tailpipe. If it was the same crew installing these hidden compartments, then perhaps—

"Finn, where are you?" Dale's voice echoed around the empty camp.

Shit. Finn went completely still and watched as Dale's booted feet walked slowly past. Time had got away from him. The last thing he needed was to be caught underneath Brian's truck.

"One of the drivers just radioed in and said they're back on the road. They'll be here in five minutes," Dale called.

Finn didn't move, willing Dale to keep walking. Which he did, striding along the side of the truck, then taking off at a tangent, heading back toward the mess tent.

Finn scrambled out the opposite side of the truck and hightailed it into the bush, keeping the truck between him and Dale's direct line of sight. When he was far enough in, he turned around and stalked back toward the camp, calling out,

"I'm here." He made a show of doing up his zip and fastening his fly, as if he'd just answered the call of nature.

Dale turned and frowned as he caught sight of Finn.

"Good, let's get the cattle ready." He beckoned him over and Finn broke into a trot, remembering to brush the dust off his clothes just as Dale turned his back to lead the way to the yards.

He gave Brian's truck one last, longing look. He needed to get back under there. Soon.

CHAPTER FOURTEEN

Indy lay awake on her camp bed, watching the leaves cast shadowy ripples in the moonlight across the ceiling of her tent. Waiting. Hoping. Everyone else had retired to bed half an hour ago. Would Finn fulfill his promise and come to her tonight?

They'd hardly spoken all day, both of them busy with work. And while Indy hadn't been actively avoiding him, she was terrified that people would see her response every time he came near. That they'd see the way she lit up when he was around. But the promise in his eyes this morning had kept her going all day. She could get through not speaking to him for all the long, daylight hours, as long as she had the guarantee of spending another delicious night with him.

But Finn had seemed distracted all evening, and she wondered what was going on in his head. Was it something to do with her? Or was it something to do with his undercover job? Had he new information from his supervisor?

Tired of waiting, Indy got up and went to open her flap, peering out into the darkness. The other times Finn had been prowling around the tent, she'd seen him as he slipped through the trees, a ghostly figure. Straining to see through the dark, she could make out nothing that might hint Finn was on his way. Had she read his body language wrong this morning? Or had he simply changed his mind?

A movement caught her eye, just before a figure appeared in front of her. It was all she could do not to let out a scream.

"It's only me," he whispered, taking her by the arm.

No wonder she hadn't seen him. Tonight, he was all dressed in black, reminding her of a fugitive, or a cat burglar.

"What are you up to?" she asked.

He put a finger to her lips and led her back inside her tent. "I've got to do something. But I promise I'll be back soon."

"What? What do you have to do?" She didn't like where this was going. Especially if it meant he wasn't about to get naked and repeat last night's performance. She'd been driving herself half-mad, thinking about the things she'd liked to do to him tonight.

"It's better if you don't know," he replied quietly. "I found something this morning. But I need to go back and double check it. If I'm right…" He let his words drift away.

"Can I help?" If lending him a hand helped whatever he had to do go quicker, so he could come back to her tent, then she'd be more than happy to join him.

"God, no." He sounded distressed by the very idea.

"Why?" She narrowed her eyes at him. "Is it dangerous?"

"Not really. As long as I don't get caught."

"Has anyone ever told you how infuriating you can be?"

"Maybe once or twice." He gave her a devilish grin and reached his arms around her waist, pulling her hard against his body. "I won't be long. How about you keep the bed warm for me?" His lips descended on hers, and for many moments Indy forgot she was mad at him. Forgot everything except the feel of his mouth and his body pressed against hers.

"*Do* wait up for me," he said, and disappeared out of the

tent.

Indy stood in the middle of her tent, biting her lip. She argued back and forth with herself inside her head. Finn was a trained police officer. He knew what he was doing. It wasn't her place to interfere. She was a civilian, with no combat training and no idea how to help him if he did get into trouble. He'd told her to stay here, and he'd be back soon. But the waiting was killing her.

With a small huff of frustration, she put some clothes on. She couldn't stand the idea that Finn might be putting himself in danger and she was sitting around in her tent like some helpless female, when she could be out there, doing... What? She had no idea. Indy was a woman of action. If something needed doing, she did it. This situation was no different.

Pulling on her boots, she crept through her tent flap. The nighttime bush would normally be filled with the small sounds of nocturnal animals and insects going about their business. But it was quiet. Too quiet. As if the surrounding bush was holding its breath. A shiver of premonition slid over Indy's skin. The smart thing to do would be to stay put. But she'd never been one to do the smart thing.

She had no idea which direction Finn had taken. The stock camp was dark and silent. Barbie whined, and she walked over to pat her on the head. Both dogs were staring in the same direction, to the left-hand side of the camp. The camp was set up in a rough circle, with the mess tent and fire almost in the middle, then everyone's individual tents or trucks on the outskirts at rough intervals, like the spokes of the wheel. Some liked to keep their privacy and kept a larger distance between them and the next bivouac. To her right, Dale, Mack, and Bindi had arrayed their tents in a clump. Indy was loosely a part of the Stormcloud group, but she'd set up her tent a little way into the bush. She liked the shade offered by a giant ironbark, as well as the seclusion. To the left, Brian and Rosie were the next couple around from Indy's tent. She could just make out the square shape of their truck, which they'd reversed beside a stand of acacia bushes. They were one couple who valued their privacy. They'd angled their truck so that the annex under which they sat faced away from the main camp.

According to her dogs, Finn had gone in that direction. The next encampment around from Brian was Dave, Carrot, and Finn's. With the water tank and shower as a buffer between them. Indy had thought Rosie may have chosen the spot to be close to the amenities, but it was also a good screen, now she thought about it.

He wouldn't have gone back to his own tent, would he? Which left Brian and Rosie's place. She told her dogs to be quiet, and instead of heading straight toward their truck, she took a wide loop, creeping carefully through the dry grass and shrubs. When she was close enough, she hunkered down behind a large saltbush and studied Brian and Rosie's temporary home. Nothing moved, and there were no lights on inside, it all seemed completely normal. Had she chosen the wrong target? Was Finn off sneaking around the Scanlon truck instead?

A flicker of light at the base of the truck caught her eye. Was that…? It looked like a flashlight, but was gone as quickly as it had appeared.

Bloody Finn. He was up to his old trick of clambering about beneath vehicles.

Sudden insight struck her. Was he looking for the same hidden boxes he'd found underneath the other cattle truck? It made a strange kind of sense.

A dark figure rolled out from underneath the rear of the truck, scampered on all fours along the side to the first wheel arch, and then disappeared again. There was more flickering of the flashlight.

What was he doing? Indy guessed he'd been right about not needing any help. She should probably go back to her tent. Whatever he was doing, it didn't seem that dangerous. As long as he didn't wake Brian or Rosie—

There was a thump from inside, and Indy froze.

The door clanged open, and Brian came down the steps. In the moonlight, she could see he was barefoot, and wearing only boxer shorts. He had something in his right hand. Was it a flashlight?

"Who's under there?" Brian demanded.

Shit, he must've heard Finn. She hadn't perceived a sound, but then she was quite a distance away.

Brian got down to his hands and knees and a strong beam of light pierced the darkness beneath the truck. "I can see you," Brian said. "Come out here now. And don't try anything, either," Brian added, his voice oddly low and menacing. That didn't sound like the Brian she knew. He was normally so friendly, always ready with a joke to lighten the mood. Then she saw the gun in his other hand, pointed directly at the shape that was now wriggling out from underneath the wheel.

Where the hell had Brian got another weapon? Hadn't the police already confiscated a handgun from him? What did it mean that Brian had more than one gun?

Finn wriggled out on his stomach and got to his knees. But he had a balaclava covering his face.

"Put your hands where I can see them," Brian growled. Finn hesitated, but then raised his hands above his head.

Rosie poked a sleepy head through the door. "What's going—"

"Shut up," Brian hissed. "And get out here and give me a hand."

Indy was shocked at the way he spoke to his wife. But

Rosie didn't seem to notice.

"Grab some rope from the box over there." Brian gestured to the neatly stacked storage containers beneath the annex. Strangely, Rosie did as she was told, not questioning Brian, and not questioning the fact he was holding a strange man at gunpoint. She scuttled toward the box, her bare feet not making any sound in the red dust.

What the hell was going on here?

Why wasn't Finn speaking? Why didn't he just tell Brian who he was? And why were Rosie and Brian acting this way? Almost as if they knew what Finn was up to. Almost as if they'd been expecting this to happen. Indy couldn't stay hidden any longer. She stood and began walking out of the bush. This needed to be sorted out. Once Brian knew it was Finn, he'd put away the gun, and—

Finn suddenly dove sideways while Brian was distracted watching Rosie. He hit the dust and then crawled as fast as he could toward the rear of the truck.

Brian swore and plunged after Finn, grabbing him around the waist just as he was about to turn the corner, knocking him to the ground. Thank God he hadn't tried to shoot Finn.

What did Finn think he was doing? The two men sprawled in the dust, grunting and straining. Brian must've dropped his flashlight when he went after Finn, and now it rolled on the ground, making crazy, flickering shadows.

Indy ran toward the scene. "Brian, get off him," she yelled. "It's Finn, you idiot. Get off him and let him explain."

But Brian ignored her. Instead, he rolled over and managed to get on top of Finn, putting his elbow against Finn's neck.

"Stop that," Indy yelled again, really frightened this time.

"Shut her up, will you?" Brian hissed, staring past Indy's shoulder.

Before she had a chance to turn around, Rosie had her by the throat, and was trying to pull her to the ground, one hand covering her mouth to stop her from calling for help. What the fuck? Mild-mannered, softly-spoken Rosie was trying to squeeze the life out of her? Indy suddenly forgot about Finn and began to fight for her own life. She might be small, but she was strong. Rosie was taller than her, thin and lean, but she wasn't as desperate as Indy. Instead of clawing at Rosie's arm in an attempt to dislodge it, Indy reverted to the dirty fighting tactics she'd learned working with the jackaroos over the years, watching them scrapping and fighting. There'd been one man, the manager of the station she'd been working at one time, Andy, who'd also shown her a few tricks—to help her protect herself, he'd told her. She brought her booted foot down on Rosie's bare toes, eliciting a muffled howl from the other woman. Rosie's hand slipped from covering her mouth, and Indy began to yell at the top of her lungs.

Even if no one in the camp had heard Indy when she called out the first time, they must've heard that. Now she suddenly understood why Brian and Rosie were trying so hard to keep quiet. If no one else came to investigate, then they wouldn't be any the wiser when Finn and Indy disappeared without a trace.

A shaft of clarity hit Indy like a bright light going off in her brain. Finn had found something incriminating underneath their truck. A link perhaps to the drug trade, and perhaps even Wombat's death. And now Brian and Rosie would do anything to keep him quiet. Which meant keeping her quiet, as well.

The blow to Rosie's toes hadn't completely set Indy free, and the other woman still hung on for dear life, her other hand clawing at Indy's face.

Indy landed her elbow into Rosie's ribs, letting out another scream when Rosie's nails bit into her cheek. The bitch was trying to rake her eyes out. Twisting her head back and forth, she grabbed a handful of Rosie's hair and yanked as hard as she could. Indy had never been in a true fight before. Certainly not a fight for her life. But if she could wrangle a wild bush micky bull to the ground for branding, then she could handle this one little woman.

With another vicious kick, she scraped her boot heel down on Rosie's shin. It wasn't enough to dislodge her completely, but she stumbled backward, and her grip on Indy's throat loosened just enough for Indy to turn and face her opponent. She lashed out with all her might, punching Rosie in the face. Once, twice, three times, until Rosie let her go to protect her face. More of Andy's long-ago tuition came back to her, and Indy grabbed Rosie by the wrist and twisted it up behind her back, the way he'd had shown her how to do all those years ago. She never thought she'd ever use this move. But it seemed to work like magic. She'd turned the tables, and now had Rosie at her mercy. All the fight seemed to go out of the other woman, and she sagged against her, sobbing.

She'd won. She could hardly believe it, but she'd won her first-ever fight.

Indy had lost track of what was going on between the two men rolling on the ground, but when she turned around, what she saw froze her blood in her veins.

Finn and Brian were still wrestling, the gun lying a few feet away in the dust, as if it'd been knocked out of Brian's hand. As she watched, Brian broke free and lunged for the weapon, rolling on his back and bringing it up to aim it directly at Finn's chest. Finn also froze midway to standing. His balaclava had come off sometime during the scuffle, and she could see his handsome face clearly in the beam from the flashlight.

"Stop it!" she shouted at the top of her lungs. "Brian, stop this lunacy. It's too late. If you kill Finn now, you won't get away with it. You'll go to jail for the rest of your life. And so will Rosie."

Brian snarled, but didn't take his eyes off Finn.

"She's right," Finn panted. "I'm a cop, Brian. If you shoot me, you can rest assured my team won't stop until they catch you."

"Fuck," Brian yelled. The gun wavered, and Indy hoped their words were getting through to him.

The sound of pounding feet announced the arrival of Dale and Mack, who rounded the back of the truck in a flurry of dust.

"What the hell...?" Dale stopped dead, taking in the scene in front of him, Mack pulling up short behind him.

"There are too many witnesses, Brian. It's over." Finn got to his feet and took a few steps toward Brian. "Give me the gun," he demanded, waving at Dale and Mack to stay where they were.

Indy's heart leapt into her throat. Brian could still shoot him; he was taking an awful chance.

Then Brian did something completely unexpected. He sat up and pointed the gun at his own temple.

"I'm so sorry, Rosie," he said quietly.

Indy gasped in dismay.

"No!" Rosie screamed. "Don't you dare do it. Don't you leave me. I love you." Rosie struggled in Indy's grasp.

"This isn't the right way to do it, man." Finn took another step towards the man sitting on the ground.

"You don't understand," Brian ground out. "I was only doing it for Rosie. For the extra money we needed to buy our property. No one was supposed to get hurt. But he tried to double-cross us. It wasn't supposed to end this way. I don't want to go to jail."

"Please," Rosie pleaded with her man. "Please don't do it. I need you. You can't leave me alone." The woman was almost hysterical in Indy's arms. Indy wasn't sure what role, if any, Rosie had played. But her heart went out to her. No wife should have to witness her husband like this. No wife should have to plead for his life.

Brian looked up and saw Rosie collapsed in a heap at Indy's feet. He lowered the gun and began to sob. In two strides, Finn was by his side, removing the weapon, disarming it, and tucking into the waistband of his jeans.

Once Finn had the gun secured, Indy let go of Rosie. She got to her feet and flew into Brian's arms, both of them sobbing like children.

"Holy fuck," said Dale. "Do you want to let us know what's going on now?"

"Sure," Finn replied, putting his hands on his knees and bending over. "As soon as I get my breath back. And as soon as you call Nash and his boys to come and arrest these two. Keep an eye on them, will you?"

Indy made her way over to Finn and flung her arms around his neck, not caring who was watching. She could hear more people approaching, but for now, her focus was on Finn. He wrapped his arms around her waist, and held her close, perhaps realizing how badly she needed to feel his warm, very-much-alive body against hers.

"Why can't you ever do what you're asked?" he chided softly into her ear.

But she wasn't going to react, instead, tipping his chin up with her fingers, so she could look directly into his face. "Please tell me you're okay?"

"I'm okay," he replied. "A few bruises, nothing broken."

"Jesus, Finn," she breathed. "You nearly gave me a heart attack when Brian pointed that gun at you."

"I nearly gave you a heart attack?" His face took on a look of absolute shock. "When you turned up my heart jumped clean out of my body," he growled. "I'm a trained police officer, Indy. I can look after myself."

"Didn't look that way to me tonight," she responded,

staring up at him, daring him to argue.

He clenched his teeth, but Indy saw the moment he decided to drop the topic, when he rolled his eyes and asked, "What about you?" He touched her face tenderly. "I can't believe you followed me. I can't believe you took that risk."

"I couldn't just sit there." She knew she was trying to justify it to herself. Would she have done the same thing if she'd known what was going to go down? Probably. Giving a shrug of detachment, she raised a cheeky eyebrow. "Better to beg for forgiveness than ask for permission."

"I'm going to change your name. To something like Spitfire, or Firecracker, or Captain Marvel," he mocked gently. But she could see the pride shining in his eyes.

This was turning out to be one helluva night. In the small recesses of her mind, Indy felt regret settle. There would be no hot sex for her and Finn tonight.

CHAPTER FIFTEEN

Finn watched the convoy of police cars wind their way up the dirt track, away from the stock camp. It'd been a wild twenty-four hours, and he drew in a deep breath for what seemed like the first time since he'd discovered the methamphetamine hidden under Brian's truck. The sun was just setting over the horizon, bringing darkness hurrying to cloak the outback.

Nash and Constable Willow had left hours ago, taking Brian and Rosie Wagner with them, to be formally charged at the Dimbulah station. Forensics had been out to inspect the crime scene, and impounded the truck and all of Brian and Rosie's belongings, which had been packed up and driven back to Cairns for further investigation. Detective Sampson and his supervisor, Detective Sergeant Coldwater, were the last to leave, taking the rest of the phalanx of police officers with them.

Standing at the end of the road, Finn could actually say he was glad to see the last of them. It'd been a long, intense day. Emotionally and physically draining. A great catch, according to Coldwater; a huge coup, according to his boss. But his body ached in places he didn't even know existed after his fight with Brian, and now exhaustion was taking over.

Indy came up to stand beside him, slipping an arm around his waist. "Dinner's ready. You must be starving." It was true, he'd hardly eaten all day. He felt a powerful urge to bury his face in Indy's hair, draw in the smell of her, the essence of all that was good in this world.

"How are you feeling?" she asked quietly. "You should be celebrating, you just caught the bad guys. But you seem...a little down."

Finn wasn't sure how he felt. This seemed like a hollow victory. He'd come to know and like the married couple, and found it hard to reconcile the fact they were drug dealers, living right under their noses the whole time. That Brian was an accessory to a murder. It was the hardest part of his job as an undercover detective. Trying to maintain distance was sometimes impossible. To understand your target, you had to get close to them. And he had got close and was now feeling the backlash.

"You're right," he agreed. "I'm not in the mood to celebrate. It doesn't feel right. Even though Brian and Rosie are criminals, they're also our own people."

"It's interesting to hear you say that." She leaned her head on his shoulder. "Does that mean you consider yourself one of us now? A lowly cattle musterer?"

She was trying to lighten the mood, but there was a grain of truth to her words. He was caught between two professions, and he wasn't sure he could even answer her question at the moment. He would always be a detective; it was his calling, his bound duty, but he also felt an affinity for the land. For the simplicity and satisfaction of hard work and long days.

He pulled her into his chest and kissed her. She tasted sweet, of the coffee she'd just consumed, and other things, like decency and authenticity. Indy was one of the most honest people he knew. He drew a bit of that purity into his soul before letting her go.

"But I am starving, and whatever Bindi is cooking smells delicious."

"It's just a barbecue tonight," Indy explained. "It's probably the fried onions you can smell." She took him by the hand, leading him back toward the camp.

"Time to face the music," he muttered, as they drew close to the circle of light around the mess tent. He went to drop Indy's hand, but she wouldn't release him, the look she sent him over her shoulder, saying she wasn't going to hide it now, and they could think what they liked. The group gathered around the fire was just that little smaller, a gap where Brian and Rosie would normally sit. The sight hit Finn in the solar plexus. They were gone because of him. No. He needed to keep reminding himself they were gone because of their own actions.

Helping himself to a plate full of steak and sausages, he nodded at Steve and Dale standing at the back of the mess tent. Steve had choppered in this morning with Aaron, and both men would be staying to see out the last remaining days of the muster. Steve acknowledged Finn, his gaze thoughtful. Finn tried to ignore the awkwardness in the air. People were still coming to terms with who he was and what he'd done.

"Wow, you sure are a surprise," Dave said, as Finn took a seat around the campfire.

There had been so many revelations today, Finn wasn't sure where to start with Dave's statement.

Everyone knew he was an undercover cop.

Everyone knew he was investigating an international drug ring.

Everyone knew Brian had been involved in Wombat's death and would go to jail for a very long time.

Everyone knew he and Indy were...an item.

Which surprise was Dave talking about?

"Who would've thought we were sharing a tent with a pig
—er, cop?" Dave corrected himself at the last second.

Finn grimaced. So that was what was eating him. And
Carrot, too, by the way he curled his lip and glared at him
from beneath lowered eyebrows. The boys were pissed at him
for keeping secrets. And he couldn't really blame them. He'd
conned them into giving him a job under false pretenses,
even if he had carried out that job pretty damn well.

"Yep, sorry about that." He cocked his head to one side.
"But I want you to know, while everything else might've been
a sham, you guys are my friends. And I don't want that to
change."

"Yeah, but what if we'd been the ones smuggling drugs?"
Carrot asked darkly.

The barb struck home. Carrot had him there. Because he
knew he would've turned them in, just like he had with the
Wagners. Maybe Carrot had a point, maybe it was impossible
to make friends when you were an undercover cop.

Scanner looked up from his plate, watching the
interchange with interest, his two daughters doing the same.

"He was only doing his job," Indy retorted, taking a seat
next to Finn. "Don't judge him too harshly."

"Yeah, well, it looks like you haven't judged him harshly at
all," Carrot sneered.

"Oi. That's enough of that." Dale strode into the circle.
"This guy just brought down part of a large drug ring. He's
doing his bit to protect our country from people who want to
exploit it. And us. You guys lay off." Dale stared down Dave
and Carrot until they lowered their gazes and muttered a sort
of apology.

Trust Dale to get it right. He was a great boss. An
upstanding man. Finn would be sad to leave his employ. Finn
didn't want to turn around and look, but Steve must still be
standing in the tent, perhaps watching the proceedings with a

sharp eye. But it was good that he hadn't interfered, letting Dale manage his crew.

The rest of the Stormcloud crew took their seats around the fire, and everyone tucked into their food. Finn could feel the aura of tension running through the group. Perhaps it was time he addressed their questions while they were are all gathered together.

Washing down his last bite of steak with a much-needed beer, he coughed to get everyone's attention.

"Let me tell you what I know," he started without preamble. Mike was probably going to ream his ass for divulging this information, but this crew had a right to know. After everything they'd been through, they deserved answers. Especially Steve and Dale, as this whole thing had played out on their property. Brian and Rosie had told most of this through their hysterical tears as they waited for Nash to arrive. The rest he had gleaned as he listened to Coldwater and Sampson question the couple. Dale and Mack had heard some of it as they helped him guard the couple after they'd called the police.

"But first, can I ask you to keep this all to yourselves, as what I'm about to tell you is classified? It's part of our ongoing investigation, and if any of this got out, it might compromise everything we've worked for." He waited until everybody had acknowledged him with either a nod or a word of affirmation before he continued. "Brian and Rosie have been selling drugs on the side for the past year and a half, maybe longer."

Beth Scanlon gave an audible gasp, then she and Maddie exchanged a look. She was the first to figure out that it meant the contracting couple had been dealing out of the stock camp this time last year. Right under their noses. And no one had suspected a thing. It was a sobering thought.

"But I liked Rosie," Beth stuttered. "She was my friend.

How could she do something so…dishonorable? I don't…"

Maddie reached out and put a hand on Beth's knee. It was always hard when you found out the people you thought you knew well on the outside were completely different on the inside.

"Yes," Finn continued. "Much longer than anyone expected. Clearly, they knew no one in this particular stock camp was interested in buying," Finn hurried to add. "But that wasn't true for other camps where they worked. They made a lucrative business as mobile drug dealers. Selling to anybody who was in need of a hit. You may think remote, country towns don't have a drug problem, but they do. Brian would often sell to smaller dealers in each town at exorbitant prices and then they'd be on their way."

Steve shook his head slowly. "I feel like this was partially my fault. I never thought I'd have to vet my contractors," Steve said, with a despondent frown.

"You couldn't have known." Dale lifted his chin in his stepfather's direction. "This isn't any of our fault."

"Dale's right," Finn confirmed. "The reason most drug dealers get away with it is because they blend in. They're exactly like you and me. Except for one vital point. They don't have strong enough morals to say no to easy cash." How could he explain this so that Steve didn't feel guilty? "Brian and Rosie were a little different from most dealers. They weren't also drug users. They were selling an item for greed alone, and not because they needed to use it, as well. Meth users, or addicts, tend to stand out. You can usually tell there's something a little off with them. But that wasn't the case with Brian or Rosie. So don't go beating yourselves up that you didn't notice something was wrong." Finn hoped that put Steve's mind at ease. But knowing the owner's own high moral standards, he'd probably question himself forever. And would probably also be more circumspect when taking on contractors next time.

"Why did they do it?" Beth asked. "It's so hard to wrap my head around."

"To help them buy that property they had their hearts set on. It would've taken them another four or five years of hard slog to be able to afford it by doing contract mustering. Rosie was desperate to settle down. She wanted to start having kids." Finn lifted one shoulder. Wasn't it the same story the world over? "But it seems Brian was the mastermind, and Rosie went along with it when she found out how much money they could make. Brian said he was only doing it for Rosie. And Rosie said she was only doing it for Brian." Love sucked sometimes. Made you do stupid things. He was sad that this couple's love had led them to do something so desperate.

"So where does Wombat fit into all this?" Scanner asked, clearly not caring about the motivations behind the criminal couple, more interested in the gory stuff.

Finn took another swig of his beer before he answered. "Wombat was the middleman. He supplied Brian and Rosie with the drugs they needed to on-sell. Problem was, Wombat told them he didn't have any meth for them this time around. They knew it wasn't true, because Brian had been in touch with his contact the day before, who assured him the drug drop would be made by Wombat. The night Wombat was murdered, Brian called his contact to complain, and he said he had someone in the area who would come and *sort it out*." Enter Ronaldo.

"Yeah, well, that's one way to sort out a problem. Kill the guy," Carrot scoffed.

"Yes, it was certainly an overuse of force," Finn agreed. "And I think Brian will confirm these facts once they've questioned him thoroughly. But it seems things got out of hand. Ronaldo wasn't supposed to kill Wombat. According to

Brian, he and Ronaldo were just supposed to scare him enough to hand over the drugs to the Wagners. Brian lured Wombat into the bush, where Ronaldo surprised him. Ronaldo demanded he hand over the rest of the drugs immediately. But when Wombat refused, saying they were missing, that they'd never been in his truck in the first place —which everyone knew was a lie—Ronaldo *lost his shit* according to Brian, and went bat shit crazy, pulling out a concealed machete and hacked the other man to pieces."

"Yeah, we saw his handiwork up close and personal," Indy chimed in. "I think bat-shit crazy pretty much sums it up."

"But what was this Ronaldo doing here in the first place? How did he just mysteriously appear out of the bush?" This was Steve, trying to get the conversation back on track.

"That's where things get a little sketchy. We believe Ronaldo was sent to watch Wombat, because the gang already suspected him of skimming off the side. And possibly keep an eye on the other truck drivers, as well. Which is why he was situated in that camp not far away."

"But how did Ronaldo end up dead? If he killed Wombat, then who killed him?" Dale asked, deep frown lines showing his confusion. "Oh, God, don't tell me it was Brian?" He leaned forward, elbows on knees, and stared at Finn, aghast.

"I don't think so," Finn replied. "Like I said, it's all a little confused, but Brian was adamant he never killed anyone. Brian said Ronaldo was alive and well when he left to return to his secret camp. Mighty pleased with himself, by the sounds of it. Whether there was another man in that camp with Ronaldo and when he found out what he'd done, he took revenge. Or whether the gang found out how badly he'd fucked up, and sent someone to sort him out, we're not sure yet."

"But we're in the middle of the outback. You don't just send someone to sort something out," Dale argued. "It's not like we're in the city, and you can just hop in a car and drive around the corner." He shook his head and banged the edge of his plate with his finger to make his point. "My vote goes to there being a second person in that camp."

Finn probably agreed with Dale, it was one of the major puzzle pieces his team were trying to fit together. They'd already rehashed this topic many times since he, Mack, and Indy had found the corpse, but were no closer to having an answer.

Possibly even more important was the identity of that second man. Finn thought about the silver lighter sitting guilelessly in his jeans pocket. He still hadn't told Mike about the find, or his suspicions. He'd thought about telling him, but it was all too insane earlier today, when Finn had talked to his sarge over the sat phone. Mike had jumped on the first plane out from Sydney to Cairns, where he was going to meet with Coldwater and Sampson. He also hoped to get a chance to interrogate the Wagners himself.

Finn was going to call him again tonight, after everything had settled down, to catch up on the day's fast-moving events. And try to slip Garrett's name into the conversation, make sure there'd been no further sightings. Finn would love to know how his brother had got mixed up in this gang, and what his role was, but he was unlikely to find out, now. He guessed his brother had hightailed it out of the area. If he'd even been there at all. Even though he was sure the lighter belonged to Garrett, it wasn't indisputable evidence that he'd been in that camp. Someone could've stolen the lighter, or Garrett could simply have given it away. And Finn couldn't really tell Mike now that he'd tampered with the evidence. Taking the lighter was a huge no-no. He'd definitely receive a reprimand, and it could possibly hurt any further chances of promotion. If Garrett was a part of this drug gang, it'd come out soon enough. Finn decided to hold his tongue.

Mike was probably going to ask Finn to come to Cairns. In Mike's view, his undercover job was finished here now. But Finn wasn't so sure. He wanted to stay for another two days until the end of muster. Just to make sure the Stormcloud crew were kept safe. Until that mystery second person was located, Finn wouldn't rest easy. Mike would argue that it wasn't his job to keep them safe, but Finn would argue it was. The sarge would have everyone working twenty-four-seven on the case. They had plenty of clues, they just needed to put the puzzle pieces together now. Mike would be working frenetically to crack the case before the syndicate decided it was too risky and fled back into the dark corners of Italy, or even around the globe.

Indy nudged his knee, bringing him back to the present. Her eyes sparkled in the firelight and his chest tightened at her beauty in that single moment.

If only he could be one-hundred-percent sure he was staying for the right reasons. Was he just trying to convince himself that his job wasn't truly over? Or was Indy the reason?

"I agree there was probably a second person in the camp," Finn said, forcing his thoughts back to the current conversation. "As soon as my team works it out, I'll let you know."

"That'd be great," Carrot mumbled sarcastically, as if he didn't really believe Finn.

"All this talk about murders and drug trafficking is doing my head in," Dale said, standing up and stretching. "And after our severe lack of sleep last night, I'm gonna hit the hay early; don't know about the rest of you."

"So, we're back out to muster tomorrow morning?" Scanner asked. "Same as always?"

"Yep, everything is back to normal," Dale confirmed.

"I'll help Bindi with the dishes, and we won't be far behind you," Mack said, capturing Bindi's hand and pulling her to her feet. She smiled at him so sweetly, a smile meant only for him. It gave Finn a jolt. Not jealousy, exactly, more like a yearning to have something like that. That special connection between a man and a woman. He could have that with Indy, if he wanted. But what would he have to sacrifice to make it happen?

"So, the million-dollar question is, are you staying on to complete the muster?" Steve asked Finn, bringing him back from his musings. The Scanlon group, who were all about to leave the campfire, turned and stared at him with interest, as did everybody else.

"Yes, sir, I'd like to, if you'll have me. I like to finish a job once I start."

"Good man." Steve nodded approvingly. "Now that we're two people down, your help will be appreciated." He and Dale disappeared into the dark together. Finn knew they wouldn't be heading straight to bed, as they had indicated. There were always jobs to do for someone in charge, such as switching off the generator that drove the shower, checking on the horses one last time. One of Dale's nightly rituals was to visit the cattle yards, just to make sure they were secure for the night.

Indy's knee nudged his own again, and he looked over to see relief in her eyes. He should've realized she would've been wondering this same thing.

Two more days. It meant he had two more days to spend with Indy. What he did with that time was the question at the top of his mind. He needed to talk to her tonight. Needed to tell her how he was feeling. If only he could figure that out himself.

"I'm going to help with the dishes as well," Indy declared, getting up and gathering other people's plates.

"Don't you dare," Bindi said from behind her folding table.

"Mack will stay with me. After the night you guys had last night, you need to get some shuteye. Go to bed, girl, I've got this." Bindi jutted out her chin, and even Finn could tell she wasn't taking no for an answer. He also didn't miss Bindi's suggestively raised eyebrow as Indy walked past her, plainly indicating she thought Indy may have more than just sleep planned for tonight.

"Okay, if you're sure?" Indy placed the plates in front of Mack, who was filling a bowl with steaming water. Bindi waved a dish towel to shoo her away. "All right, I'm going," Indy laughed.

Just before she stepped out of the circle of light to go find her own tent, Indy turned to send a searching look toward Finn.

He nodded once in reply. Yes, he would come to her. His cock rose at the thought of what they might do together tonight.

Dave leaned over, shaking him out of his contemplation of Indy's swaying hips fading into the gloom. "Sorry, mate, I didn't mean that earlier, this is all just a bit of a shock, you know. You're still me mate. And you're still one of the best bloody motorcycle riders I've ever met."

High praise indeed.

"And don't worry about him." Dave nodded in Carrot's direction. "I'll talk him around."

"Thanks," Finn replied.

Even though the secret was out about him and Indy, Finn still hesitated to make it obvious he was following too quickly behind her. He would sit here with Dave and Carrot for a few more minutes, then he needed to go and call Mike. He wasn't looking forward to this conversation. But after that…he was definitely looking forward to the time he could slip into Indy's tent.

CHAPTER SIXTEEN

Indy lay in her camp bed, waiting for Finn. She was tired, had been awake for nearly forty-eight hours, and the fatigue had settled into her bones. But she needed Finn more than she needed sleep. Needed to hold him against her, have him make love to her, cradle her body afterwards. To help block out the horrors of the past day. To prove there was still some decency left in the world. And to prove that Finn was still the man she thought he was, beneath that cold, hard exterior he'd shown last night. In her heart of hearts, of course, she realized Finn was a police detective, with all the clichés that went with the title. Judging right and wrong in terms of black and white. Ruthless in pursuit of justice. A formidable physical force to be reckoned with. But it'd taken watching him in action last night to bring the reality to her. The look of pure focus on his face as he arrested Brian, ignoring the way the man still blubbered. Eyes steely and hard as he read Brian his rights, and slipped the handcuffs on Rosie's wrists.

Her mind wouldn't stop spinning. There'd been no doubt in Finn's mind that he was doing the right thing. If the shoe had been on the other foot, would she have been able to arrest Brian and Rosie? She didn't think so. And perhaps that was why she could never become a police officer.

There was also the other side to Finn, the side she was coming to know. The highly affectionate, slightly goofy one minute, serious and thoughtful, the next, tender and skilled lover. The guy with the look of complete joy on his face as he shot after a micky bull on his motorcycle. Hard working, and dependable, easy going, fitting into the muster crew so easily. Becoming friends. With her and the others.

Or was that all a cover? She wished she knew.

It was hard to reconcile the rugged, outdoor man Indy had come to know, with the slick, professional, city bloke Finn must be normally when he was on the job.

Even with all this swirling around in her head, she must've fallen asleep, because suddenly someone was touching her cheek and her eyes flew open to see Finn kneeling next to her camp bed.

"Sorry. That last call to my supervisor took longer than I expected." His voice was quiet, and he was a dark, amorphous shape in the dim night.

She grabbed a handful of his hair and pulled him to her, lifting her head to meet his mouth with hers. This is what she'd been waiting for. Finn and her, finally alone together. He tasted exactly like she remembered, warm and spicy; a little like coming home. A flare of heat darted through her veins as he kissed her, accompanied by a welcome ache between her thighs.

"I missed you," she said, when she finally released him.

She wasn't going to ask him about what his sergeant had said. She didn't want to think about dead guys, fly-ridden bodies in the bush, friends who turned out to be betrayers. All she wanted was to lose herself in Finn for a few hours, get drunk on that visceral response he elicited.

"I missed you, too," he replied, the light of seduction turning up the corners of his mouth.

She pulled him down for another long, lingering kiss,

leaving him in no doubt of what she wanted.

"Look what I've got," Finn said, breaking the kiss and digging in his jeans pocket, producing a handful of little silver packets. "I had to ask Dave," he admitted sheepishly. "I think I took his whole supply."

"Better that than no sex," she replied. "I'm sure we could've got innovative without them," she added with a smirk. But she was glad Dave had come through. There was no way she was going to have unprotected sex so soon after her recent surprise pregnancy. Not even with Finn; not even with the way she felt at the moment. The miscarriage was still too raw. But like she'd said, there was more than one way to have fun. Now she knew she was safe, she could relax. "But it's always good to know we can also rely on the good old-fashioned missionary position."

"I'll have you know, I have a lot more in my repertoire than just the missionary," he retorted. Looking down at his hand, he counted the silver packets. "Four," he announced with glee. "Four different ways we're going to do it tonight."

"Good. I plan on using them all," she whispered into his ear, trailing her fingernails up beneath his shirt and lightly scratching the skin.

Finn seemed to catch her sense of urgency, as he dropped the packets on the floor and shoved her tank top up and over her head, dropping it next to the condoms, leaving her sitting half-naked in her bed.

"Such beautiful breasts," he sighed with pleasure, before dropping his head to suckle one nipple. She arched her back, pressing herself into his mouth. But then decided they needed more room to maneuver.

"Wait." She pushed him, so he rocked back on his heels, then threw her blanket on the floor and got out of the camp bed. Finn took her cue and was already undoing his belt, yanking down his jeans and rushing to tug his boots off.

She followed suit, shucking her sleeping shorts with one quick flick of her wrist. Finn stalled, his shirt half-way off, staring as she stood naked and unafraid in front of him.

After the last few days—hell, the last few weeks—she was so full of adrenaline and impatience; she felt a wildness build in her. Lying down on the blanket, she beckoned him with a crook of her finger. Hurriedly, he tossed his shirt aside and was on his knees beside her in one fluid movement.

"Have I ever told you how exquisitely beautiful you are?" he muttered, and her breath hitched in her chest at the intensity of his words.

She had no air left in her lungs to answer him.

He leaned in and flicked his tongue against the hollow at the base of her neck, finding her pulse and capturing it with firm lips. She inhaled sharply at the exquisiteness of his touch, digging her nails into his back. The bristles of his stubble—he hadn't had a chance to shave in the past two days—rasped across her skin, sending deep shivers of pleasure straight to her core.

Lowering himself slowly over her, he flattened her breasts against the hard wall of his chest, and her nipples peaked at the friction as he gently moved his body up and down. Then he rolled them both over, so he was on the bottom and now she had control. Maybe. Or maybe he was the one still in control. The skim of his large, hot hands over the naked skin of her hips had her dragging in a trembling breath. Sharp teeth nipped at her throat, then ran up her neck until his tongue flickered against her earlobe.

A low humming sound came unbidden from deep in her chest. Her body burned at his assault on the sensitive parts of her neck.

She pressed her thigh against the hard shaft of his erection and felt a small thrill when he shuddered in reaction. He took her mouth, sliding his tongue in deep, and the carnal sensation of his stroke transferred to a building need between her thighs. She began to gyrate against him, reveling in the friction, the pressure of his thigh between her legs a drumbeat pulsing in her veins.

Rising on her elbows, she panted, "Time for packet number one."

A deep, rasping laugh erupted from inside his chest; she felt the vibrations run through her, making her nipples ache with need. "In a bit of a rush, aren't we?" He grated his thigh between the notch of her legs, setting all the nerve endings in her body alight. No time to wait. She slid a hand between their bodies and grasped his cock, which twitched and surged in reaction.

"Now, Finn," she demanded, yearning and impatient.

He didn't need to be told twice. Reaching with one hand, he felt around until he found one of the packets.

"Let me do it." She took the foil square from his palm, using her teeth to rip it open. Then she nipped at his mouth with those same teeth, sucking on his bottom lip, letting him know how much she wanted it. At the same time, she slowly rolled the condom on, luxuriating in the way he jerked and groaned beneath her fingers. Turning, she straddled him again and, taking her time, she positioned herself above the tip, holding still for three beats of her heart. Then she clenched her thighs and took him in.

In the filtered moonlight, his blue eyes met hers. Trust, yearning, and possessiveness lit deep in their depths. There was a connection deeper than merely two bodies joined together. As he surged inside her and Indy cried out, tremors began to build in her stomach, in her chest, in her arms and legs. Bolts of white heat darted through her, straight to her core. There was no denying this beautiful thing between them. She moved faster, and he matched her stroke for stroke, until there was nothing but him and her, until her whole world paused. On a knife edge. And then her orgasm swallowed her. Vaguely, she heard him cry out as her muscles rippled around him and her whole body shuddered violently.

She didn't know how long she lay on top of Finn, completely drained and satiated. His hands softly stroked the length of her body as he remained buried deep inside her. When she finally found the strength, she levered up onto her elbows and stared down into his face. He ran a finger across her bottom lip. A move both possessive and caressing. She traced the strong lines of his jaw with her gaze, caught in the depth of his stunning azure eyes.

Shit. She was in trouble. She was falling in love with this man.

Now what?

Indy rolled off him and lay on her back. Finn got up on his elbow and began stroking her hair. Softly. Tenderly. The sound of a million frogs from the nearby billabong filled the air. It was peaceful, and Indy couldn't remember a time when she'd felt more content. Overflowing with feelings of happiness. Finn was everything. A spirited and curious lover. A man with high moral standards. Courageous. Fearless. Incredibly good looking. And he was here with her, treating her body like a temple, and worshipping her every physical need. What they shared was far stronger than just sex. And therein lay the true danger. She had bonded with Finn. Powerfully. Irrevocably. This was much more than a few nights of hot sex in a tent.

But try as she might, she couldn't banish the gnawing doubts about where this was going. What was going to happen in two days' time? She didn't want to break this precious bubble around them. Let them stay like this until morning, and maybe then she'd ask the questions.

Finn continued to stroke her hair as she stared into his eyes.

This relationship was so new. There were so many things they didn't know about each other. She still hadn't told him the full truth about her and Patrick. About the pregnancy, and her miscarriage. From what she knew about Finn now, she didn't think he would be frightened away by her revelation, and she knew she needed to tell him soon. But there was something holding her back. Perhaps it was the fact he had a daughter of his own. Perhaps a small part of her envied him. Wondered if he would want any more children later down the track.

"This is getting complicated, isn't it?" Finn broke the silence.

"Yeah," she agreed. "It's just that..."

"There's so much we don't know about each other," he finished for her.

How did he do that? Were they really that much on the same page?

"There's one thing I do know," he added. "Even with all the shit going on around us, I know we found something special. *You* are a special lady, Indy. And I want to spend more time with you."

It was bittersweet. Because while she agreed with him, she couldn't see how this would work. Of course, there were options. Love was about making sacrifices and compromises. She could take a job in Sydney. But the mere thought of moving into the city made her insides contract. What would happen to her horses and her dogs if she did that? She wasn't sure she was prepared to make that sort of sacrifice. Would Finn be prepared to take a job as a stock hand out here in the country, instead? She didn't think she could ever ask him to abandon his career just for her. Perhaps a long-distance relationship, at least in the first instance, until they got to know each other better, might work.

"Let's just take these next two days and see where they

lead us," she said. "We don't need to make any decisions right now."

"If that's what you want," he agreed.

They were agreeing to ignore their problems, for now. It didn't mean they'd magically go away. All Indy wanted was to enjoy Finn as long as she could.

"Now, I still count three more condoms lying on the floor over there." His serious eyes turned mischievous.

"Already?" she queried, returning his cheeky smile with one of her own. "You want to go again, huh, stud?"

"That's me." He tapped her nose with his finger and reached over to grab another foil packet. "Just call me stud, from now on." He wasn't kidding, she could feel his rock-hard erection pressed into her thigh, letting her know just how ready he was.

All her fatigue washed from her bones. Taking the chance to spend the next few hours with Finn would be worth the hours of lost sleep. She would keep this gorgeous man in her heart for the rest of her life, even if she could only have him in the flesh for a few more days.

CHAPTER SEVENTEEN

Finn blinked his bleary eyes. Rubbing them did no good. The only thing that'd fix his blurry eyesight was sleep. But he wasn't counting on getting much tonight, so his eyes would just have to suck it up. He'd run undercover ops before, where he'd gone three to four days on very little sleep, so this was nothing new.

Dave nudged his elbow and said, "Too much nocturnal activity last night, huh?"

"Yeah, the missus keep you awake all night?" Carrot sniggered. At least Carrot seemed to have come around and forgiven Finn for his sins, for which he was grateful.

Finn merely raised an eyebrow and went back to listening to the banter around the campfire, waiting for the dinner gong to sound. There was no way he was giving out details of his exploits with Indy. At least everyone had accepted he and Indy were a couple without any fanfare. Almost as if it had been a given. A bit of friendly ribbing was to be expected. He'd even seen Beth smile encouragingly at Indy, giving a wink and a nod in Finn's direction. Which made him wince inwardly, but he didn't blame the crew for needing something else to talk about besides death and mutilation.

He'd been avoiding turning his sat phone on all day,

avoiding Mike at all costs. After their conversation last night, Mike would probably still have steam coming out of his ears. Finn had practically overruled his supervisor's command to return from the field, refusing to leave until Friday night, when the muster would be over, and everyone would go their separate ways.

Like he'd predicted, Mike wanted everyone back in the office to work non-stop on bringing these guys down. Mike thought they had a solid lead as to the man in charge of the whole operation. The GPS tracker they'd planted in the drugs, which'd been sitting in the port for the past few days, was showing the drugs had moved. It'd led them to a house in the outer suburbs of Townsville, where they'd arrested a man who turned out to be a courier; a middleman who would distribute the meth to various dealers. But the courier had broken down much more easily than they expected and given them some names. Most of them were dealers he worked with, but one he'd assured the cops was the name of someone big in the drug ring. An Italian businessman living the high life in Broome, but with rumored connections to the underworld, as well as mafia connections back in his home country. The team was making connections and talking to sources to confirm the details. But if the lead proved correct, they'd be launching a raid, possibly within the next few days, and definitely within the week. Mike wanted Finn there to take part. Finn wanted to be there, also. Not wanting to miss his chance to be part of such a historic takedown.

Finn had argued back and forth with the sarge, trying to come up with a concrete reason he needed to stay and see out the end of the muster. Mike had eventually grudgingly agreed, but made it on one condition. If the raid was scheduled to take place sooner, then he wanted Finn's ass back ASAP.

Two cattle trucks, both with double trailers, had rattled

into camp just as everyone was taking their seats around the fire. Bindi had sighed and laid out two more plates for dinner. "They always seem to manage to time it just right," she grumbled.

But who could blame the truckies? Bindi's cooking seemed to be getting a good reputation out here. And perhaps that reputation was overturning the rumors and innuendo caused by two murders at the camp. Finn had no way of knowing if these truck drivers were clean or dirty. Now they had garnered the information they needed, the task force was letting the drug gang continue to run unhindered, until they were ready to pounce. So, these trucks could well be loaded with methamphetamine. It was no longer Finn's duty to check, however, and he was glad about that. All he was doing now was monitoring the crew's safety and making sure nothing untoward happened in the next two days.

Which was good, because all Finn could think about right now was grabbing a hot shower to finish off this long day, and falling into bed with Indy.

The two truck drivers joined them, introducing themselves as Brandy and Clive. A husband-and-wife team, who often drove together. Interesting. Finn had to keep reminding himself it took all types to make the world go round, and it was very different out here in the country. Brandy was a tiny woman who at first glance resembled a child, walking along beside her large, hirsute husband. Until she finally turned around to face them all, and her large breasts seemed completely out of place on her petite body. The question, *were these two hauling drugs tonight?* ran through his brain, but he was so tired that, for once, he didn't really care.

It was nice to have two fresh faces in the mix. They brought in news from the outside world. But they also said that Stormcloud Station was the talk of the outback, with speculation flying about the two bodies found so close together. Very little information had been released to the public. And luckily, they were so remote that the media had pretty much ignored them. Preferring instead to get their updates directly from Senior Sergeant Johnson in Cairns. Except for the few brave souls who'd ventured out to Dimbulah to try and track down the story. They hadn't lasted very long in the heat and flies and the lack of information being sent their way. So far, it seemed there'd been no hint of the true nature of the crime, or that drug smuggling was involved. Which put Finn's mind at ease.

Indy plonked herself down in the chair next to Finn, fresh from the shower. He couldn't help it, he lifted his nose, and breathed in deep. "You smell good," he whispered.

"I know," she whispered back, touching the tip of her tongue to her front teeth and giving him a seductive smile that only he could see.

They still had one condom left from last night. But after that was gone... Finn considered asking Carrot if he had any to spare. Not for the first time, Finn berated himself for not bringing any protection. But it'd never crossed his mind he'd need them out here.

"I borrowed something from Bindi," she said quietly in his ear, and his heart leapt. He knew exactly what she was talking about.

"Nice," he replied with a wink.

They chatted over dinner, and of course the truckies wanted to hear all about the double murder. Finn listened as the rest of the crew were only too happy to fill them in on the details. He was bone tired, and all he could think about was sleeping next to Indy. This might be sacrilege, but he may have to forego the sex for some sleep. But at least if he was doing it next to Indy, it'd be the next best thing.

While everyone was still discussing the intricacies of how a man could be murdered in such a gory manner, but yet no one in the camp had heard anything, Finn leaned over and spoke to Indy. "I'm just going to take a shower and do a quick tour of the camp. Then I'll be over to you in half an hour or less."

"I'll be waiting," she said, lowering her gaze coquettishly. He didn't need any more invitation than that.

With a renewed bounce in his step, he gave his plate to Bindi and made off for his tent to collect a set of clean clothes. He hadn't done any washing for over a week, and was running low on things to wear. Washing facilities out here were basic, at best. An old wringer washing machine had been set up near the shower, plugged into the generator that supplied the pump for the water. But you had to stand and watch it the whole time, otherwise it chewed your clothes and Finn hadn't found the time. Perhaps he could do a couple of shirts and some boxer shorts in the shower with him.

Quickly visiting his tent, he grabbed his flashlight, some clothes and his shampoo, and headed for the shower. He really should've done it earlier, the air had a decided chill in it, now the sun had gone down. Using his flashlight to find his way in the dark, he whistled something happy as he rounded the back of the water tank.

A rusty old spotlight had been set up above the shower, but when Finn flipped the switch, nothing happened. Bugger, the bulb must have blown. He needed to tell Dale to come and fix it. But he was here now, and his flashlight would do the trick. The shower was a small cupboard like structure, open to the sky, with a foot-high gap running around the bottom where the water ran off into a gulley. He stepped inside and shut the door. Maneuvering in the small, cubicle-like space wasn't easy, but he found a spot on top of the wall where could rest his flashlight. Stripping off quickly, he folded his clothes and pushed the pile underneath the bottom of the cubicle, placing his hat on top, then turned on the tap and stood back, waiting for the hot water to flow through.

Suddenly, the flashlight disappeared, and his world was plunged into darkness.

Shit. It must've fallen off the wall. Now he'd have to go out there stark naked, and search around in the dark until he found it.

He fumbled around until he found the latch and opened the door. A figure loomed in front of him, then a bright light flashed in his eyes, blinding him.

"Evening, bro."

That voice.

It was Garrett.

"What the hel—" Something struck him on the side of the head and his world went black.

CHAPTER EIGHTEEN

Where the hell was Finn? Indy was getting tired of waiting. He said he'd be half an hour, at the most, it was now over an hour, and her impatience was building, turning into a licking flame of anger and doubt. What could be keeping him so long? He'd mentioned that he wasn't going to talk to his boss tonight, but maybe he'd changed his mind. Or perhaps he changed his mind about coming to her tent? No, he wouldn't do that. Finn was a decent man; he wouldn't hang her out to dry like that. Certainly not after that look he'd sent her just before he left the campfire, like he wanted to devour her whole. Perhaps he'd got caught up chatting to David and Carrot. But by the sound of it, everyone had gone to bed.

Dammit. She got out of bed and wandered over to lift the flap of her tent, peering outside into the darkness. She'd left the small tent light on low to help Finn find his way. Where was he? Should she go and look for him? Taking a few careful steps, not wanting to step on anything nasty with her bare feet, she walked to the corner of her tent and peered around the edge. All the lights in the camp were out, except for hers, which confirmed her theory that everyone was asleep. She wrapped her arms around her middle, the cool night air nipping at her bare skin.

That did it. She was going to look for him. As she turned around to go back into her tent, the snap of a twig brought her head up.

"Finn, is that you?"

A figure stepped out of the gloom, and she gave a sigh of relief as she recognized Finn's broad shoulders, and his quick, easy step.

"Yeah, babe, it's me," Finn replied. Before she knew it, he'd removed his hat and scooped her up in his arms, and kissed her, his tongue delving into her mouth, hungry and urgent. She wanted to melt into him, but something stopped her. Perhaps it was the remnants of anger that he'd made her worry unnecessarily. Whatever it was, she pushed him away.

"I thought you were going to have a shower," she said, when he released her mouth reluctantly. He sure didn't smell like he'd had a shower. Exactly the opposite, in fact. Almost like he hadn't showered in days, the smell of dry sweat a little overpowering.

"Sorry, babe, I was going to, but something's come up. We need to leave. Now."

"Oh, no." She put a hand to her mouth. "What's happened? Why do we need to leave?"

"I'll tell you on the way. But you need to get dressed. Quick, now." He patted her on the bottom, pushing her toward the open tent flap.

He followed her inside, his features thrown into sharp relief by her small light. He looked worried as he tugged his hat down deeper over his brow. Was there something different about his face? She searched his eyes for a second. That same brilliant blue they always were. His strong jawline and sharp aquiline nose all so familiar. Same clothes she'd just seen him in earlier tonight. Nope, it was definitely Finn.

"What about everyone else?" she asked, hurriedly pulling a T-shirt on over her tank top.

"Nah, they're all safe. It's you I need to get out of here. You're the one in danger."

Oh, God. That didn't sound good. "What sort of danger?"

"I heard someone from the gang is coming to get me. And you. They found out about you helping me, and they want to get rid of us both." Finn banged his hat agitatedly against his thigh.

"Oh, Jesus," she breathed. She dragged her jeans on over the top of her sleep shorts, Finn avidly watching her every move. Normally, she liked it when his hungry gaze flicked up and down her body. But tonight it felt a little…inappropriate. Especially given what he'd just told her.

"Where are we going? How did you find out? Have you told your boss yet?" Sitting down, she tugged on her boots.

"Nah, I haven't had time. I was talking to Clive, and he said something that made me suspicious. Look, I'll answer all your questions later, we need to get moving." He made shooing movements with his hands, hurrying her along.

"Coming." She grabbed her jacket at the last second, knowing it would get cold outside soon, and preceded him out of the tent.

"Where are we going?" she asked, suddenly wondering what his plan was. Finn didn't have a vehicle of his own, he travelled with Dave and Carrot in their truck. Unless he was planning on using his motorbike. "And are you sure we shouldn't wake Dale and Steve? At least tell them we're leaving."

She didn't really feel like Finn had any sort of proper strategy worked out. She knew she shouldn't doubt him, but still.

"I left a note," he replied, but she thought she detected a slight hesitation in his answer.

"A note? Who for? Do you mean Dave?"

"Yeah, I left a note for Dave. Come on, babe, we need to

go." He took her by the hand and led her directly into the bush.

What was with this *babe* thing? Finn had never called her *babe* before. For some reason, she didn't like it. And what was this story about Clive telling him something that made him suspicious? Not a lot of this was making sense, but for now, Indy had no choice but to go along with it. She'd get to the bottom of it soon enough.

They battled their way for a long time through the bush. Indy thought they were heading in a northerly direction, toward Repeater Hill, but she couldn't be sure. The moon had yet to rise tonight, leaving them only starlight to navigate by. She should've thought to bring a flashlight. Actually, why hadn't Finn brought a flashlight?

"Where are we going?" she finally asked. This was becoming ridiculous. Escaping on foot from the stock camp wasn't going to work. They were miles from anywhere. They'd end up getting lost. Wouldn't it be better to go back and ask Dale or Steve to drive them out? Finn was the trained police detective here, but she was beginning to doubt his sanity.

"I've got a little hideout, just over this ridge," he replied.

He what? Why hadn't he mentioned anything about this before?

"The boss always told me I should have a bolthole, if I needed it."

"Oh, okay." She let him grab her hand and tug her along again. That all sounded... plausible. So why was her skin crawling? And why did his hand feel clammy in hers? Her feet began to drag, and she stumbled a few times over logs and rocks.

"Nearly there," Finn encouraged.

They headed up a short, steep incline. This must be the ridge Finn was talking about. The trees opened as they crested the top, and Indy got a quick glance at the surrounding bushland before they headed back down the other side. Finn pulled her along eagerly until they were practically jogging down the other side.

"Slow down," she cried. She was going to take a tumble in the dark if he kept up this pace. Why was he in such a hurry? And why was he not listening to her?

The ground leveled off beneath their feet, and she sighed in relief. Leaning back, she managed to pull her hand away from Finn's grasp, just as he announced, "We're here," and suddenly stopped in front of her.

It was hard to tell where *here* was in the dark. They seemed to have come to a standstill on the edge of some sort of dirt track. She could see the pale line of cleared bush stretching away to either side of them.

"I think," he added, staring into the dark is if trying to get his bearings. "Are we far enough north?" he muttered to himself.

Far enough north for what? But she didn't voice the question. Instead, she delved into her memories, and decided this could possibly be the track that led to the secret bush camp where she, Finn, and Mack had discovered the body. They'd been heading in the same direction, but when she and Finn had done this on their horses, they crossed the ridge through a saddle higher up Repeater Hill, and so had missed the track completely. With all the traffic from the police investigation, the unused route had become more pronounced.

"Yep, this is right," he confirmed. "Now, we just have to wait."

"Wait for what?" Indy was becoming increasingly irritated by Finn's lack of communication.

"Oh, come on, babe. Don't be like that." Without warning, he grabbed her by the waist and pulled her hard against his chest. "I thought you trusted me."

"I do," she replied. "But—"

His mouth descended on hers, cutting off the rest of her words. Lips hungry and demanding pressed against hers, his tongue flicking in and out, delving so deep she felt she might gag. His erection pressed into her stomach, hard and pounding through his jeans. He definitely wanted her. It was weird and a little off-putting. This was neither the time nor the place to be thinking about sex. She wanted answers, not kisses. She shoved him in the chest.

"Finn, get off me. What are you doing?"

But he didn't let her go. "Mm, you taste good. Better than I imagined."

What was he talking about? "Finn, I mean it. Get off me." She struggled in his arms, but they merely tightened around her.

"What's wrong, babe? I thought you liked this. I thought you liked me."

"I do you like you," she spat. "Most of the time. I just want answers, that's all. Let me go, Finn, you're scaring me."

"Perhaps you should be scared." His voice was suddenly deep. And slightly menacing.

"What?" She froze in his arms.

"You really believe I'm Finn, don't you?"

"Yes, why wouldn't I?" She'd stopped struggling, but his arms remained like tight bands around her middle.

"Didn't Finn ever tell you about me?"

Indy's mind began to roil. It was all beginning to make terrible sense. Finn had mentioned a brother. But he never told her his name. And he'd never said…

"Yeah, that'd be right." A disgusted sound rumbled in the back of his throat. "Of course, he didn't say anything. He's ashamed of me, that's why. We're twins, and yet he can't stand me."

Her heart felt like it was about to beat out of her chest cavity. Indy sagged against this man who wasn't Finn, her legs no longer able to hold her weight. Finn had a twin brother. And he'd never told her. Even worse, it looked like his brother was on the wrong side of the law.

"Ah, you're a smart one, hey?" He bent his knees slightly so he could stare her in the face, starlight reflecting from his eyes, tipping his hat back so his nose was mere inches from hers. "I can see you're putting two and two together."

He studied her for a few moments, sharp, perceptive gaze boring into her skull. "I can see why he likes you. You're feisty. Brave for a woman. A decent person, by all accounts."

She was still trying to wrap her head around this… deception. How had she so easily fallen for him?

"But you're wearing his clothes. His hat…" she stuttered to a halt. She'd recognize Finn's hat anywhere.

"Yeah. He loaned them to me."

"He did nothing of the sort," she retorted.

"It doesn't really matter if you believe me or not," he replied with a shrug. "Because I've got you, and I'm not letting you go."

"Yes, you are." She spat in his face, stomping on his foot as hard as she could at the same time. But it did no good, he still had her about the waist.

"You little bitch. You're gonna pay for that," he said, slowly drawing his sleeve across his face to wipe away the spittle.

"No!" she screamed the word in his face, then brought her knee up into his groin. But he twisted at the last second, and she missed connecting fully with his genitals. Even so, he buckled, and let out an *oof* noise, but managed to hang on to her. A hand smashed across her face and pain bloomed, instant and colossal, almost blinding her. Then her knees were kicked out from beneath her and she landed on the gravel so hard it knocked the wind out of her.

He was on top of her in an instant, still moaning like a wounded lion.

"Settle down, you bitch," he snarled in her face. "Or I'm gonna have to make you settle down."

But she wasn't listening. All she could think was she needed to escape. Needed to escape this man who pretended to be Finn. Still fighting to breathe, she strove to get a leg free, at the same time clawing at the man's face.

"Stop it," he bellowed, hitting her across the face again with such force she thought she blacked out for a few seconds. That old cliché of seeing stars was actually correct. Bright lights flickered in front of her eyes as she struggled to stay conscious.

"That's better," he crooned as she lay immobile, almost senseless. He stroked a finger down the undamaged side of her face, and she flinched away from the contact.

"Don't," she snarled. Or at least she tried to snarl, it came out as more of a slobbery wail through her split lip, which was already beginning to swell. She couldn't see out of one eye as it became puffy, too.

"Or what?" he taunted, his mouth crushing hers as he kissed her again. Pain speared through her injured lip, and she tried to bite his tongue, but he forced her teeth apart and ravaged her mouth. The weight of him holding her down surprised her; their size difference suddenly apparent. Funny, she'd never considered how heavy a man could be before. Finn had lain on top of her when making love, but she'd never realized just how much he supported his own weight. This guy was pinning her to the ground, and she didn't think she had the strength to push him off. The smell of his unwashed body was making her stomach churn. How could she have thought Finn would ever smell like this?

"You're in no position to stop me," he rasped, as he came

up for air. Indy realized there was something different about this man's voice. A slightly deeper tone than Finn's. More domineering. How had she missed it before? Then she felt it. His growing erection throbbing against her thigh, and she was so disgusted she nearly vomited. He was getting off on this. The sick, twisted pervert. She wished she'd kneed him twice as hard. Kicking out with her feet, she tried to dislodge him, managing to roll to the left and get one elbow beneath her. The hard gravel bit into her back and shoulders, but she ignored it.

"Oh, no you don't." His forearm landed on her windpipe, and he pushed down, hard, until she couldn't breathe. She stopped struggling and began to tug at his arm, ripping her fingernails with the effort.

"If you lie still, I'll let you go," he said calmly.

She was beginning to see stars again, and so she stopped struggling and stared up into his face, desperately hoping he meant what he said. If she passed out, it would all be over. She wouldn't be able to stop him. Would never escape.

"Good, girl," he said softly, and released some of the pressure, but not all. She could breathe now, but she knew he had the power to change that in an instant.

She felt one of his hands slide between them, while his other arm remained firmly pressed against her windpipe. What was he doing? *Oh, God*. He was undoing his belt buckle, pulling down his zipper. Then he fumbled with the fastener on her jeans.

"I don't normally like to force a woman. I prefer if they come to me of their own free will. But you're just too tempting. I want to find out what my brother sees in you."

Was he going to rape her? Was this what it was like to be raped? She'd always imagined that she'd be able to fight off any man who tried such a thing. But with her heart in her mouth, she knew that wasn't going to be the case. He was too strong.

She wanted Finn. Wanted him to come and rescue her. Where was he? Then she remembered this brother was wearing the clothes Finn had worn today. Which meant…

"What have you done to Finn?" she choked out through her partially blocked windpipe. Oh, God, had he hurt Finn, was that why he hadn't come to her tent?

"Stop worrying about your boyfriend. I can be your boyfriend from now on." He'd managed to get his jeans undone, shoving them down to his thighs, and was now tugging hers down past her hips, as well.

No. She wasn't going to let this happen. She would die first. Straining against his weight, she arched her back, twisting her shoulders in the opposite direction at the same time. It was enough to dislodge his arm from her throat, and she took her opportunity and bit his forearm with all her might, tasting blood on her tongue as her teeth ripped into his skin.

"Ow, you fucking bitch." He reared back, and she kicked him all the way off. Getting her feet underneath her, she levered up to standing, tugging up her jeans, so she could run, her feet ready to take off in a sprint into the dark surrounding bushland.

"Stop. Or I'll shoot you." Indy's back was to the voice, and she hesitated. A few more steps and she would disappear into the night. The urge to turn around warring with the urge to just go. Run into the bush and be free. The skin between her shoulder blades prickled. Should she believe him?

"I mean it," he growled. "Turn around now, or you're a dead woman."

Slowly, she spun on her heel to find Finn's brother still kneeling on the ground, but with an object that could be a gun pointed directly at her. He beckoned her, and the glint of starlight on metal made it clear, he was indeed holding a weapon.

Shit. Now what? Was he going to try and rape her again? Should she take the chance that he was perhaps a bad shot; duck, and dive into the bush to get away from him?

Indy didn't know how long they stood in a tableau, both unwilling to budge, when suddenly the glow of car headlights lit up the track. If she hadn't been so preoccupied fighting for her life, she might've heard the low purr of the engine earlier. Who was coming? Was it a rescue? A mad thrill set her heart thrumming. It was Finn. Somehow, he'd found her, and was coming for vengeance.

"Here comes our ride." Finn's brother got to his feet, the gun still trained mercilessly on her. Her moment of wild hope was dashed. It wasn't Finn. It was this asshole's accomplice, come to...what? What were they going to do with her? Kill her? Use her as a hostage to get to Finn? Well, she wasn't going to stand for either of those options.

"Pity we won't be able to finish our bit of sport," he said lightly. "But maybe later." He flashed her a smile, and for an instant, her heart lurched when she saw Finn in that smile.

She stared into the face of the man who held her captive, now lit by the oncoming headlights. So like Finn, yet at the same time, so completely different.

Would it have made any difference if Finn had told her about his twin brother? Perhaps she wouldn't have been led so easily by him. Perhaps she would've spotted the ruse immediately. But then, who was she kidding? It would have made no difference.

No matter. What was done was done. But she wasn't sticking around to see what Finn's brother and whoever was driving that vehicle were going to do to her. Watching the other man intently, she waited for the exact second he'd be distracted enough by the oncoming vehicle to look away from her. All she needed was a split second.

"At least, you'll be happy to know that you and your bastard boyfriend will be reunited."

What had he just said?

"Yeah," he gave her a twisted grin. "We already got Finn. He's all nicely wrapped up and waiting for you in the back of the car. I had to hit him three times before he went down. Tough bugger, my bro." The brother almost seemed proud of the fact, and it made Indy's stomach clench.

Was it true? Was Finn really in that car coming toward them? Not coming to rescue her as she hoped, but as a prisoner of this man and his accomplice?

"If you don't do exactly as I say, he's gonna end up as dead as a doornail." The brother did up his pants, still holding the gun on her, but they both knew the power had shifted. He had the ultimate leverage over her now. Because she wouldn't do anything to risk Finn's life. She stood meek as a lamb as they watched the car bounce toward them over the rutted track.

A white, four-wheel-drive came to a stop in front of them, and the brother motioned her in in the direction of the rear door. "Get in," he growled, all business now, no sign of the rapist left.

"Where's Finn?" she demanded, as she opened the door but saw no one inside.

"Just get in, woman," a deep voice from the driver's seat commanded. Did she recognize that voice? It was hard to tell, and she hung back, hesitating, not wanting to take that last step into the vehicle.

"He's tied up in the back," the brother added. "You'll see him when you get in." He prodded her in the ribs with the barrel of the gun, and she climbed in warily. He clambered in behind her, shutting the door, but keeping the gun trained at her stomach. Not caring about her own safety, she turned to peer into the rear cargo area. There was a shape, like that of a man curled into a loose ball on his side, and she put her hand to her mouth to stop a groan from escaping.

"How do I know that's Finn?" she asked weakly. She was demanding proof, but something inside knew it was him.

Finn's brother flicked a switch on a light in the ceiling, and even though the glow wasn't very bright, it was enough to make out Finn's dark hair and square-jawed features. This time, the groan did escape her throat. It was true. They had him. But why was he wearing nothing apart from his boxer shorts? Because the brother had stolen his clothes, she reminded herself.

"How do I know he's not dead? He looks dead." Her voice became almost hysterical. Was he dead? Because if he was…

The brother leaned over the backseat and prodded Finn's thigh hard with the tip of his gun. "Wake up, sleepyhead," he taunted. Finn groaned, but didn't open his eyes. It was the sweetest sound in the world. He was still alive, and for now, that was all that mattered.

"What took you so long?" the brother barked at the driver.

"Whaddya mean, Garrett? I've been looking for you for the last twenty minutes. You fucked up again, you came out too far north." The man in the driver's seat turned around to glare at them and Indy gasped. In the glow of the weak light, Indy made out his features.

"Swampy?" She could hardly get the word out, she was so shocked to see him. It was the same truck driver from the day Wombat had been killed. Was everyone in this whole stock camp a criminal? She no longer knew who she could trust. How had Finn and his detective team missed this connection?

CHAPTER NINETEEN

Finn wanted to open his eyes, but they wouldn't obey. Was he dreaming? Stuck in a dream where he couldn't wake up. A shiver ran through him. It was cold. The floor was hard and bone-chilling beneath him. Concrete, by the feel of it. Clearly not in his nice, snug, swag tangled up with Indy's warm body, then. So where was he? Rolling from his front onto his side took a great effort, but he managed it, wincing as the cold floor hit his naked skin. Why was he naked? Well, nearly naked, he was still wearing boxer shorts. And what was going on with his arms? It took him a few seconds to realize they were tied behind his back. An experimental shuffle of his feet told him his ankles were tied, as well.

"Finn, are you awake? Oh, God, please say you're awake." That was Indy. What was she doing here? Was he still dreaming? He forced his eyelids to open this time, but groaned, as a bright light hit his eyes and pain shot through his temple until he shut them again with a snap.

"Finn, please." The barely restrained terror in Indy's plea plucked at his soul.

"Indy?" He croaked.

"I'm over here," she replied.

Where was here? He lifted his head a few inches and

cracked open his eyelids again. It took him a few seconds to focus, his head was pounding so hard, he could hardly concentrate. They were in some sort of square room, with a concrete floor, and blank walls, a single wooden door, the only light coming from the window up high. A shaft of late afternoon sunlight beamed in through the window, hitting him almost directly in the face. Indy was propped up in one dim corner, her hands and feet also tied; her face an indistinct, pale oval in the gloom.

"Are you okay?" He needed to get over to her. With a heave, he rolled back onto his stomach, and then over again, a bit like a tumbling caterpillar. Every movement caused a sharp pain, like a knitting needle being rammed through his eye, but he found that if he kept his movements slow and controlled, it wasn't so bad. At last, he rolled once more and came to rest against Indy's thigh.

"Hey, gorgeous," he said, tilting his head back so he could look in her face. It was tear streaked and the left-hand side was bruised, her lip cut and swollen, her eye bright red, and puffy. Her hair was half out of its ponytail, sticks and leaves matted into the strands, as if she'd tumbled on the ground. What the hell had happened to her? "Shit. What have they done to you?" He tried to sit up, but it was a vain effort, and he had to lie still for many moments before the pain level in his head subsided once more.

"I'm okay," she assured him. "At least we're both still alive. I think they drugged you. You've been asleep for a long time. It's nearly dark now, and I've been trying to wake you for hours. You can worry all you like about my injuries later. Right now, we need to get out of here. Before they come back."

"Before who comes back?" he asked groggily. Drugging him would account for the cotton wool still clouding his brain, and the weakness in his limbs.

"You don't remember?" Why did she suddenly sound so unsure? "Somebody hit you. Don't you remember who it was?"

"No." He went to shake his head and stopped just in time before another needle spiked through his brain. Wait... A memory came back, sharp and clear as crystal. Garrett calling his name, right before he was knocked unconscious. "Garrett," he whispered.

"Yes," Indy confirmed.

"But why...?"

"I don't know. But he seems to be holding a grudge against you."

That might be putting it mildly. If his team succeeded in bringing down this drug ring, and Garrett was involved—which it seemed highly likely he was—it'd put an end to his lucrative business; at the very least, put a large dent in his career as a drug smuggler. And then there was that look on Garrett's face as he'd walked away the day he'd come to visit Kayleigh. Perhaps if Garrett was holding a grudge, Finn brushing him aside like that certainly hadn't helped. It took his bruised mind a few moments to catch up.

"Wait, so you've met Garrett?

"You could say that, yes." Her lips tightened into a firm line of disapproval. And something else he couldn't quite fathom.

"Oh, God. I'm so sorry. I should've told you. I was going to tell you. But it's...complicated."

"So I gather," she replied smoothly. "Time for all that later."

"Agreed." He groaned and tried to sit up again, this time using the wall, slowly shuffling until he was upright next to Indy. "I can't believe I dragged you into this. There aren't enough words for my apology."

"I know." Her mouth lost its twisted grimace and softened

as she turned her head to look at him. "Again, there'll be time for that later, Finn." Now he was level with her, he got a good look at her face, and he winced. Someone had hit her. More than once, by the looks of it. If he found out Garrett had harmed her, he would *never* forgive his brother. "I've got some more interesting news. Swampy was driving the vehicle that transported us here," she said.

Finn blew out a long breath. "Wow. Mike won't be happy when he hears he missed that one."

"Yeah, I've had a bit of time to think it over in my head. He played the part pretty well," Indy agreed. "Pretending to warn us about his missing mate, Wombat, when really he must've known what was going on all along. It's no wonder he was in such a hurry to get out of the camp once the police arrived."

"Yep," Finn mused. "But Brian told us it was Ronaldo who murdered Wombat. I'm not sure how Swampy fits in. Maybe he's just a driver, nothing more. Maybe it was sheer luck he wasn't transporting drugs that day and his truck was clean. Or maybe he was there to keep an eye on Wombat. Who knows?"

"I've considered all that, and more," Indy consented dryly. "But my gut tells me he's a whole lot more involved than just as a simple driver."

They stared at each other for many silent seconds, digesting their predicament.

"How's your head?" she asked, a tiny frown creasing her brow as she seemed to remember he'd received a head knock. "You might have a concussion."

More than likely, but she didn't need to know that. A little concussion wasn't going to stop him from trying to escape. "I've got a headache," he admitted. "But I'll live." If she could ignore her injuries, then so could he. It was time to change the subject and work on getting out of here. "Any idea where we are?" he asked without much hope.

"I'm not sure." She shook her head and then shuffled around as if trying to find a more comfortable position. It was cramped sitting up with your arms tied behind your back. "They blindfolded me. But I reckon by the length of the trip, and by the sounds of the size of the city, we might be in Cairns."

He inclined his head slowly. That might make sense, if they only knew why they'd been abducted in the first place. Leaning forward, he examined the bindings around his ankles. Large, plastic zip ties. Damn. If it'd been rope, they might've had a chance to untie the knots. But zip ties were almost impossible to break out of. It was why a lot of police used them as a backup to their handcuffs. He wriggled his hands behind his back experimentally, but the plastic bit into his skin with every movement.

Indy, who was watching him investigate his bindings, said with a note of defeat, "Believe me, I've already tried to get free. Your brother seems to know what he's doing when it comes to holding people captive," she added bitterly.

He nodded, but wasn't ready to give up just yet. A quick examination of the rest of the room showed it was completely bare, but tucked up high on the ceiling in one corner was a state-of-the-art security camera. They were being watched. What would happen if he moved around? Would he call attention to them? He was about to find out.

Grunting and shuffling, he inched his way up, leaning his shoulder against the wall, and pushing with his feet until he was standing, balanced precariously. Taking small, precise hops, he worked his way toward the window. He needed to see what was outside. At the least, it might give away their location, and at best, it might offer a way of escape.

He was just tall enough that the bottom of the window was at eye level. It looked as if they were in some sort of basement. The window hovered barely above the ground, and outside, he could see earth and a few patches of dead grass stretching away to peeling fence in the background. A suburban backyard, by the looks of it. A neglected backyard; nothing was growing, only a dead shrub in the back corner, a couple of overturned plastic chairs, and a small shed huddling by the bush. Which gave him no clue as to where they actually were.

"Looks like we're in a residential house," he whispered to Indy. "But I'm not sure—"

The door flew open, and Garrett strode in. "What do you think you're up to, bro?"

"Garrett, you bastard. Let us go," he snarled, turning to face his brother and nearly falling flat on his face when his tethered ankles locked together.

"Nice to see you, too." Garrett gave a wink and settled himself on the floor next to Indy as if he didn't have a care in the world. She glared at him and shuffled away, her lip curling in dislike. Ignoring her blatant animosity, he grinned broadly and said, "And how about you, babe? How are you fairing?"

Indy fixed him with a look that would curdle milk and refused to answer.

"I have to admit, I'm a little jealous of your girlfriend," Garrett continued, resting his head against the wall and looking up at Finn through half-closed eyes. "She's a feisty one. Got some guts. Pity she's so gullible when it comes to you. She followed me through the bush like a half-starved lamb. It was so easy to fool her, it surprised even me."

"Why, you little fucking—"

"Ah, ah, ah." Garrett held up a hand and wagged a finger in his direction. "Losing your temper won't get you anywhere. Apart from perhaps a bullet to the stomach." He reached behind him and pulled out a gun from his waistband, resting it in his lap, the threat clear to both of them. Indy gasped and looked to Finn, her beautiful brown eyes wide with fear. Finn reined in his anger, keeping it under tighter control. She was already scared enough, him losing his shit would just scare her even more.

"Why don't you come sit down, and we'll have a chat?" Garrett patted the concrete next to him.

So, Garrett wanted to play a game, did he? Right. Finn had always been able to beat him at checkers, Monopoly, Scrabble, just about any board game you cared to mention. Maybe Garrett had forgotten how good he was at games. If only Finn could figure out the rules, then he might be in with a shot.

He hobbled over to the corner and tried to sit down, but it was almost impossible with his hands and feet tied, and he ended up in a heap on the floor. Wriggling around, he finally got his legs out straight and sat up, inserting himself between his brother and Indy, making it clear his brother was to get no closer. Ignoring the fact that he was practically naked, trying not to feel intimidated by his lack of clothing, he fixed Garrett with his stare.

Indy's gaze flickered between the two of them, as if weighing them up. Finn was used to the scrutiny, most people stared when they first met a set of identical twins. It was human nature, as they attempted to work out who was who. Finn wondered what Indy saw. Did she see the similarities? Or did she see the differences? He hoped it was the latter. He hoped she understood just how divergent the two of them were.

"Right, let's get on with business then, shall we?" Garrett leaned forward.

Finn wanted to smack that smug grin on his brother's face, and he was just about to snap out some sort of derogatory comment when he saw Garrett's gaze slide to the camera and then angle his body a little more to the side; the move so quick Finn nearly missed it. Someone else was watching what was going on in this room. And if Finn wasn't mistaken, Garrett didn't want whoever that was to see what he was doing. Could the other person hear what was being said? Finn couldn't be sure, but he thought probably not.

"What the hell do you want from us?" Finn demanded. "And take these bloody restraints off."

Garrett pursed his lips, not looking for a second like he was about to do as Finn had asked.

"It took me a long time to realize, but you always loved to be in charge, didn't you, bro? Always had to be the one in control. Well, not anymore." Garrett speared him with a steely, blue gaze, and it hit Finn. His brother had been jealous of him all along. When he had no need to be. They were equals, or had been, at one stage. If only Finn had become aware of this seething envy earlier, perhaps he could've done something about it. Was it somehow Finn's fault that Garrett ended up the way he had? Could he have done something to change this outcome? Helped Garrett in some way get through their father's death a little easier. But Finn had been hurting just as badly, and Garrett had shut himself off so completely, it was almost impossible to penetrate that shield; even for those who cared about him. Staring into those dead eyes, he sensed his brother was too far gone. Even if he might've made a difference back then, there was nothing he could do for him now.

"What's going on here?" Indy broke in. "Is this some kind of sick, sibling rivalry? Because if it is, you can both go to—"

"Far from it, *babe*," Garrett cut her off, nearly shouting the last word. "There ain't no sibling rivalry here. This is me telling you what to do. End of story. Now shut up. I'm going to do all the talking, and you're going to listen." He picked up the gun and waved it threateningly. She blanched at the brutality in his tone, and the barrel of the weapon now pointed at her.

"It's okay, Garrett. Indy didn't mean it," Finn cut in. He sent her a quelling look; it was one thing for him to provoke Garrett—it was his prerogative—but he didn't want her doing it, as well. He shuffled a few inches closer in a vain attempt to protect her.

Garrett watched his little show of gallantry with narrowed eyes. Instead of commenting further, he went on as if this was all a simple business deal. "I'm not going to tell you where you are, so don't bother asking," he said. "As you can see, it's getting toward sunset. You've been missing for nearly twenty-four hours, and needless to say, your friends are getting worried about you. But we needed to give them time to confirm that you two are missing. That way, they'll take us seriously when we call them."

"Call them?" Indy butted in again. "What? Are you going to let us go?"

Garrett continued, as if she hadn't spoken. "You're...going to make a phone call, and then..." Why was Garrett hesitating?

"A phone call to whom?" Finn asked with an icy tone.

"To your boss." Again, there was that slight hesitation. What was Garrett about to ask?

But Finn was lost. What in God's name was Garrett hoping to achieve by calling Mike Rogers? Unless he wanted a swift arrest. And then to spend the next twenty years in jail for abducting a law enforcement officer. Because that was the only outcome Finn could see.

"You're going to tell them where you are. Tell them you escaped, but you're injured, and you need them to come get you."

Finn's mind whirled. There seemed to be no reasoning behind this. "What? Why?"

"Because I told you to, that's why," Garrett snarled, and

waved the gun. But there was something slightly off. Something Finn couldn't put his finger on. Garrett was watching the door, as if waiting for something. "You're going to make the call and say exactly what I told you. Nothing more, nothing less. That's all you need to do, it's pretty simple, really."

"Why would you let me do that?" Finn insisted. "Why would you let me call in the cavalry?"

"That's none of your business. Look, *bro*," Garrett spat the word as if he had a nasty taste in his mouth. "You do what I tell you, or your girl here is gonna die." Garrett got to his feet, seemingly tired of the argument, and pointed the gun at Indy.

At that same instant, Swampy barged into the room. "Stop bloody pussy footing around, and get on with it," he shouted. "We're running out of time. It's getting dark, and we need to get out of here. The boat leaves in an hour." The big man was just as Finn remembered, long beard bristling, and huge belly preceding him through the door. He wore a dark-blue, workmen's cotton singlet that didn't quite cover the gap between his rolls of fat and the waistband of his dirty shorts, his tattooed biceps on display.

The whole dynamic in the room seemed to shift. And Finn realized with sudden clarity that Swampy was in charge. He was who Garrett had been afraid of. But no. Now he studied his brother, he could see it wasn't fear, it was contempt that hovered just below the surface in Garrett's eyes. Contempt and greed. What was Garrett up to?

"Nice to see you again, Swampy," Finn said, his voice low and guttural. He'd love to know what part this bastard was playing in this whole scenario. Who did he report to? Or was he the boss? Finn doubted it; the man wasn't smart enough. He was just a grunt-man, higher up on the hierarchy than his brother, obviously, but not the boss. The other man ignored him.

"Here." Swampy shoved a cell phone at Garrett. "Get him to make the damn call. Everything else is set. Let's do it, and get out of here."

An ice-cold sliver of fear embedded itself in Finn's stomach. There was something terribly wrong going on here. There was no way these two were just going to let Finn's team come and rescue them. A horrible premonition almost made him gasp in shock. They were up to something. They weren't going to just allow a bunch of cops to come storming in and seize the day. Were they setting a trap? Using him as the bait.

Garrett caught the phone and held it up, punching in some numbers. "I'm on it," he replied evenly. "I'll get it done. Go and bring the car around. I'll be out in a minute."

Swampy hovered next to the door, as if wanting to get on with the job, but not sure whether he should leave Garrett. Some sort of war of dominance seemed to be going on between the two men. Garrett was the first to break the stare. But as his gaze slipped away, Finn didn't miss the clench of Garrett's fists. Swampy might think he was in charge, but his brother obviously thought differently.

"Just make sure you do," Swampy growled, and slammed the door behind him, and Finn released a pent-up breath.

Garrett hunkered down next to Finn, holding the phone up to the side of his face. "When I put the call through, just say what I told you to. Tell them you don't know where you are, but they should be able to track this phone. Tell them it's a burner you managed to steal when you escaped."

"I'm not going to say anything," Finn growled. "You're setting some sort of trap, aren't you?"

"So what if we are?" Garrett flung back. "The die has been cast. There's no getting out of this now, Finn. You pissed off too many people. You and your whole team. And they need to die."

"So, you're going to murder us all in cold blood?" Finn asked. His suspicions seemed to be true.

"What's going on?" Indy asked. She'd been sitting back watching the interplay, probably trying to figure out what was going on, just like he was. But it'd obviously become too much.

"Make the call, or I'll kill her," Garrett threatened, but there was something about his threat that Finn didn't believe. A twitch of his eyelid, a certain slant to his chin.

"What?" Indy squeaked, fear twisting her face, which drained of all color. She wasn't privy to his insider knowledge, so she didn't know what he was thinking. Finn could still read Garrett, sometimes, at least. And he knew there was a chance.

He made a conscious effort to ignore Indy. Ignore how her beautiful eyes begged him to do something. Ignore how he wanted to take her in his arms one last time, hold her body against his. Her fear and confusion were palpable. But if he were to save her, he needed to get this right.

Garrett glanced once more at the camera in the corner. Perhaps hoping Swampy wasn't watching. Was that why he'd told the other man to get the car? So he had a few moments alone with them?

"I don't believe you," Finn sighed, and fidgeted. "You're not going to shoot her." His arms were going numb behind him, and his back was aching as he tried to maintain a sitting position. "And what does it matter, anyway? She's either going to die now, or later. I'm assuming what you have organized is meant to kill us all? Is that right?"

Garrett looked away for a second, as if debating. "If you make the call, you have my sworn promise, I'll take her out of here when I leave." Garrett turned to stare him directly in the eye.

This was an interesting development.

Should he believe his brother? Did he have the choice? They were never one of those sets of twins who had an almost-telepathic connections. They'd been close when they were younger, but those days seemed a distant memory. For at least the last ten years, it felt like he and Garrett had been at odds; on opposite sides of a war.

"And do what with her?" Finn asked.

Garrett saw him hesitate. Then a light entered his eyes, as if he had an answer to this stand-off. "She's my ticket out of here. I'll set her free once I get to the docks. I promise she won't die in this house. But that's all I can give you."

It was a bribe. Garrett was bribing him with the one thing he knew might work. But would he go through with his promise? Would he release Indy after he'd made his escape? It sounded like he was going to use her as some kind of hostage, to make sure he made it to the docks—whatever that meant. Was there a ship due to leave tonight? Perhaps loaded with cattle or cargo, and a way for Finn to escape unnoticed?

"What happens if I don't make the call?" Finn asked defiantly, angling for more time. Time to come up with a solution. Time to get out of this no-win situation.

"If you don't make the call, then I will kill her," Garrett stated bluntly. "And then I'll shoot you. Look, bro, take the deal. This way you get to save the girl. If you don't, then you'll both die, anyway."

Finn stared at his brother, not comprehending how he could be so cold and calculating. How this could mean so little to him. Indy was right, Garrett was holding a grudge, but this was one, gigantic, enormous grudge. Finn had thought he no longer knew his brother, but now it was driven home like a sledgehammer beating into his brain. His brother was a psychopath.

As Garrett watch Finn waver, he reached into his pocket and pulled out the engraved silver lighter. Finn had forgotten about it, with everything else going on. It took him a second to remember that Garrett was wearing Finn's jeans, and must've discovered the lighter at some stage.

"Thanks for finding this for me, bro." He sniggered and leaned down. Finn's blood turned to ice. Garrett had just confirmed that he'd been in that secret bush camp. Did that mean...? "I looked everywhere for this. It's my favorite. Stupid of me to drop it, really. I was a bit worried it might incriminate me, if you know what I mean. But it looks like you kept it safe."

And suddenly Finn knew with a profound clarity that his brother had been the one to murder Ronaldo. A heavy weight settled in the pit of Finn's stomach. If Garrett was capable of that kind of cold-blooded act, then he was capable of just about anything. Had he been ordered by someone to kill the other man? Had they had a disagreement that ended in murder? It didn't matter why Garrett had done it. All that mattered was that he had. It made him shudder to think Garrett had been that close to stock camp, and he'd never even known.

Why hadn't Finn turned the lighter in for evidence as soon as he found it? He knew he should've. That stupid sentimental streak of his had no place in a murder investigation.

But there was no time for self-reproach, as Garrett leaned even closer, an intent gleam in his eye. "But that's not why I brought this up. I want to make a deal with you." His brother flicked the switch and moved closer, holding the lighter between them, so they both focused on the brightly burning flame.

"I promise I'll set her free. I vow to be true to our twin flame," Garrett intoned.

Finn flinched away from his brother, but he couldn't escape the light of the fire. He wanted to shout *bullshit* in his brother's face, but then a memory caught him, and he stopped.

It was a stupid pact they'd made as kids. They must've only been seven or eight when they'd played with that box of matches. Lying in the long grass in their neglected backyard, hiding from their mother, who was on the rampage, trying to get them to clean their rooms. They'd been setting miniature fires with dry blades of grass held between thumb and forefinger, lighting them and then watching them burn until they almost singed their fingertips.

They'd been skylarking and joking, egging each other on, until Garrett had unexpectedly become serious. Plucking two long blades of grass, he handed one to Finn, and then made him hold it up against his own.

Setting the twin blades ablaze, they'd watched the entwined stalks burn, as Garrett recited, "Together, forever, we'll always have each other's backs." Then Garrett had hissed at Finn. "Say these words after me. I promise never to forsake my brother. I promise to keep the flame alive."

Foolishly, Finn had repeated the words, in shock that his brother had come up with something so profound. Then they laughed and dropped the burnt grass just before the flame touched their fingers.

It was a silly child's vow, made back when they were too young to know how cruel life could be; how different they'd eventually become. Finn had almost forgotten the whole thing, but clearly Garrett hadn't. How ironic, because Garrett was the one who'd ultimately broken the pact, the one who'd chosen the dark path. The one who'd fragmented their family. And yet here he was, offering Finn his promise. And a choice, of sorts. A choice to perhaps save Indy's life. At the cost of his own.

"What about Swampy?" Finn demanded. From what he could tell, Swampy was in charge. If he didn't agree to

Garrett's terms, Indy would still be in danger.

"I'll handle him. I promise I will get her out of this alive." Garrett leaned in and touched Finn on the leg. It was the first time his brother had touched him in over ten years.

But Finn wasn't fooled by this sign of good faith. He was only saving Indy to get what he wanted. He needed Finn to make that call, and if the only way to get him to do that was to save the one thing that was precious to him, then Garrett was no idiot.

What if Garrett didn't set her free? Or what if he simply wanted Indy for himself? Was this perhaps another form of revenge, to take his woman away from him? Whatever the reason, Finn didn't have the time to mull over the different options. He was out of time and out of choices.

Finn sagged against the wall. "As long as you promise to let her go. I'll make the call."

He couldn't believe he was doing this. Couldn't believe he would willingly put his own team in danger. But when it came to that unthinkable choice between saving Indy—the woman he loved—or sacrificing himself, it was a no-brainer. He just hoped he wasn't agreeing to sacrificing his team members, as well.

Garrett was offering him this one ray of hope. This one dispensation. And it'd have to be enough. He had to trust that a tiny piece of the old Garrett was still in there somewhere. The one who would hold to the promise he'd made to his twin brother.

"No. Finn. What are you doing? You can't do this?" Indy shook her head wildly from side to side. "I won't let you." A single tear slid down her cheek, and he watched it fall. She was so bewitching, even when she was crying; especially when she was crying. He would do this. He would save her.

CHAPTER TWENTY

Indy struggled against Garrett, refusing to go with him. She wasn't leaving Finn. She wasn't. Tears were flowing freely down her cheeks. She couldn't dash them away, because her hands were still tied behind her back. Garrett had been smart enough to only release her feet, dragging her out of the basement and up the stairs, locking the door behind him as they went.

"Why are you doing this? That's your brother in there. Don't you care about your brother?" she screamed.

"Me and Griff ain't seen eye-to-eye for a long time, now," Garrett mumbled. "It's a little unfortunate that things had to end this way. But it was always going to be me or him. Only one of us is going to win."

"I don't get it. You're identical twins. Aren't you supposed to be soulmates, or something?" How could he do this? To his own brother? It was incomprehensible to her.

"In a perfect world, maybe." Garrett shrugged. "Look, I promised Griff that I'd see you safe. But if we stay here much longer gabbing, then you're gonna be as dead as he is."

"Dead?" The word felt like ash on her tongue. It was her worst fear confirmed. Garrett and Swampy meant to kill Finn somehow. She'd gleaned that much from their conversation.

And in amongst it all, Finn had also bartered his life for hers. "You're going to kill him?"

He gave an exasperated sigh. "Like I said, it's out of my hands. I'm doing Griff this one favor. And you might just be an asset to me, as well. But if you don't move now, then I'll leave you hog-tied in here, and you'll die in the explosion, just like everybody else." Garrett swore under his breath, and she knew he hadn't meant to let that last detail leak.

Explosion. So that was what he had planned. A bomb of some kind, perhaps. And by everyone else, she assumed Garrett meant the rest of Finn's detective team. This was a trap, and they'd be walking right into it. Finn must know that. So why had he…? He was letting Garrett take her…to use as some sort of hostage, by the sounds of it. Was that any better than dying in an explosion? But Finn must have a reason. He didn't do anything without a reason. Was it just to save her life? Or did he have something else up his sleeve?

She took a deep, shuddering breath. Her fear was turning to rage. It bubbled up her throat, and it was all she could do to stop it from erupting in a spout of hysteria. A streak of white fire lit through her, stealing her breath with its ferocity. If her hands hadn't been tied behind her back, she might well have tried to rip Garrett's heart out. Instead, she bottled up that anger, keeping it ready, like a simmering cauldron, for when she needed it.

She'd listened in shock as Finn agreed to make the phone call to his boss, Garrett holding the phone to his ear for him. When she tried to interrupt, Finn had shaken his head vehemently, and Garrett had slapped his hand over her mouth, and glared at her.

She'd listened as Finn told his boss the story Garrett wanted him to spin. Something about him escaping, hiding out and being injured. Asking Mike Rogers to send the team to retrieve him. Adding to the enticement that the two criminals weren't far away, and if they hurried, they may well make an arrest at the same time. Finn's voice had been flat and devoid of emotion, not meeting her eyes. She wasn't sure how he could do this to his friends and colleagues. Betray them like this.

Garrett had cut the ties around her ankles and pulled her to her feet. "Outside, you." He yanked roughly on her arm.

"Wait. At least let me say goodbye," she pleaded. She might not understand what Finn was doing, but she couldn't just leave him there.

Garrett grunted, but held her by the arm as she leaned down to look Finn in the face, her loose hair tumbling sideways over her cheek. Her heart threatened to burst from her chest at the thought this might be the last time she ever saw Finn. He needed to know how she felt about him. But there was no time. There were no words. Something unexpected and powerful surged through her. It made her speak the words she hadn't thought she was ready to say.

"I love you," she whispered.

A tender press of his mouth against her cheek. "I love you, too," he rasped in return.

Then Garrett had wrenched her around and pushed her through the door. They'd climbed a flight of stairs and were standing in some sort of kitchen. Dusk was falling outside; it'd be dark in a few minutes. Indy's quick perusal of the kitchen and the other rooms she could see through the open doorways was of an empty house. Derelict and rundown. Linoleum peeling on the floor, the cupboard doors hanging open. Was this a hideout? An empty house they were using as a bolthole? She'd heard Finn repeat the address to his boss over the phone, but it didn't mean much to her, apart from the fact she'd been right about them being in Cairns. It didn't really matter where they were. She could figure that out later. All she needed now, was to escape.

Snarling like a trapped animal, she said, "You should just leave me here. I don't want to go anywhere with you."

"Stubborn fucking woman," Garrett snarled back. "You're coming and you ain't got no say in it."

Indy heard an engine outside the kitchen window, and looked up in time to see a set of headlights appear as a vehicle swung into the driveway out front, Swampy at the wheel. It was the same white four-wheel-drive he'd been driving when they'd abducted her. Perhaps he'd hidden it out of sight, in case the cops were already looking for it. The driveway ran down the side of the house, allowing the car access to the backyard, and Swampy drove the vehicle right through until it was almost at the back door.

"He's here." Garrett's face hardened, as if he were steeling himself for what was to come. "You need to keep your mouth shut and do as I tell you," he commanded.

"And what if I don't?" she yelped.

"Then you'll die, like I said before." Garrett never even had the decency to look at her, as he spoke, just peered out the window at the encroaching dark.

Indy considered Garrett as he stared at the car idling in the backyard. It would do her no good to stubbornly insist she wasn't going with him. She believed him when he said that if she stayed in the house, she would die. And if she died, then so did Finn. Which meant the only way to survive was to go along with his plan. For now. And if she survived, there was a small chance she could also help rescue Finn. It was a long shot. But it was all she had. She couldn't wait until Finn's team arrived, because they would just barge in and set off the bomb. She needed to warn them, as well.

Her shoulders drooped, and she closed her eyes for a brief second. Was she really going to give in?

As if Garrett felt her concede defeat, he tugged her along by her bound wrists, down the short hallway. And she let him lead her. Out the back door and down the two steps onto the dusty ground.

"What's she doing here?" Swampy asked, opening the driver's door and peering out, leaving the car idling.

"I'm taking her to the docks, as added insurance. In case the cops pull us over before we get there." Garrett kept his voice down, and glanced over the fence, is if afraid a neighbor might hear him.

Swampy looked unconvinced. "That's not the damn plan, and you know it. We don't need a hostage." But he also kept his voice down, his gaze darting about in the gloom.

"It might not be *your* plan, but mine is better. A hostage can't hurt." Garrett's tone turned pleading. "Come on, you know I'm right. Once we get to the docks, we can shoot her and drop her over the side. No one will find her body for days. And if the sharks find her first, well…" Garrett lifted his hands in a show of indifference.

Indy didn't like where this was going. This didn't sound like a plan to set her free.

The fat man stared at Indy for ten full seconds, stroking his beard as if in deep thought. "Fine, bring her along. She'll end up dead, either way." He waved the pair of them toward the rear door. Indy dragged her feet, scuffing along in the gravel of the driveway. Should she make a bolt for it? If she got free of Garrett, she could sprint down the driveway and be gone. Although her bound hands would hamper her running.

"Keep walking," he whispered in her ear, as if he sensed her treacherous thoughts, pushing her inexorably toward the vehicle.

"Have you set the motion sensors?" Swampy asked, just as Garrett opened the door.

"Oh, ah…" Garrett glanced over his shoulder at the house.

"You fucking idiot," Swampy roared, then quickly lowered his voice and continued, "How could you forget the most important step? Without those sensors, the fucking bomb won't trigger." Swampy stepped all the way out of the car, muttering under his breath, saying something like, if you wanted a thing done right, you gotta do it yourself. "Get in and wait for me," he added.

Garrett pushed Indy into the rear seat, but didn't immediately follow. Instead, he watched as Swampy went back into the house. As soon as the large man disappeared inside, Garrett slipped into the driver's seat, shutting the door silently behind him. Indy watched as he put the car carefully in reverse and then waited. What was he doing? It almost looked like...he intended to leave Swampy behind. She was alone in the backseat. She could make a break for it now if she wanted. Instead, she decided to see how this played out.

Swampy appeared on the top step, cautiously closing the door behind him. Then he looked up and saw Garrett in the driver's seat.

Garrett gunned the car, reversing quickly down the drive, the tires squealing as they hit the bitumen, and then he swung the car around, so it was headed down the street. Indy watched Swampy as realization dawned on his face. Fury erupted in his features, and he chased the car, lumbering down the driveway after them, his fat legs flashing like shadowy scissors in the headlights. He almost caught up to them when Garrett slowed the car to put it in first gear. Indy saw his fingers brush the door handle before Garrett slammed down the accelerator, and they left him standing in the middle of the road.

"Ha ha, the fat, old toad," Garrett crowed as he sped down the street. "He'll never get away quick enough. This place will be crawling with cops soon. Let's see how he likes that. The Italian don't take it real well when his employees fuck up. Swampy's on the fast track to the bottom of the ocean now."

Indy was confused. Garrett had left Swampy on purpose. So...what? So, he could be apprehended by the police? Was Garrett planning some kind of coup? Wanting to knock Swampy off the top spot? And who was The Italian?

There was no time to consider the ramifications of Garrett's power struggle maneuver, however, she had to save Finn. She made some quick calculations. How long until Finn's team got there? She had no real way of knowing, because she had no idea where they were situated. In reality, they could be anywhere from ten minutes to half an hour away. Slowly and carefully, she undid her seatbelt, hoping Garrett didn't notice. She needed answers. And then she needed to get back to the house as quickly as she could. Following closely the directions Garrett was taking, she demanded urgently, "What do the motion sensors do?"

"What?" Garrett glanced at her from the front seat.

"In the house, how do the motion sensors work?" She willed Garrett to slow down, the farther they drove, the longer she'd have to run back.

He smirked for a second and she was scared he wasn't going to answer her. "Not that it matters, but they're set, so that if anyone opens a door or goes through a window, they'll trigger a bomb to go off fifteen seconds after the house is breached. Why?" Garrett asked. "Do you want to know exactly how your sweetheart is going to die?" he mocked.

"A booby-trap," Indy whispered, ignoring his jibe. The timing would allow most, if not all, of the team who'd come to rescue Finn to be inside the house before it detonated.

"Exactly." Garrett flashed his teeth, as if he were enjoying the simple cruelty of it. He really did have a twisted mind. He really was the complete antithesis of everything Finn stood for. Vaguely, Indy noted Garrett slowed to take a right-hand turn, then accelerated again.

"How do you turn it off?" she asked.

"You don't." He sent her another surprised look. "They're set using a keypad inside. Once it's set, there's no going back. It's just…kaboom." Garrett smiled as if he liked the idea of a large bomb going kaboom.

"Kaboom?" she repeated dazedly.

"Yep, you got that one right, babe." Garrett smiled as he turned around another right-hand corner.

"You bastard." With a snarl, Indy let all her bottled up rage loose in a burst of fury. She clawed her way forward, and put her bound hands over Garrett's head, positioning the plastic tie across his throat.

"What the fu—" the rest of his words were choked off as she pulled tight, and the car began to careen across the road. He wasn't wearing a seatbelt, either. If the car crashed, both of them might end up dead.

"Stop the car!" she screamed.

But Garrett didn't seem to hear her, as he took his hands off the wheel, and battled to haul her arms away. The vehicle slowed when Garrett removed his foot from the accelerator, but it was still hurtling down the road at speed. Shit, what did she do now? Perhaps she hadn't thought this through properly.

Garrett made a harsh gurgling sound as he fought for breath. The vehicle skidded and hit the curb, bouncing off and careening toward the opposite side of the road. They were headed straight for a house, a brick letterbox and a carport looming in their direct path. Indy clung tight, not letting go of her strangle-hold around Garrett's neck, bracing herself behind the seat for impact. There was a loud thud and a splintering of glass and wood, and Indy was thrown forward, smacking her forehead against the back of Garrett's head.

Garrett's head lolled sideways against the back of the seat.

He was unconscious. The whole front of the car was buried beneath a pile of rubble. The windshield was completely destroyed, the steering wheel slammed up against Garrett's chest, and the airbag had left the cabin filled with a cloud of white dust when it'd deployed. Indy couldn't see the engine, couldn't even see Garrett's feet. His legs were covered from the waist down with broken bricks and shattered wood.

Lifting her arms over Garrett's head, she shook free of the debris scattered in the back seat, evaluating herself for any injuries. Her wrists and forearms twinged painfully, having taken the brunt of the force of impact. In a way, it was probably a good thing she'd kept her tight hold around Garrett's neck, it was almost as good as wearing a seatbelt.

She didn't wait to see if Garrett was alive. There was only one objective. To get back to Finn.

Voices sounded from within the ruined house. She had to get out of here. She hoped no one had been hurt inside from the crash, but she couldn't wait around to find out. They might try to stop her. There was no time to break out of her restraints. She'd have to run with her hands still bound. It'd be awkward, but she'd manage.

But there was one thing she needed first. Reaching over the seat, she felt around in Garrett's top pocket of his shirt. Please let it be there. Please let it not have fallen out in the crash. Her fingers closed around the slim metal object. Garrett's phone.

Her door was jammed shut, and she had to kick it twice before it popped open. Keeping the phone held tight in one hand, she jogged down the road, and ducked behind the cover of a truck parked farther up the street as she heard voices. People had begun to emerge from their houses to see what all the noise was about. Taking care to stay hidden, she threaded her way between the front gardens of the next three houses until she came to the T-intersection. She allowed herself a single glance backward to the smoking wreck, a small crowd gathering beneath the sallow glow of the streetlight. If she was supposed to feel guilt about leaving Garrett, perhaps dying or even dead, she didn't care. She only had room in her heart to care about one thing, and that was getting Finn out alive.

What would Finn think when he found out she'd caused his brother to be hurt? Garrett was his twin, after all. If he died in that car crash, would Finn blame her? Finn already told her they weren't close, and after what Garrett had done to both of them tonight, she saw that as unforgivable. But Finn might see it differently. Losing a sibling, a twin brother, would still leave a terrible gaping hole in his life. Leave a scar. For Finn's sake, she sent a silent prayer that Garrett was still alive. But for herself…not so much. All she could do right now was hope that Finn could see she'd done her best, and he wouldn't hate her later for acting on instinct in the heat of the moment.

Turning down the road, she was now finally out of sight, and could make her way back onto the bitumen where the running was easier. Streetlights were just flickering on, as dusk draped heavily over the suburban road. Cowboy boots weren't made for running, the solid heels clacking noisily on the bitumen. And even when she held her hands beneath her chin, clutching the phone tightly, it was impossible to run fast and stay balanced, so she slowed it down to a fast jog. One more left-hand turn and then it was straight down the next road for about five hundred meters.

What would she find when she got there? She doubted Swampy would have hung around. If what Garrett had said was true, and there was no way to turn off the sensors once they were armed, then Swampy couldn't get back inside. And he surely wouldn't wait around for Finn's team to arrive.

Nonetheless, she'd take it easy once she got close. No point in getting caught again.

There was the house. She'd imprinted the front façade into her memory banks. No front fence and no garden, just dead grass, letterbox leaning to the left, house set far back from the road, bright-red front door, sagging roofline hinting at the disrepair inside.

It'd probably taken her ten minutes, at least, to get back to the house. She slowed, then came to a stop outside the tall fence of the house next door. Time to make a call and stop Finn's team from dying.

Garrett's phone was locked, but that didn't matter, she could still access the SOS function. Holding the phone awkwardly to her ear because of her bound wrists, she waited until a recorded voice said, "You have dialed emergency triple 000. Your call is being connected." And then finally a real person came on the line. "Police, ambulance, or fire?"

"Police," she said, keeping her voice low, just in case Swampy was still lurking around.

A police dispatcher came on next, asking for her address and the nature of the emergency.

"I need you to get a message to Detective Sergeant Mike Rogers. This is important. His life and the life of his team members might be in danger," she whispered over the top of the dispatcher as he tried to interrupt her. "They've been called out to a house," she rattled off the address. "But it's a trap. The house has been rigged with a bomb. You need to tell them not to enter the house, under any circumstances." As she spoke, Indy studied the front yard, and she peered around the side of the fence, down the long driveway. Nothing moved. Was the coast clear?

The dispatcher was still requesting her name and more details. It struck her that she sounded crazy, that he might think she was a prank caller.

"My name is Indy Solomon. I've been working with…" she

hesitated and then remembered to say his proper name, "…
Detective Griffin Carmody on an undercover case. You need
to get a message to Mike Rogers. Stop him storming this
house." She spoke succinctly and clearly, trying to make the
man understand. "When you get in touch with him, he can
call me back on this number." With that, she ended the call.
She'd wasted enough time, when all she really wanted was to
make sure that Finn was still okay; to get him out of there in
one piece.

It still shocked her when she thought about what she said
to Finn right before Garrett had led her away. She said the *L*
word. It'd felt right at the time. And it still felt right.

And he'd said it back to her.

It scared her. She hadn't planned on falling in love. Not
after what Patrick had done to her.

Could you even fall in love after only a week? Even though
it was stupid and way too fast, Indy knew she'd fallen head
over heels for Finn, probably from the very first day. He
seemed to get her somehow. Somewhere down deep, they
understood each other. Like she'd never *felt* for anyone
before.

She knew absolutely zero about loving a police detective.
Just the thought of it made her heart flutter in her chest, like a
trapped bird in a cage. Was that panic? Or was it something
else? They had a good chemistry together. The sex had been
great. Fantastic. Empowering. But she hadn't really thought it
would go any further than that. Until she'd said the word out
loud. Love. It'd been like the slow, stealthy stalking of a
predator hunting its prey. These feelings for Finn had grown
day by day, without her realizing it. Now a giant swell of
emotion threatened to bury her beneath an avalanche of
feelings at the thought that Finn might die.

And she knew, in that instant, that she would do anything
to save Finn—no matter the risk. Because he was worth it.

The rush of blood was a dull roar in her head at the thought. But she knew he meant too much to her to just stand around and wait for the cavalry to arrive.

She was going in to save him.

To hell with the consequences.

Her need for Finn was an inexplicable thing, but it continued to grow, even now as she stood deciding her next move. The depth and power of their intimacy daunted her, but she knew her desire for him went way beyond the physical. Which was why the thought of standing idly by while Finn was trapped inside the house was completely unacceptable. She had to do *something*.

Sneaking down the driveway, she hugged the side fence, keeping to the unlit shadows. The backyard was dark, and Indy used her memory from when Garrett had placed her in the car. There was a window about halfway along the foundations of the house, down low near the ground, which Indy hoped was the window Finn had peered out of earlier, while they'd been trapped in the basement. She might be able to get him out that way. If the window wasn't booby-trapped, as well. Maybe they'd missed that one. There was a small shed in the back corner. It might hold something she could use, either to break out of these zip ties, or to help her rescue Finn.

As carefully as she could, she snuck in the direction of the shed, keeping to the fence line, eyes wide, watching for anything. A movement, a figure. But there was nothing, and she finally made it to the small building. The door stood slightly ajar, and after checking it was empty, she slipped inside. Using the flashlight app on Garrett's phone, she quickly searched the space. Cobwebs hung heavy in the corners, and dust and filth caked every surface. It hadn't been used in years, probably much the same as the house.

There was a little bench hugging one wall, and there were

items scattered on it, all covered in the same grime. Brushing aside the cobwebs, and suppressing a shudder when a black spider scuttled away, her fingers found something cold and metallic. Lifting a pile of dirty rags, she found a rusty, old hacksaw. Eureka. Clamping the handle between her knees, she sawed at the plastic zip tie, and within seconds, she was free.

Oh. Sweet. Jesus. The relief of having her hands free was like nothing else in the world. She rubbed at her wrists, which were chafed and raw from the bindings. Then she rolled her shoulders experimentally back and forth, easing the cramped muscles from where she'd held her hands in front the whole time.

If she could somehow get the hacksaw into where Finn was being held, he might be able to free himself. And then they could work out a way for him to escape before the house blew up.

She searched quickly through the rest of the stuff on the bench. She grabbed a hammer and a screwdriver, not sure how they would help, but they might come in handy.

All of a sudden, Garrett's phone, which she'd tucked into the back pocket of her jeans, began to ring, and she dropped everything in her hands in shock.

With a curse, she took out the phone and slid the button to answer.

"Miss Solomon?" A deep voice asked without preface.

"Yes," she answered hesitantly. "Who is this?"

"It's Detective Sergeant Mike Rogers."

"Oh, thank God." She let out a gust of relief.

"We're en route to the house. Are you still there?"

"Yes, sir. I'm outside in the backyard. Finn is still trapped inside. And the house is booby trapped with a bomb. But I believe he is safe," she added as an afterthought.

"Yes. Thank you. We got the information from dispatch.

Are you sure about the bomb?"

"Ah…" She wavered. Swampy and Garrett had seemed pretty definite. She didn't doubt them. But she also had no solid proof there was a bomb in the house. "I'm pretty sure, sir."

"Right," he replied. She could hear someone giving orders in the background, and the sound of a siren wailing. "I want you to stay where you are. We'll be there in two minutes. And please don't touch anything."

She didn't respond, not wanting to make a promise she might not keep. Perhaps if she could let Finn know she was here, that Mike was on his way.

"Miss Solomon?" Mike's voice snapped her back.

"Yes, yes, I'll be waiting." She ended the call and put the phone back in her pocket.

Gathering up the dropped implements, she stepped out of the shed and into the backyard. Just as Swampy descended the back stairs in a hurry, pulling the door shut behind him.

She stopped to stare at him.

As soon as he saw her, an evil grin spread across his fat face. "Too late, now, girly," he crowed. "I just tripped the device. Figured I may as well get one of you. I know you warned the coppers." Swampy was still moving, getting as far away from the house as he could. "That fucking Garrett betrayed me, but I'm off to get him next. His life ain't worth squat now, that little prick."

Indy's gaze swapped between him and the derelict building, not really understanding what Swampy had just done.

"Go on. I'd love to see you dive in there and try and save him. But you ain't got long, five seconds maybe." He was jogging toward her as he spoke, his large belly wobbling with the effort. "Because you either die in the explosion, or at my hands. Take your pick."

"What?" Indy couldn't believe it, her mind scrambled to make sense of what was happening. "You can't. How did you...?" She dropped the tools and darted around him, even as he grabbed for her. He turned with a snarl and started to lumber after her, but she ignored him as she ran toward the house.

She was halfway across the yard when the house exploded, sending a searing orange fireball reaching for the sky. Glass shattered, and wood and metal flew in all directions. Indy was knocked to the ground by the impact. On instinct, she covered her head with her hands as burning embers and pieces of wreckage rained down on her.

CHATPER TWENTY-ONE

Indy coughed, the smoke and dust were so thick she couldn't see a foot in front of her.

"No! No! Nooooo." The words were ripped from her throat in a horrified cry. She was just about to save Finn. Swampy had ruined it all. This wasn't how it was supposed to end.

Standing up, she pushed away the refuse lying all around. The smoke began to clear, and she stared at the ruined house in front of her. Flames licked out of the window from what had once been the kitchen. Part of the roof was blown completely off, and smoke billowed from the windows facing the front. The house was still partially standing. But no one could've survived that. Indy was numb. Her whole body was just…numb, like she couldn't process what was happening. She couldn't be too late to save Finn, she just couldn't. He'd been in the basement. Perhaps he might've survived the blast, somehow.

Rushing toward the house, she called his name. "Finn. Finn, answer me. Are you there? Please, answer me." Her last words came out as a sob. The little window that led into the basement, just along from the stairs coming down from the backdoor was completely gone, covered by the steps which had collapsed in a pile of rubble. She sank to her knees and began to sob for real.

There was a sound behind her. A deep, rumbling sound. Like somebody laughing.

Slowly, she got to her feet and spun on her heel to see Swampy closing in on her. His beard jiggled up-and-down with his unconfined mirth.

"I got that bastard," Swampy roared. "He won't be doing no more detective work. And you're next, you interfering little bitch."

"You," she hissed.

"Yeah, me," Swampy crowed. He raised an eyebrow in her direction, and then grinned at the burning house, is if pleased with a job well done.

Finn was dead. Her world went red. A ferocious need to maim, kill, blew through her like an incendiary fire. She didn't care that he was aiming to kill her. Instead of turning to run, she charged at Swampy as if possessed by the devil.

He only had time to give a shout of surprise, before she dive-tackled him, and took him out at the knees. His enormous bulk hit the ground with a sickening thud.

She bared her teeth and leaped for his throat, like an animal possessed. He was big and heavy. Much heavier than her. And as she tried to land a fist in his face, he brushed her hand aside, like it was a mere nothing, then he slammed his own fist into the side of her head. Intense pain bloomed, and for a second, she thought she might blackout. In that instant, Swampy yelled and reared up, catching her head between his two meaty hands and bringing it down on the ground beside him, smacking her forehead against the dirt. This time, stars shimmered in front of her eyes. Or was it just flames from the fire?

He rolled her over and then Swampy climbed astride her, his huge size no match for her small frame. It felt like he was crushing her with his weight; it was hard to breathe. But she wasn't going down without a fight. This man had killed Finn. Adrenaline was surging through her like a wave of hot lava. She'd use that strength.

Remembering a move she'd seen a girl do once in a movie, she swung her legs up and around him, managing to get one booted heel beneath his chin. The other leg wouldn't fit around his huge girth. But one foot might be enough. The hard heel of her cowboy boot wedged into the fleshy part of his gullet, and she heard his croaky cry cut off, as she rammed her foot as hard as it would go, muscles in her thigh screaming. Using her other foot as leverage, she pushed against the ground, lifting her hips and squeezing tight with her thighs, digging her elbows into the dust as she arched her back. His fingers tore at her arms, her chest, reaching for her face, but she held him away, and he finally toppled backwards, slamming against the ground in an effort to break free as he gasped for breath.

Not waiting, she rolled to her side and pounced on top of him again. A blind fury of hate, and blood, and burning fear surged through her.

She was going to kill him. He'd killed Finn; he deserved to die. Revenge wouldn't bring Finn back, wouldn't bring back the dream of the two of them sharing a life together. But if she had to live without Finn, then this man was going to die.

Somewhere behind her, someone was yelling, but she didn't turn around to see who it was.

Rough hands grabbed her under the arms and lifted her away from the man lying on the ground.

"Leave me be," she screamed. "I'm gonna kill him. He murdered Finn."

But the arms were too strong, dragging her away from Swampy, her heels leaving twin divots in the dust. In her peripheral vision, she saw two more men dive on top of Swampy as he attempted to get up.

"Settle down, Miss Solomon," a gruff voice commanded. "Let us handle this. I'm Detective Sergeant Mike Rogers, and we're here to help."

"No. No," she sobbed. "You're too late. We're too late. Finn was in there when the house blew up. He's dead," she wailed, collapsing in a heap on the ground, her knees no longer strong enough to hold her weight. Mike knelt down and put a comforting arm around her shoulders. She wanted to shrug him off, but she no longer had the strength.

"Hey, Sarge. You need to come and look at this," a deep voice echoed out of the night, coming from somewhere in the front yard. Indy tuned him out, too lost in her own grief to even wonder what he was calling the sarge for.

"I'm busy," Mike replied, not removing his arm, which was beginning to feel like it was the only thing anchoring her to this world.

"No, boss, you need to see this," the man continued to request his presence. "I think it might be Detective Carmody. I believe he's alive."

Indy lifted her head, hope flooding through her.

* * *

Finn dragged in another lungful of air. Sweat was pouring freely down his back as he pushed himself up another step. Two more, and he'd be at the top. Who would've thought dragging yourself up a flight of stairs by your elbows and knees could be this taxing? Perhaps he was still suffering a concussion. No, that was a definite, his cognitive abilities were not up to scratch. And also suffering from whatever they'd drugged him with, which must be still circling around his system.

His shoulder ached like a bitch from where he used it as a battering ram to knock down the door at the base of the steps. It'd taken him four hits to finally splinter the door enough to knock it away from the lock. Thankfully, the door was made of typical, cheap fiberboard. If it'd been metal, he would never have escaped the basement. It was nearly dark outside; the sun having set half an hour ago. Which meant there was only just enough light inside the house to make out walls and doorways, but not the details.

Finn moved carefully and slowly, checking every square inch of ground before he moved forward. He didn't know what kind of booby trap Garrett and Swampy had set, but he was guessing it was possibly a bomb of some kind. If the criminals were planning on murdering a bunch of cops, the best way to do it was to explode the whole house. He'd studied bomb making, detection, and how to defuse a simple incendiary device as part of his training.

There were many ways to trigger a bomb. The easiest way was to have someone push a button. A person would have to be nearby and be able to see when the detectives entered the house to do this. But he'd heard the vehicle drive away after a loud altercation. And then silence. From the little info Garrett had given him, it seemed like everyone was leaving. Going to the docks, it sounded like. Which left the idea that the bomb would have to be triggered internally. There were all sorts of ways to set up an ambush. Pressure pads under the floor; but that seemed a little too high tech for this duo. A simple tripwire set across an entrance or hallway, but they were easier to spot and could possibly be avoided. Which left the other common and simple-to-construct method of sensors around the door and windows. It was the technique a lot of household security systems used to detect break-ins. Easy to hide, unless you knew what to look for.

With all of these thoughts in mind, Finn had carefully made his way up the stairs. He wasn't going to sit here like a helpless kitten. He was going to fight until the end. And save Mike and the rest of his team from annihilation.

He'd taken a calculated risk when he'd bashed his way

through the basement door. The door could have been wired, but there was nothing obvious on his side, and from the quick glance he got as Garrett hustled Indy through the door, he could see nothing on the other side, either.

He dragged himself up the final two steps, and lay panting, getting his breath back, while at the same time studying his next move. A hallway ran directly from the stairs toward the front of the house, doorways leading off left and right. The first doorway to the right led into a kitchen; he could just make out the peeling linoleum floor and the edge of some cupboards from his position on the ground. There had to be an entrance leading from the kitchen out to the backyard, because that was where the voices had come from right before the vehicle pulled out of the driveway.

For a second, Finn lost his train of thought as images of Indy crowded his mind. The tears tracking down her face as Garrett hauled her to her feet. The despair and anguish in her beautiful brown eyes as she'd turned to glance at him over her shoulder before Garrett pushed her through the door.

Finn was going to kill Garrett when he got out of here. If he got out of here. The traitorous fucker. But he'd have plenty of time for that later. All he could hope now was that Garrett had kept his word, and got Indy well away from here. Was she safe? He wouldn't put it past Garrett to use Indy as a human shield if need be. But Finn had had no choice. He knew Indy probably hated him for what he'd done. For making that phone call and putting his own team in danger to save her. But he couldn't live with Indy's certain death on his conscience. This way, he'd been able to get her out of imminent danger. He hoped she would forgive him one day.

With a deep breath, Finn levered himself onto his knees and elbows and began to shuffle carefully down the hallway. Time to get to work. Mike had said he'd be there in twenty minutes. Finn calculated that had been fifteen minutes ago.

They were due here soon, and he needed to stop them from coming inside. Crawling into the kitchen, he located the rear door, but it was too dark inside to make out anything clearly. With a grunt, he used a cupboard and then a countertop to heave himself up to standing, and awkwardly hopped over to study the door frame.

Yep, just as he thought. Now he was close enough to see it in the dim light, the door frame had wires running around the inside. Hopping over to peer out the kitchen window, he could see the same white wires tucked into the window frame. It was a dodgy job, but it didn't need to be perfect. By the time Mike and his crew noticed there was something odd about the window, it'd be too late. But how was he supposed to get out without triggering the bomb? If Garrett and Swampy knew anything, then they'd probably set a delay on the trigger, allowing more people to flood through after they breached the door, killing the maximum number of victims. How long was that delay? Five seconds? Ten? Twenty? If he breached the window, how long would he have to get away before it blew up?

Hoping to find something, a tool or a knife, that might help him escape his bindings, he searched the kitchen. But there was nothing on the countertops, and the drawers were hanging open, empty. The house had clearly been abandoned for a while, and whoever had moved out had taken everything with them.

Where had they hidden the bomb? He half-heartedly opened and closed a few cupboard doors. But even if he found the explosives, it was too dark for him to try to defuse the bomb.

He considered the kitchen windows. If he were to throw himself through those, he'd have to first clamber up onto the countertop, which would be tricky. He could do it, but if he didn't break the window the first time, he'd be losing precious seconds while he tried again. He looked at the door. Same with that. If it took him as long as it had to break through the basement door, he'd probably be fried before he even got out.

Time was ticking down, he was aware he had less than five minutes up his sleeve. But if he was going to jump through a window, if that was his only avenue of escape, he needed a larger window that he could bodily throw himself out of. Shuffling back into the hallway, he headed for the front of the house. There might well be a living or dining area in this direction, with more accessible windows.

He was right. The large front room was empty, much the same as the kitchen. Disused and un-lived in. The main door sat between two large picture windows. Approaching the front door, he could see it was wired, as well. Hopping to the left, he peered through the window without touching the pane of glass. Wired. They'd done a thorough job. It looked like every access way was booby-trapped. He stared out into the dark front yard, which was much the same as the back. Dead grass, a few neglected trees, a leaning mailbox. Right below the window was an old garden bed with a row of half dead hedges. It wasn't much of a soft landing, but it would have to do. Wishing he had more clothes on wasn't going to help now. He was going to have to jump through the window practically naked.

A flash of movement caught his eye. It was there, and then it was gone. Someone was hiding out there in the gloom near the front corner fence of the house next door. Someone moving stealthily, not wanting to be seen. Was it Mike and his team? Had they arrived earlier than expected? Or was it someone else? Swampy, or someone from the drug gang? Whoever it was, they couldn't be allowed to enter the house. He had to do something. It was now or never.

He shuffled backward a few steps. Lined up his target and

sucked in a deep, calming breath. He could do this. He began to hop forward, bracing for impact. But the second before he crashed through the glass, he thought he heard the rear door open. It was too late to stop his forward momentum, and all he could do was tuck his head between his shoulders, and hope like hell he wasn't too late to stop the bloodbath. And that this didn't hurt too much.

Glass splintered around him. He landed with a sickening thud; the wind knocked out of his lungs. Spears of pain sliced through his shoulder, which took the brunt of his fall, and then his back and legs burned as he tumbled through the hedge below, glass raining down on top of him.

Even as he landed, he opened his mouth to yell a warning, but nothing came out. It took him precious seconds, as he lay on the ground, gasping like a landed fish.

"Run," he croaked. "Get away." But his voice was feeble and raspy. He hurt all over, like he'd been set on fire, like a million wasps were stinging his bare skin.

He tried shouting again, "The house is going to explode! Clear the area." But again, it came out on a hoarse, wheezing breath.

He should probably follow his own advice and get as far away from the building as he could. Fighting through the knee-high bushes, he rolled until he felt the dirt beneath him. Then he kept rolling over and over, his skin alight with pain as tiny bits of glass shrapnel grated against his defenseless skin.

"Run," he yelled each time he rolled. "It's going to blow."

And then it did.

The house erupted in a fireball, the heat so intense it singed his eyebrows, burned the hair from his legs. A blast wave hit him, the hot surge of air so strong it took his breath away, and pushed him so that he rolled a few more times in the dust.

Then everything went quiet. Apart from the roar and

crackle of the flames as they devoured the house. But Finn could hardly hear, the blood pounding in his ears was so loud.

Shit. Shit. Double shit.

That was intense. A small part of him hadn't quite believed this house would blow. Hadn't quite believed that his brother would go that far. But this proved beyond a doubt that Garrett was evil, right through to the core. Somewhere inside he wanted to grieve, wanted to rant and shout at the world that it wasn't fair. That he and his brother were supposed to be best mates. Supposed to grow up together, have a happy family each, and live in a house just down the street from each other, then grow old together. He was grieving the loss of that dream.

Finn didn't want to move. Every single part of him hurt. He could feel blood trickling down his back, down his temple. But he had to get up. Had to get going. Needed to find Indy. That was top priority; all he could think about. The docks. That's what Garrett had said. And so that was where he was headed.

With a groan, he got up on one elbow.

"Stop. Don't move," an authoritative voice demanded. "Stay right where you are." Finn froze as the muzzle of a rifle appeared in his face. "Put your hands up," the voice growled, and Finn tilted his head up and caught sight of a police uniform. Oh. Thank. God. For a moment, he thought it might've been Swampy, come to finish the job.

"My name is Detective Constable Griffin Carmody," he said slowly and clearly. As clearly as his raspy throat would allow, at least. "I was being held captive in that house. I just escaped through the window. And I can't put up my hands, because they're tied together."

The muzzle wavered, then flashed up and away as the police officer bent down to stare into Finn's face.

"We've been looking for you, Detective Constable."

"Yeah, well, better late than never," Finn sighed, and lay his head on the ground, no longer having the strength to hold it up.

"Let me get those ties off you." Finn heard the man shout something to a colleague standing in the road. "And an ambulance," the officer added as an afterthought, trying to hide his grimace, and Finn wondered how bad he really looked.

The officer returned a moment later with a large pocketknife to cut away the ties, then helped Finn to sit up. "An ambulance is on the way, sir," the young constable said, offering him a bottle of water, which Finn took gratefully. Until that exact second, he hadn't realized how thirsty he was. A blanket was draped around Finn's shoulders as he downed half the bottle in one gulp. "My name is Constable Bradley Webster. I've let the sarge know you're here."

Finn listened to the officer talk excitedly. "We thought you might have been one of the criminals when you came crashing through the window like that. You were lucky we didn't shoot you. And then when the house exploded, we lost sight of you for a while there. I can't believe you survived that." The young man glanced at him in awe.

"I don't want an ambulance," Finn said, slowly pulling himself to his feet.

"But, sir…" the officer gave him a horrified glance.

"I need some clothes, and I need to borrow a car."

"Have you seen yourself?" Constable Webster gestured to Finn's chest and then his legs. Finn glanced down for the first time. Oh, wow. He did look a mess. Hundreds of tiny cuts covered him from head to toe, a couple of deeper lacerations, but most of them were flesh wounds from where he'd rolled on the tiny bits of glass after he crashed through the window.

"I'm fine," Finn said, even though he could feel his

shoulders and back, which'd taken the brunt of the fall, stinging like he'd been lit on fire.

"No, you're not, Griff," a familiar voice said from behind. "You're not going anywhere except to the hospital." The sarge stepped in front of him.

Then a mini tornado barreled into Finn, nearly knocking him to the ground.

"Indy?"

Where had she come from? What was she doing here?

"Finn," she cried. "Is it you? Is it really you?" She pressed her sweet body tight against his and he didn't care anymore how much his cuts and bruises stung. He hauled her to him.

The sound of her voice made his chest expand until he felt like it might burst.

She was here. With him. Safe.

They were both safe.

Indy's fingers curled into the hair at the back of his neck and she pulled him to her, clinging as if he were a life-raft and she was afraid of drowning. Not kissing him, but staring into his eyes, as if she couldn't believe he was real. Protective. Yet terribly vulnerable at the same time.

"You were dead," she sobbed. "When that house exploded, I knew you were dead." Fine tremors ran through her body, and he enfolded her with his arms.

"I'm not dead, baby," he soothed, burying his face in her hair, letting her unique scent, her very essence, sink into his soul.

But she wouldn't let him go. And he didn't mind that one bit. Not even caring that the swell of emotion brought tears to his eyes. Let everyone stare if they wanted. He had the woman he loved back in his arms, and that was where he intended to keep her from now on.

CHAPTER TWENTY-TWO

The gravel driveway curved through one last stand of trees and Stormcloud Lodge came into view through the trunks of two large eucalyptus. The sight of the lodge made a sudden knot swell in Indy's throat. *Home.* She was coming home. It was an odd thought, because she'd never thought of Stormcloud as home before, not truly. But after the last few weeks, the trauma of the past few days, this place was like a balm to her soul. At last, she might've finally found a place where she belonged.

A grin tickled her lips as she watched a number of the small luxury cabins surrounding the billabong emerge from the bush. Her horses. And her dogs. She couldn't wait to see all of them. Dale had promised that Gypsy was back safely by Beethoven's side, and Digger and Barbie were getting fat and possibly a little bored, tied up with Steve's dogs. It was one of the first questions out of Indy's mouth when she'd seen Dale the morning after the explosion. Was someone looking after her dogs? Did they have enough water? Had they been fed? But she needn't have worried, Dale told her Bindi had adopted them almost as her own.

"Happy to be back?" Dale asked, watching her smile.

She glanced over at him in the driver's seat, big hands

confident on the wheel, handsome face a touch pensive as he studied her.

"I mean… I just want to make sure you're okay." The frown lines between his eyes deepened.

Dale, Steve, and Mack had driven straight to Cairns when they'd first heard the news that she and Finn have been found alive. After many hours talking to the police, and Mike Rogers in particular, Steve and Mack had been persuaded to return to the stock camp, to help finish dismantling it and return everything to the station. But Dale had stayed, determined to be by her side until she was ready to come home. And he'd been apologizing profusely over and over, ever since, as if it'd been his fault she'd been taken from the camp. Which it hadn't, there wasn't anything he could've done. It was her own stupid fault for falling for Garrett's tricks.

After a visit to the hospital the night of the bombing— where they'd dressed Finn's larger wounds and given her the once-over to make sure she had no major damage—it'd taken three days of talking until her throat hurt, endless interviews with endless different detectives, going back to the crime scene at least three times to clarify points where the cops hadn't believed her, signing countless forms and sitting in countless offices, waiting, until she'd finally been allowed to come home.

During that whole time, she had only seen Finn twice. For a blissful few hours at the hospital, where she and Finn had huddled close on a hospital bed because he wouldn't let her go. Or was it because she wouldn't let him go? Then the clamoring voices demanding their statements to the cops had become too loud, and Finn had finally given in, his strong sense of duty driving him to agree to answer their questions. Telling her to do the same, he'd promised they'd be back together soon. The second, and last time, she'd seen him, had been this morning at the Cairns District Police Headquarters, where Mike Rogers had set up a temporary task force. Finn had pulled her aside into an empty office and she wrapped her arms around his waist and laid her ear against his chest, listening to the comforting, solid thud of his heart. Then he'd told her he needed more time. Just a few more days, that was all.

Finn wasn't allowed to reveal much. All she knew was that Detective Sergeant Rogers and his team were about to carry out raids across various cities and towns in the north of Australia. And Finn had asked to be included. It was important to him, she understood that. Important for him to help capture and bring down the chief figures from the drug gang he'd been hunting. A form of closure for him, and a huge coup for his team. It was part of why she loved him, his dedication to his job, his fierce bravery, his determination to make the streets a little safer by destroying that drug supply line. He'd waved away her concern about his injuries, saying they wouldn't hamper him, and he needed to do this.

He'd kissed her then, deep and powerful, letting his mouth tell her what his words couldn't. Leaving her with his promise on her lips and in her heart. She'd felt hopeful, slightly dizzy, and a recognition of something big. But also, terror. An irrational fear. But of what exactly, she couldn't put a finger on. Afraid that he might not feel the same way? Afraid this thing between them was too unstable to last? She didn't say the words again. Didn't tell him she loved him. That single word might rip her fragile heart apart. For those few moments when she'd thought he was dead, she'd suffered such devastating emptiness. It made her realize just how deep her love for him went. But she needed to know if he felt the same. And she couldn't tell him all these things in the middle of a sterile office at the Cairns police department.

She'd stared into eyes the color of blue topaz so beautiful it hurt, and she'd let him go.

She hated not knowing where he was. What he was doing. Of course, he'd given her his word he'd come visit her as soon as he possibly could. But…she wasn't sure what that meant, exactly. Would he even come? Of course, he would, she was being silly. The two opposing thoughts warred back and forth in her mind all day.

And then there was Garrett. He was still in a coma in the hospital. The doctors were unsure as to when, or even if, he'd wake up. The twins' mother was by his side, but Finn wouldn't talk about how he felt about his brother. About his involvement in the drug gang. About whether he cared if Garrett lived or died. A knot of worry twisted in her guts every time she thought of Garrett. It was her fault he was in the hospital. But she had no idea how Finn felt about that, either.

Dale was still frowning at her, awaiting an answer.

"What? Oh, yes," she said lightly. "I'm fine." And she was fine, physically. Or at least, would be soon. She'd sustained superficial cuts and bruises, most of them while she'd been fighting with Swampy. But they were already healing. "And yes, I'm happy to be home."

"Good, because everyone is desperate to see you. Look, there's Bindi, standing on the top of the steps, waiting." Dale pointed and Indy saw the dark, diminutive figure of her friend. Mack came out to stand behind her, the sound of the car clearly drawing him outside. Soon, there were other figures waiting for the vehicle to pull up in the parking lot. Skylar and Sasha had joined them, Sasha waving joyfully in welcome. Daniella, Julie, and Daisy had also emerged, followed by Alex and a few curious guests. The small crowd clapped as she got out of the car. Indy hung her head, unsure of this hero's welcome. She was no hero, she'd just done what needed to be done, like any of the rest of them would have.

Hesitating, half out the car door, she felt Dale's hand on her shoulder. "Come on," he encouraged. "They've got a bit of a celebration organized for you. And you deserve it. If what Nash told me is true, you and Finn possibly helped to bring down one of the largest drug cartels operating in Australia. Take your fifteen minutes of glory," he added. "Because, before you know it, I'll have you back out there working your butt off." He grinned, white teeth flashing. "You're one of the family now, in more ways than you understand. A lot of us have been through a few nightmare scenarios of our own, and now you've joined the club. We joke about it here. But it's almost like a badge of honor, the way Stormcloud men and women have to fight to get the love they deserve."

"Oh… Wow." Indy wasn't sure what to say. It was the most profound thing Dale had ever said to her. She'd always viewed him as her boss first, and her friend second. But she could see she'd got it wrong. To Dale, she was as much part of his family as the rest of his staff.

Indy had heard all the stories of how Dale and Daisy had bonded after he'd rescued her from a flooded creek, and Skylar and Nash had survived a helicopter crash. And Julie and Aaron, the most unlikely pair Indy had ever seen, had to fight off a crazed stalker to get their happily-ever-after. Mack and Bindi, too, had come through an attempt on Mack's life— even though he didn't like to talk about the scar on his left hand. It was true, she was joining the ranks of men and women who'd been through hell and back. With one major exception. She wasn't sure where she and Finn stood; where their relationship was headed. It left a hollow ache behind her breastbone every time she thought about him.

"So, are you coming?" Dale was still standing with his hand on her arm, as she wavered, half in and half out of the vehicle.

"Yes, of course." Pushing thoughts of Finn to the back of her mind, she stepped the rest of the way out of the car and squared her shoulders to walk up the steps.

"Steve and Aaron send their apologies; they've had to take the helicopter out to check a broken fence. But they'll be home soon," Dale said, as he trailed her up the staircase.

There were a few people missing from the crowd that Indy would've liked to have seen one more time. She was sad she hadn't had a chance to say her goodbyes to the rest of the muster crew. Once they found out she and Finn were safe, Dale told her that Dave and Carrot had quickly moved on to a job on another station farther west, bemoaning the fact they were down to two again, and joking that perhaps they could lure Finn away from detective work. He'd made a damn good stock hand, and once he realized that he'd missed his true calling, he'd come crawling back to them, Dave had said. The Scanlon family had spent a few days resting and recuperating at Stormcloud, but they, too, had moved on. Sue, the eldest Scanlon sister, was pregnant and due to give birth in a few weeks, so they were heading south to make sure they were there in time for the happy event. Indy hoped they sent her a photo of the new baby. Brian had been released on bail, awaiting a trial date, and their truck had been impounded. She was sad for Brian and Rosie; they'd destroyed something wonderful. They could've had a large, wonderful life on a property of their own if they'd waited a few more years. Now they would be confined to a small life, where Brian spent at least the next few years in jail. Indy wondered if their marriage would survive.

Bindi was the first to greet Indy, wrapping her up in a bearhug. "God, we were so worried about you."

"Yes," Julie echoed, joining in the hug. Indy wasn't normally much of a hugger, but she relaxed into them, liked the feel of it, the way they embraced her, made her feel like part of the circle. Then everyone was talking at once, everyone wanting to touch her, talk to her, wish her well.

Until Daniella clapped her hands. "Let's take this inside, everyone. Give the poor girl some room to breathe," she said.

It was coming on to mid-afternoon, smoko time at the lodge, Daniella ushered the guests back to their tables, which Indy could see had been set up a bit like a high tea, with piles of small, delicate cakes, silver cutlery, teapots, and matching teacups.

As they made their way through the dining room, she quirked an inquiring eyebrow at Bindi, who rolled her eyes and said quietly into Indy's ear, "Daniella's idea. She wanted us all to be here when you arrived home, and she needed something to entertain the guests this afternoon. So, Skylar and I have been run off our feet, getting it ready."

"It looks amazing," Indy said admiringly.

"Yeah, it tastes amazing, too," Mack confirmed.

"Really?" Dale turned greedy eyes toward the feast. He was always hungry, and he'd do just about anything for Skylar's cooking.

"Don't worry, bro, I saved some for you." Skylar punched her brother on the shoulder.

Alex pulled out a stool from beneath the long countertop in the kitchen for her with a gallant sweep of his arm, while everyone else clustered into the kitchen, taking up positions leaning against the wall, or snagging one of the other stools, all talking loudly.

Skylar placed a plate of cupcakes in front of Indy and a large mug of tea, then looked at her expectantly. The kitchen went quiet. "Well, go on," Skylar prompted. "Tell us all the gory details. We need to hear everything."

Indy glanced around the kitchen. This was what it meant to be part of a family. The give-and-take. The expectation, but also the support. She'd never felt anything like this before.

Dale's words from earlier came back to her. She was part of the Stormcloud family now. Without any brothers or sisters of her own, Indy hadn't really known what she'd been missing, until now.

It suddenly made her want to have a family of her own. Something she'd never really had while growing up. A way to re-frame her future, so it was completely different from her past. It was the first time she'd really dissected the idea of having a family. For the short time she'd been pregnant with Patrick's baby, she'd quickly come to terms with the idea of having an infant. But that wasn't the same thing as having family, she realized that now.

And she wanted a family with Finn.

But did he want the same thing? He knew she didn't have any family left, but they'd only discussed it briefly, so there was no way he could realize just how important it was to her. And even if he did, how were they going to make it work? He already had a daughter. Gorgeous, little, four-year-old Kayleigh. How would she fit into this picture of the perfect family? He might not even want any more kids. It was getting harder to see a way out of this maze of complications. She knew Finn was worth holding onto, but she really needed to talk to him, to find out what was going on in his heart.

CHAPTER TWENTY-THREE

Finn drove as fast as he dared on the gravel roads. *Slow down*, he told himself. It wouldn't do to crash the rental car when he was this close. He was nearly at Stormcloud, and his heart beat a little faster with every kilometer. It'd been four days since he'd last seen Indy. Four interminably long days, where he'd spent most of the time strategizing, planning, ignoring the pain of the myriad of tiny cuts all over his body, and finally executing their plan. But always at the back of his mind was Indy.

It was getting close to dusk, and Finn knew the wildlife would be coming out soon, and the roads would get dangerous. He flipped on his headlights just in time to see the sign announcing the Stormcloud entrance one kilometer up the road. He wasn't sure what to expect. Even though he'd spent time with the muster crew, he'd never been to the lodge itself. He'd heard lots of good things, but he wondered if it would live up to the hype.

Turning into the driveway, he was surprised to find it wound deep into the scrubland, taking him almost into the foothills of the escarpment. After ten minutes, over a small rise, the lodge appeared through a copse of trees, and Finn's breath caught. It *was* everything people had said it was.

Reclining back into the side of the shallow hillside, it was made of local timber, using sustainable architecture, and it almost looked as if it'd emerged fully formed from the bush. As if it belonged there. Understated, but classy. It oozed natural charm and hinted at the luxury to be found inside.

The lights were on inside the lodge, casting a soft glow out onto a grassy slope that led down to a picturesque billabong. Indy had been right. This place was stunning. People moved around inside the building, and Finn decided it must be mealtime. As he found a spot in the parking lot, a couple drifted past him, holding hands, heading up the stairs and inside. Probably guests going in for dinner. Damn, had he chosen a bad time to arrive? Indy would probably be busy helping to serve or in the kitchen. It was all-hands-on-deck when they were fully booked, or so she'd liked to tell him. He should've called ahead, but he wanted to surprise her.

Finn got out and stood beside his car, trying to figure out his next move. Should he go in the front door? Or be more discreet and find a rear entrance?

He decided the back door would be preferable. Skirting the bottom of the stairs, he made his way around the corner of the building. He was just reaching for the handle of a door that looked like it might lead inside when he heard a loud gasp behind him.

"Finn? Is that you?"

He turned to see Indy coming down the steps from a separate, smaller building. The staff quarters, perhaps. She opened and closed her mouth a few times, as if trying to speak, but no words would come.

"Hiya, gorgeous." He turned and was relieved to see her look of confusion morph into one of pure joy.

She leaped down the stairs and bounded into his arms, clinging to him for all she was worth. A couple of his wounds twinged, but he managed to swallow his grimace as her hungry mouth found his, and she raised up on her toes to press herself more fully against him. The hollow ache that'd existed in his gut when he'd said goodbye to Indy in Cairns was replaced by a growing drumbeat of warmth and desire. Replaced by her. She was what he'd been missing. She was the missing part that made him whole.

"I hardly recognized you with that suit on," she finally murmured, releasing his mouth, and drawing back to look at him.

"I brought some work clothes," he mumbled in reply. "Would you like me to go and change?"

"No. I'd like you to keep kissing me." She grabbed him by the hand and went to lead him to the small building she'd just exited.

Then, as if remembering something, she said, "Wait. Stay here for a second." She dropped his hand and went in through the rear door of the lodge. Ten seconds later, she was back, a wry grin tugging at her lips. "I just had to tell Skylar you were here, and I was going to be…indisposed for a little while."

He grinned back as she took him into the staff quarters, shoving open a door halfway down the hallway and dragging him inside. He barely had time to register that this must be her bedroom before she pushed him down onto the bed, landing on top and kissing him. His cock stirred as her tongue stroked skilfully inside his mouth. She was every bit as hungry for him as he was for her. Even as they kissed, her fingers fumbled with the buttons of his white shirt, pushing at his suit jacket, trying to dislodge it from the shoulders.

At least she still wanted him physically. That bit hadn't altered.

A tiny part of him had been worried something might've changed in their four days apart. Worried that she'd decided he wasn't worth the risk anymore. Wasn't worth the complicated baggage that being a detective brought along with it. A detective with a four-year-old daughter. It was still a question that needed to be answered.

The suit jacket was restrictive, so he shrugged it off, along with his shirt, and her hands eagerly explored the hard planes of his chest, urgent and demanding.

"Oh, shit. I forgot," Indy exclaimed as her nimble fingers touched the edge of a bandage covering the back of his shoulder blade. "I'm sorry." She tried to sit up, apology written all over her face.

"Well, I'm not," he growled, nipping at her bottom lip. "They're just scratches, and they're feeling so much better now I'm with you."

"If you're sure?" Her eyes lost their contrition and she let her hands wander again, nails digging gently into the ridges of his stomach. "I've missed you so much. Missed doing this so much." She dropped her head and let her tongue travel around the sensitive skin of his nipple, and across to the other one. Then she dragged it lower, and her hands fumbled with the fasteners on his trousers.

His cock felt as if it were made of granite. He might well explode too early if she kept going like this.

"Slow down," he murmured. "I'm not going anywhere." He artfully flipped them both over, so he was now on top, and he deliberately made his kisses slow and deep, taking his time to taste her, and she moaned into his mouth as he slid his hands underneath her shirt and over the soft skin of her hips.

"I don't want to slow down," she whispered under her breath, and he grinned like a Cheshire cat.

She was this wild, beautiful thing, and he wanted to hold on to her forever. But she was right in one aspect, perhaps they needed to get naked. He was half-way there, but she needed some help. Tonight, she was wearing a light-blue button-up shirt with the Stormcloud logo on the pocket. It took him no time at all to snap the buttons open and remove it, revealing a white-lace bra beneath. Mmm, she was so beautiful. He pressed a kiss in the hollow of her collarbone, and between her breasts. Sliding first one, and then the other strap of her bra over her shoulders, he became almost mesmerized by the swell of her breasts beneath the lacy fabric.

With a grunt of impatience, Indy arched her back and released her bra strap, throwing the piece of underwear into a dark corner of her room, and he looked his fill of her perfect breasts. Running his hands across the silky surface of her stomach, he tried to imprint every curve, every dip. He wanted to learn everything there was to know about her body.

But Indy was getting impatient again. She ground one thigh against his erection, sending white-hot arrows of desire spiraling through him. And now, so was he.

He popped open the buttons on her jeans and pulled them off in one swift movement, her panties following a second afterward.

Reaching into his pocket, right before he tossed his trousers on the floor, he said, "I came prepared this time." He waved the fistful of condoms and then dumped them on the bedside table. The room was practically dark now, the sun having set in a gaudy display of oranges and pinks over the mountains as he'd pulled into the driveway. But he wanted to see Indy, so before he lay down on the bed, he twitched the curtains closed and flicked the little bedside lamp on. Now he could see her in all her glorious perfection.

Both of them naked now, he lowered himself slowly over her body, glorying in the feel of her thighs against his, her breasts beneath his chest, his cock pressed into her stomach.

"Where's the condom?" Indy asked, voice husky and full

of urgency.

"Already?" he queried.

"Yes, already." She took his hand and guided it between her legs, where he could feel she was hot and ready for him. He didn't have to be told twice. It took him five seconds to rip open the packet and sheath himself, then hover on his elbows above her.

Lifting his eyes to hers, he plunged inside. She moaned and raised her hips to welcome him in. Oh. So. Good. Indy. And him. So good together. It was like she took him to another plane. Where intimacy and desire combined.

They climbed the peak together as he thrust, slowly at first, then faster and faster. Until Indy dug her nails into his shoulders and he could no longer contain himself as great shuddering breaths took him over the brink.

He didn't know how long he lay with his head between her breasts, still buried within her, her hands tangled in his hair. But when he finally lifted his head and stared into her eyes, he saw her looking back at him with such tenderness, he couldn't help but say the words.

"I love you." A sudden lump formed in his throat. Because it was the simple truth. He'd already said the words days ago, he was just cementing them into his mind; into her heart.

Her hands stopped their gentle exploration of his neck and shoulders, and she clenched her thighs around him.

"You do?" Her face screwed up in a comical frown, half bemused, half pleased. Almost as if she hadn't expected him to say it.

"Of course, I do." He laughed. "You're the most amazing woman I've ever met. You changed my life the day you galloped into it on that bloody horse of yours. You're the strongest woman I know. The bravest and the most loyal. You tried to take down Swampy, a desperate criminal, twice your size, when you thought he'd killed me." Finn could still hardly believe her story, but Mike had backed her up, and he really shouldn't have expected anything less. "You touched my heart and now you've got my soul, too, Indy Solomon."

Tears shimmered in her eyes. "You don't know how glad I am to hear that. I was worried…"

He smoothed the hair back from her face. She had no need to worry. "I'm all in, Indy. No more half measures. I'm in this all or nothing. Whatever it takes to make this work, I'll do it," he added, not bothering to keep the possessive note out of his voice.

"Are you sure? I mean, I'm sure I want to be with you. I want to see where this takes us."

"Yes, I'm sure. I signed the divorce papers yesterday. Soon it'll be official." He wondered why he'd been so hesitant to do it before. He and Chloe were never getting back together. But Indy had been the true solid reason he'd needed to put pen to paper. He wanted no impediments to them being together.

"Really?" she breathed. "That's good." She nodded, then bit her bottom lip. "But…what about Kayleigh?"

He had an answer for that question, too. In the little spare time he'd had over the past few days, it was practically all he'd thought about. "Kayleigh and Chloe have built a life in Ireland. They won't be coming back to Australia," he admitted. It was a bitter pill to swallow, but it was the simple truth.

"Have you considered moving to Ireland to be near them?" she asked.

Yes, he had. It was true, at one stage he'd considered doing that for Kayleigh. But it would never work. He knew that now. "Kayleigh is my daughter, and I miss her every day. But as much as it leaves a hole in my heart, I can't move back to Ireland. My life is here. This is where I want to live. I would resent it if I moved, resent them for making me do it, and I would hate to feel any kind of resentment toward my daughter."

"Are you sure?" she asked again, not unkindly. But there was a core of strength in her tone, as if she needed to be one-hundred percent sure he wasn't going to change his mind.

"Yes. I'll go and visit her, and when she's older, I'm hoping she might come and stay during school holidays and the like. You can come with me, if you like."

"To Ireland?"

"Yes, I'd love to show you around. And I'd love you to meet Kayleigh, she's a little pocket rocket, so full of energy and sunshine."

"I'd like that," Indy agreed, turning trusting, dark eyes up to his. "And I'm sure I'll like her, too."

"We'll find a way to make this work. I'm ready. As long as you're ready, we can do this together. You and me against the world." He fist pumped the air in mock celebration, and she giggled at his comical enthusiasm.

Then she sobered and said, "I love you, too, Finn." And his heart nearly exploded at hearing those words.

Much later, they lay tangled together in the sheets. Lying face to face, Indy's soft exhalation of air every time she breathed out tickling his face with a featherlight touch. It was late, they'd heard first Bindi and Mack come in to the staff quarters; they had a master suite at the end of the building, and Finn had recognized Mack's deep voice. And then the front door had banged again, and Indy told him it must be Sasha and Alex also turning in for the night.

"I haven't even asked you how your brother is," Indy said softly into his ear. He could tell by the slight hitch in her voice she was almost afraid to ask. He hadn't been sure she was even awake, her breathing had slowed and her eyes had been closed for a while now.

He drew in a deep breath as guilt stabbed him in the gut. "He woke up yesterday," Finn replied. "I talked to Mum on the phone, she's been by his side in hospital the whole time. She's absolutely shattered by this whole thing. Not only finding out that one of her precious sons is a criminal, but that he's going to be spending the rest of his life behind bars."

And that he tried to kill his brother, Finn thought. His mother still didn't know all the details of that night, and he didn't want to be the one to tell her. But someone had to.

Finn hadn't been to see Garrett in the hospital, yet, and wasn't likely to, either. He still hadn't worked through all his conflicting emotions, and he was scared he wouldn't be able to stop himself from punching his brother in the face the second he saw him. His conflicting emotions stretched to his poor mother, as well. He had no idea where to start with her, either. He knew he owed her the truth, that he'd known about Garrett's criminal occupation, and he'd kept it from her. He was sorry now that he hadn't told her sooner, as her grief and pain almost bordered on mania, and she was partially blaming Finn for everything that'd happened in her attempt to understand why one of her cherished boys was under police guard in the hospital. Which was unfair, but not totally unreasonable, given she only knew parts of the story. But he couldn't go to her yet. Not while she was still so protective of Garrett.

And not while he still wanted to tear Garrett limb from limb.

At least his younger sister, Caroline, was helping to support their mother. Caro was as shocked by all this as his mother, but she seemed to accept it with a lot more composure, as if she somehow suspected what Garrett was capable of.

In Finn's mind, Garrett was irredeemable. He'd done the unthinkable and tried to kill Finn. The only small saving grace was that he'd taken Indy out of the house before it blew up. But that act had been more to save his own hide than out of any compassion for his twin brother. To use Indy as a human shield, if necessary. And Garrett was also a murderer, if Finn's suspicions were proven correct. Finn had confessed to the sarge about the lighter, and how he'd withheld vital evidence. Mike had been mad enough to chew nails, and for a few moments, Finn thought his job was on the line. But Mike had finally accepted it as the possible breakthrough they needed to help solve Ronaldo's murder, and had calmed down. A case against Garrett for Ronaldo's death still needed to be put together, so there was no mention of the charges. Yet. But how his mother was going to take this additional development, was anybody's guess. Not well, he decided.

"Oh, your poor mum," Indy said, bringing up a hand to stroke his face.

"Yeah. I need to talk to her."

"You do. And Caroline. And Garrett," Indy prompted hesitantly.

"Not sure I'm ready for Garrett, yet. Maybe not ever," he growled. He knew she was only trying to help. Knew that by not facing his brother, he was leaving things to fester, but he needed to get his emotions back under control before he did that. And seeing Indy, holding her close and satisfying his desperate need to know she was safe and well again, it went a long way to helping him do that. Knowing that his brother's treachery hadn't had any lasting ill effects on her.

Indy stared at him for a long time, not saying anything, merely stroking his hair softly. At last, as if she realized that pushing him on the subject of Garrett wasn't going to help, she changed the subject by asking, "And what about the drug bust?"

That was a much more agreeable topic, because he had good news on that front. "You'll probably hear about it on the news tomorrow." Mike was due to give a media interview in the morning, where the huge undercover bust would be revealed.

Finn rolled onto his back to ease his right shoulder, which'd taken the brunt of the shards of glass when he'd smashed through that window. Now that the high from their erotic pursuits had settled, he was beginning to feel his injuries again, and he was stiffening up. But it'd been worth it. And he'd become good at hiding his pain, otherwise Mike probably wouldn't have let him take part in the raids, either. But again, that'd been worth every ache and small agony, to be able to capture the head mastermind behind the whole drug gang.

"But yeah, we got them. Remember when I rolled beneath that truck and you had to act like a dumb bimbo to stop the truckie driving over the top of me?"

"Yes, I remember it well." Indy raised an eyebrow at him.

"Mike's team stopped that truckie and took him into custody." They'd also put a tracker in with the drugs, which'd been left in a container at the docks. Eventually, a few days after the drugs had been dropped, they'd managed to nab a dealer as he came to collect the stash. But he was small-time, a peripheral part of the drug ring."

Finn continued with his story. "At first, he said he didn't know anything. But then, after Mike offered him a deal for a much-reduced jail sentence—the guy has a young family in Brisbane—he finally came up with some names. And one of them was Swampy. Said that he was his contact. But he only revealed that information on the day of your abduction. If we'd known earlier..." Finn ground his teeth together. If they'd known, perhaps they could've started tracking Swampy earlier. And stopped Garrett from abducting Indy. It was one of the myriad of reasons Finn still wanted to kill his brother.

"Swampy turned out to be the key to this whole thing. His real name is Dwayne Carey, and he was the right-hand man in this whole trafficking operation. Employed by an Italian businessman to do his dirty work. We finally put all the puzzle pieces together, corroborated the link between Swampy and the Italian man we already suspected of being the head honcho of this drug ring, and we had enough evidence to make our arrests." The hard part was now going to be the long, drawn-out court case to prosecute The Italian —these guys were as slippery as eels when it came to getting a conviction, but Finn believed his boss had enough evidence to make the charges stick.

"Oh, wow. I would never have guessed," Indy replied. "Swampy didn't seem... I don't know, intelligent enough." She pursed her lips and lifted her eyes to the ceiling. "But I guess you can't judge a book by its cover."

"Exactly. All that dumbass-truck-driver persona was just a cover, he's a mean son-of-a-bitch. But he fooled most people, even me, so it was a good act." He gave a cynical grunt. "The ironic part is, if Garrett hadn't double-crossed Swampy by taking you and driving off with the getaway car, we would never have caught either of them. They had a boat waiting at the docks, filled with cargo and ready to sail to Indonesia. They would've got away scot free." And possibly have taken Indy with them, but Finn didn't like to even consider that scenario.

"Details are still sketchy, the doctors won't let us interrogate Garrett properly yet. But it seems Garrett had a plan to overthrow Swampy and become the right-hand-man instead." Funnily enough, Garrett's greed had been his ultimate undoing. If Garrett hadn't proceeded to play out his little coup attempt that night, if Swampy had been in the car with him like he was supposed to be, then Indy would never have escaped. "And Swampy was so incensed at Garrett ditching him, that he decided to change up the plan. Decided to kill me by exploding the house while he still could. He had some stupid idea that perhaps you and Garrett were in cahoots, and were going to warn the cops about the booby trap. So he wanted to finish me off; killing one cop was better than none. And I'd also seen his face, would be able to identify him, if I lived. But that was his first and last mistake. He didn't count on you showing up, my brave, little, ninja woman."

Indy took a while to digest all this startling information, and he watched the different emotions play across her face. Finally, she snorted, "I'm no ninja. Just a good, old-fashioned cowgirl who knows a trick or two."

He smiled. That she certainly was.

"Did Swampy know Garrett was your brother?" she continued.

"Yeah, but once Garrett had proven himself to be the criminal he is, and once he'd persuaded Swampy how much he despised me and wanted me dead, Swampy decided he could use him as an asset. Garrett might be able to garner insider information that could be helpful. Which in the end proved wrong. All Garrett wanted was to weasel his way up the criminal ladder."

Concern was etched in the lines around her eyes. "He wanted you dead? Garrett actually said that?" Indy asked, ignoring his other revelations.

Finn shrugged, but the motion hid a much deeper pain. "Seems like he did."

"That's a lot to deal with," she said softly. "I still can't believe you're twins and you're so…different."

He couldn't either. But he was over talking about Garrett.

"You have a bit of a white knight streak in you," she said, with a cheeky grin.

"A what?"

"You need to rescue everyone," she chided.

"It's not everyone I want to rescue," he said gruffly, pulling her in for a kiss, telling her with his body that she was the only treasure he wanted to keep safe.

"I'm not saying it's a bad thing," she replied with a laugh when he finally let her up for air. "It's what makes you, you."

He'd never thought of it like that before. He wasn't sure he had a *white knight complex*, or whatever it was she'd said. But he did have a desire to help people. And he thought he'd inherited that personality trait from his father. His dad had been a good firefighter, strong and fearless. He knew that, because his whole team had come to see the family after his dad died. One of the guys had taken him aside and told him how brave his dad had been, and how it was the greatest honor in the world to die while trying to save someone else's life. Finn must've taken his words to heart, but he didn't remember a huge epiphany or anything like that. It'd just grown on him day by day that helping people who were unable to fight their own battles, by bringing down the bullies and low-lives in the world, was a good thing.

"Should I still call you Finn?" she asked, voice soft and melodious. "Or are you Griff?"

"Yeah, I like it." He loved the sound of his name on her lips. She'd known him as Finn from the start, and he liked that she wasn't from his old world. Liked that she didn't know him as Griff. It allowed him to be a different person around her. A better person. A fresh start.

He wasn't sure exactly how they were going to make this work yet. But he was committed. And so was she. He wasn't prepared to live without her in his life, and he'd do just about anything to keep her. Nothing was a deal-breaker when it came to Indy.

But for tonight, he had some immediate plans that just couldn't wait. And they involved using a few more packets from that stash of condoms on the table.

Rising on his elbow, he waggled his eyebrows suggestively

at her. "And I like it even more when I hear you scream my name at the top of your lungs."

"There won't be any screaming tonight, Finn," she answered subduedly. "Sasha and Alex are two doors away; I'm not going to—"

He cut her off by claiming her mouth with his, and running his hand between her thighs, eliciting a moan from deep in her chest.

EPILOGUE

Indy sipped her drink and stared out over the billabong from the edge of the veranda. The air was warm, and smelled of a heady mix of the dusty outback and gum leaves, the sky full of stars so bright and crisp. A few revelers dotted the grassy slope, lit by the flickering flames of torches dotted around the edges. Some had even wandered down to the edge of the water, lured by the plop of fish surfacing to catch insects.

It was the perfect night for a perfect engagement party. Nash had finally asked Skylar to marry him. Everyone said it was about time, but Skylar was a complicated woman, and Nash hadn't wanted to rush her. They'd been living together for nearly two years now, and that was more of a commitment, in Nash's mind, at least, than a piece of paper. Of course, the party was held at Stormcloud, and of course, Skylar had done most of the catering—with lots of help from Bindi and Julie. Daniella had kept this weekend free of guests, so the staff could all join in and enjoy the party. It was mid-November and accommodation bookings were beginning to taper off anyway, in preparation for the wet season.

She could hardly believe it'd been a little over six months since the whole drug bust. It felt like just yesterday. But then it also felt like a dream, something that'd happened to someone else. A lot of things had changed since then.

Finn came up from behind, and wrapped his arms around Indy's middle, sneaking a kiss to the side of her cheek as he lay his chin on her shoulder. "Watcha doing?" he whispered.

She rested against his firm chest, tipping her head back, so she was cheek-to-cheek with him. "Not a lot," she replied. "Just appreciating the beauty of this place."

"Mmm, it is divine," he agreed. "But not as divine as you are in this dress." He ran a hand surreptitiously over her hip and cupped her bottom through the silky fabric. "Allows me much easier access than those jeans you usually wear." His fingers trickled down the back of her thigh until they were playing with the hem, lifting it slowly up her leg.

"Finn, don't." She playfully slapped his hand away and checked to make sure no one had seen them.

He'd already shown his appreciation of her summery dress earlier this evening, when she'd first emerged from the bedroom and his eyes had gone as round as saucers. He hadn't been able to keep his hands off her—and to be fair it was only the second time he'd ever seen her in a dress, the first time had been on their inaugural date because Finn had wanted to make their dating an official thing—running his hands up her legs beneath the short hem and then finding the lace of her new underwear she'd bought especially for tonight. It was a shimmery, pale-green dress that she'd let Bindi talk her into buying online, and now she was glad she had. Finn had promptly swung her up into his arms and carried her into the bedroom, soon quieting any protests she might've had with his clever mouth and nimble hands. They'd ended up being ten minutes late arriving at the party, but Indy didn't think anyone had noticed her slightly flushed cheeks or Finn's audacious grin.

She and Finn were leasing a little property on the outskirts of Dimbulah. It was a small cottage, with a large, airy veranda running around three sides, and a set of old, but very comfortable, cane chairs out front. Where Indy loved to sit with Finn after a long day and sip a beer, watch the world go by, and talk about their different days at work. The cottage came with a few acres of land out the back, where she could keep Gypsy and Beethoven. Both her horses were currently stabled at Stormcloud, but she'd bring them home over Christmas, when Stormcloud shut down during the height of the wet season. Finn had built Digger and Barbie a comfy kennel each by the back door, and they loved the freedom of their huge backyard to roam free.

"Shh," she said, turning in his arms at the sound of someone tapping on a champagne flute. "It's time for the speeches."

Finn gave a low groan, but moved to her side and captured her hand with his, raising his beer to his lips with the other, and taking a big slug. He was looking handsome and relaxed in black trousers, and a dark-blue, button-up, short-sleeve shirt that showed off his biceps nicely. Indy itched to run her fingers over his freshly shaved jaw, but had to content herself with merely a glance, instead. By silent agreement, they decided to stay where they were, out on the veranda and watch from the back of the crowd.

Everyone turned to look at the enormous stone fireplace at the center of the great-room, where the two families were gathering on the raised, stone hearth so they could be seen by everyone in the room. Indy was glad of her heels tonight, which allowed her to see over the heads of all the guests threading into the room through the wide-open French doors.

First up to speak was Daniella, who looked surprisingly relaxed in a floor-length indigo dress that suited her svelte figure perfectly, Steve standing at her shoulder, trying not to look uncomfortable in his pressed white shirt. Daniella looked fit to burst as she motioned Skylar and Nash up to stand next to her. She waited until a hush fell over the room, then she spoke loud enough so even Indy could hear out on the veranda.

"Welcome to Stormcloud, everyone. Thanks for coming to help us share this wonderful event of Nash and Skylar's engagement." Daniella had to stop, as the catcalls and whistles of encouragement from the crowd became too loud. But she wasn't bothered, and as soon as the noise died down, she went on. "I'm Daniella, and this is Steve, and we're the parents of the bride-to-be, just in case any of you didn't already know." More whistles and loud comments, which only made Daniella smile. "And please let me introduce Nash's mother, Cheryl, and his three sisters." Daniella made room for Cheryl to join them on the raised platform, and together they introduced Aimee, Ashley, and Cody, who were gathered below the step with happy smiles on their faces.

Dale, Daisy, Julie, and Aaron stood next to the sisters, also watching their own sister and brother-in-law-to-be, and grinning delightedly at their embarrassment as Daniella began to gush about how talented Skylar was as a chef, and how much Nash had come to mean to them as a family. Indy could see where Nash got his surfer curls from. While his mother's hair was greying now, Indy could see how striking her hair might've once been, echoed in her offspring's glorious curls. Nash's sisters were just as spectacularly good-looking as he was; the family was blessed with great genes.

Then Steve took over, with a few anecdotes about Skylar as a child growing up and getting into all sorts of trouble, often involving food—combining new and interesting ingredients that didn't always go together—and adding a few stories about Nash in the time after he'd joined their family circle, not forgetting to mention how lucky Nash and Skylar were to have survived the helicopter crash that ultimately brought the two together.

It was a typical engagement speech by doting parents of the bride, full of love and joy at the union, and Indy couldn't help the large smile that lit up her face at the shared deep affection throughout the room. She tuned out the voices, preferring to watch people's faces and capture their emotions, as they smiled at the young couple, wishing them well in their life together. Friends and work colleagues, as well as locals from in town. Nash was well known and liked in the town of Dimbulah, and everybody wanted to see him and Skylar happy. All the families from both sides, Skylar and Dale's two half-brothers, were there, and of course, all the Stormcloud staff.

Indy tuned back into the speeches when Nash cleared his throat.

"I'm not big on words," he said, suddenly awkward in front of the large group of people. "And I don't always say clearly how much Skylar means to me. But I'm sure she knows I couldn't live without her. I don't need her to marry me, to know how much she means to me. We made an unbreakable commitment a long time ago, and I'll always honor that commitment, piece of paper, or not." Nash took Skylar's hand and raised it to his lips. "You and me against the world," he said, clear blue eyes fixed on hers. "Nothing can break us when we're together."

"Nothing can break us," Skylar repeated softly, staring back at Nash, looking for all the world as if she were lost in his eyes, as if the rest of the room no longer existed.

A lump formed in Indy's throat. Nash always came across as calm, in control, and easygoing. But the intensity with which he was staring at Skylar right now had Indy's heart beating fast. It was almost as if Nash were putting into words the exact way she felt about Finn. And it was the strength of that love that'd see them through. Through all the thick and the thin bits.

She and Finn had had an unconventional beginning, but because of the fear and the danger and the angst, it'd brought them together so much more quickly than a normal love affair might've done. A bit like Nash and Skylar, actually. Indy watched Nash kiss Skylar with no reservations, as if no one were watching and she was the center of his universe. Indy squeezed Finn's hand so tight, she felt his knuckles crack together.

Everyone clapped and cheered until the engaged couple finally quit their kissing to grin at the whole room.

"Oh, before everyone goes back to enjoying their night," Nash said, standing on tiptoe so the people at the back of the room could hear him. "This might also be a good time to welcome Finn Carmody to our team." Nash tilted his glass in Finn's direction and more than one pair of curious eyes turned in his direction. "As most of you probably already know, Dimbulah police station is going through an expansion. The powers on high have decided that with all the crime going on in this little neck of the woods, we need more manpower out here."

Everyone raised their glasses and saluted Finn, who returned their acknowledgments with a serious smile. But Indy was close enough to see the slight color rising up his neck; he hated being the center of attention, which Nash already knew, and was now raising a wickedly challenging eyebrow in his direction.

The new police station was a result of a few factors. Nearby Ravensthorpe Station was closing. The town had dwindled in size—as often happened in these smaller outback towns—and there was less call for a permanent station to be housed there. Two more constables were being sent to Dimbulah station and would start in January. And Finn was the local, regional detective, liaising with the main

Cairns station, starting four weeks ago. It meant that Nash was now responsible for a larger area, and had three more staff to supervise. Which'd made Skylar so happy that Nash was finally getting the recognition he deserved, along with a nice promotion.

Another reason HQ was beefing up the Dimbulah station was an alarming uptick in crime in the region. It was a little ironic, because a lot of the increased crime they were referring to had come as a direct result of goings on at Stormcloud Station. Indy sent a fervent prayer skyward that there be no more trouble from here on in. No more drug traffickers, no more stalkers, or crazy gunmen shooting helicopters out of the sky. Stormcloud had seen enough drama and tragedy to last a lifetime.

Indy tried to listen to what else Daniella was saying, but her gaze kept sliding to Finn, standing tall and handsome beside her. She could hardly believe their dream had come true. She hadn't had to give up her lifestyle, or her love of the land. Instead, Finn had found the perfect job, so that he could join her. She was worried he might resent her, that he was taking a step away from the ladder of becoming a Detective Sergeant himself one day. But he'd assured her this was what he wanted. He hadn't known how much he missed his former days spent as a jackaroo and how it made him feel more connected to the country and to himself. It'd been Finn's idea to apply for the job at Dimbulah, and Nash had been only too happy to work alongside him; they'd developed a deep respect for each other during Finn's undercover work.

Before the job had come up, they'd continued a long distance relationship, with Finn coming to Cairns whenever he could, and her visiting him in Sydney on long weekends. But they'd both known it wasn't going to be sustainable. They needed a solution, and they'd got one, almost as if they'd been handed a miracle. They'd only been living together for one month, but it already felt right. Easy. They kept no secrets from each other.

Well, okay, perhaps just one.

Indy had decided never to tell Finn about Garrett's attempt to rape her. She knew it may not be completely fair, but she'd managed to fight Garrett off, and she knew if Finn found out, he would *never* forgive his bother. And Indy believed Finn needed to forgive him if he was ever to completely move on from that situation. Even if he never spoke to his brother again, that forgiveness was still key to Finn being able to move on. Forgive but not forget. Indy, on the other hand, couldn't forgive Garrett. Not for what he did to her, but also for what he'd done to Finn. But that was different. Perhaps with time and distance, she might come to see him as more of a pathetic soul who deserved her absolution, but not right now.

Garrett had been charged with Ronaldo's murder, which was shocking, but not surprising. He was already going to spend at least the next ten years in jail for the attempted abduction of herself and Finn. And there were more charges being laid for dealing and transporting illicit substances. Once the murder trial was over in a few months—and she felt sure he'd be convicted—he'd probably end up with a life sentence. Finn told her they suspected that Swampy had commanded Garrett to put an end to Ronaldo after he killed Wombat in a fit of rage, against Swampy's explicit orders. But Garrett was admitting to nothing, and neither was Swampy, even though the evidence was piling up against them both.

It was a sad ending for Finn's brother. You only had to look at Finn to see how much potential Garrett might've had. If only he'd followed a similar path to his twin. Finn's mother was still in shock, not quite believing everything being said about her precious boy. But at least she and Finn were back on speaking terms, and she'd forgiven him for not telling her the truth about Garrett's fall from grace back when he first suspected things weren't right. Indy and Finn were going to fly down and see his mother and sister for Christmas. A trip she wasn't altogether sure she was looking forward to, but hopefully it might help to rebuild those relationship bridges. And Finn assured her that she would like Caroline, who was the same age as Indy, a passionate animal-lover, and desperate to talk to her about her dogs and horses. But she didn't want to think about Garrett, or uncomfortable family meetings. Not now, while they were at Skylar and Nash's engagement party; it was supposed to be a happy event.

Indy shifted her feet; her heels were killing her, she needed to sit down.

"How you feeling? Shall we go home?" Finn was suddenly solicitous, grabbing her arm and laying a protective hand over her belly.

"I'm fine," she whispered, taking his hand and placing it on her hip instead, hoping no one had seen. "Be careful," she mouthed. She didn't want the cat getting out of the bag yet, it was still early days. Really early days. But when she'd peed on the stick a week ago and it'd come back positive, Finn had been over the moon. For which she was forever grateful. Her pregnancy was a surprise, but not an unwanted one. They'd discussed having a family, even while they were doing the long-distance thing. She'd unburdened herself to him about her cold, lonely childhood, and how she wanted more than that now. How she wanted to create a family of her own, with new rules, surrounded by love and acceptance. Everything she hadn't had and so much more. And lots of kids. At least three or four. To her grateful surprise, Finn had wholeheartedly agreed. Kayleigh was Finn's first daughter, but he was more than happy to add to their little brood, hopefully including Kayleigh as much as they could. Indy looked to Skylar, Dale, and Julie for inspiration. They were step-siblings who'd grown up in separate families when they were younger, but now had steadfast and strong relationships as adults. It was a positive sign that things could work out.

"Sorry," he apologized. "But I just get so…excited, and worried. You know."

And they should be worried, after Indy's miscarriage with her first pregnancy, she was wary of losing this one, too. Which was why they weren't going to tell anyone yet. It was hard to overcome her fear at the beginning, when both of them agreed to stop using protection and see what happened. Trepidation and doubt plagued her. Because what if it happened again? But she wanted Finn's baby, and in the end, she had conquered her misgivings so she could fulfill her greatest wish. She had a good feeling about this pregnancy, however. This one was meant to be.

Perhaps her last one hadn't meant to be, for whatever reason.

She'd never returned Patrick's calls or texts. She decided she didn't have anything good to say to him. Telling Finn about getting pregnant to Patrick had been hard. How losing the baby had been devastating at the time. It was the night of their first date, and she'd just blurted it out and then watched him, nervously gauging his reaction. But she shouldn't have been worried, he was supportive as well as horrified at Patrick's callous mistreatment of her and his complete disregard of the child he'd helped to conceive. He wanted to go and punch Patrick in the face, and part of her wanted to let him do it. But in the end, she'd said that part of her life was over, and she just wanted to forget him and move on. It was another reason Finn was even more attentive toward her, and her yet-to-grow belly. He knew how precious this baby was to her. As well as to him.

Indy leaned back against Finn's strong bicep. "I might just

go and sit down for a—"

"Did I just see what I thought I saw?" Bindi arrived at Indy's elbow with the widest grin on her face.

"Oh, ah…" Indy exchanged a look with Finn, but she knew there was no hiding it from Bindi's astute gaze. "We only just found out ourselves," Indy confirmed. "We're not telling anyone yet, it's too soon." Now if only she could swear her to secrecy…

"I wondered why you weren't drinking champagne. Now it all makes sense. I won't tell a soul, I promise." The petite woman bounced on her toes with excitement. "Oh, except Skylar, she'll be over the moon, and we work so closely, I can't keep a secret from her… And Julie, she's so in love with babies. I really thought it'd be her and Aaron doing the kid thing first," Bindi mused.

Indy smiled, but wished Bindi would keep her voice down. Finn was frowning, but the corners of his mouth were turned up, as if he wasn't sure what to do with Bindi's enthusiasm, either.

"And you have to tell Daniella, she really misses Kee's little daughter, Benni. Having her here last year made her yearn for the pitter-patter of little grandchildren's feet." Bindi's gaze became mischievous. "This is so going to put the pressure on Dale and Daisy. They've been married a year and they're still not popping the kids out, yet."

"This isn't a competition." Indy wasn't sure whether to scowl or laugh at Bindi.

"And Mack. You have to let me tell Mack. He's gonna want to do the manly cowboy thing and take Finn out for a beer and cigar, you know." Bindi turned her gaze to Finn.

It seemed like the genie was out of the bottle, after all. And Indy couldn't find a reason to be sad about it.

"Okay," Indy conceded. "But can you do me one favor and keep it a secret just for tonight?" The last thing they needed was to take the shine off Nash and Skylar's night.

"I can do that," Bindi promised.

"Let's go and find you that chair to sit in," Finn suggested.

"Oh, yeah. You guys do that," Bindi said. "I can hear the band starting up outside, and I need to go and dance with Mack." Bindi stood on tiptoe and kissed Indy on the cheek. "I'm so happy for you two. Seems we all got our happily ever after, hey?"

"Yes, we did," Indy agreed.

Following Finn out onto the veranda, she let him pull her down onto his lap in an empty, Adirondack-style wooden chair. She lay back against his chest and he twined his fingers in her hair. It was true; she was getting her heart's desire. A family with the man she loved.

They'd have to go and see Kayleigh soon. Finn had gone over to Ireland on his own on a hurried trip just after the drug bust, to persuade Chloe and his daughter that he was safe and well. But he also wanted to introduce Indy to his daughter and spend more time in Ireland, so a longer visit, where she and Finn could spend quality time with Kayleigh and introduce her to the idea of having a baby sister or brother, was definitely on the cards. A blended family might have its problems, but she and Finn would work them out.

Indy had never been happier in her life. She loved working at Stormcloud. She had no doubt Daniella would be amenable to some kind of arrangement once the baby was born. Raising a child on the land was the most grounded type of childhood any kid could ask for. Indy had high hopes for their future at Stormcloud.

"I'm sorry, but I might have to borrow my man Nash's words from earlier," Finn whispered in her ear. Then he spun her around so he could stare straight into her face. "Nothing can break us when we're together. I truly believe that."

"We're unbreakable," she agreed, kissing his delectable

lips, tasting the beer, but also acknowledging the desire he was funneling through to her. "Perhaps we should head home, after all," she suggested with a wicked grin.

Also by Suzanne Cass
NEW

**Stormcloud Station Series
(A Stargazer Spinoff Series)
Small Town Romantic Suspense**

Clear Skies
Starlit Skies
Crystal Skies
Dawn Skies
Tangled Skies
Outback Skies

**Stargazer Ranch Romance Series
Small Town Romantic Suspense
Combustion: Prequel Novella
Wildfire
Firelight
Snowbound: A Christmas Novella
Snowfall
Cloudburst**

**Island Bound Series
Mystery Romance (on an Island)**
Books can be read as stand-alone
**Bound by Truth
Bound by Silence
Bound by the Stars**

**Colors of the Earth Series
Small Town Romantic Suspense**
Books can be read as stand-alone
**Shadows in the Dust
Shadows in Deep Blue
Shadows of Red Earth**

* * *

Romantic Suspense
Single Title
Island Redemption
Glass Clouds
Chasing Bullets

Love in the Mountains Novella Series
Small Town Short Romance
Novellas can be read as stand-alone
Rain on a Tin Roof
Lost and Found
Rescue his Heart

Please Leave a Review

The greatest gift you could ever give an author is to leave a review. You will be helping other people to discover this book and making a difference to me as an Independently Published Author. If you liked this book and want other people to read it to, please leave a review.

About the Author

Suzanne Cass is an Australian author who writes rural romance and romantic suspense abounding with passion and danger.

Her debut novel, Island Redemption, won the Romance Writers of Australia Emerald Award in 2016. Suzanne was also a finalist in the 2019 Romance Writers of Australia RUBY award.

She had always had a fascination with the tough resilience of people who live in our amazing red-dirt outback country. When not writing about the characters that inhabit her head, Suzanne can be found roaming the Perth beaches with her border collie, or encouraging from the sidelines as her two sons play sport.

Stay in touch via my website

www.suzannecass.com

Acknowledgements

Outback Skies is the sixth book in the Stormcloud Station Series. I'm a little sad to be saying goodbye to Stormcloud Lodge, it has been a big part of my life over the past eighteen months. Although Stormcloud is a fictional luxury resort, it is based on lots of research and a little bit of personal experience, helping to bring the country to life for you, the readers. After spending so much time writing about it, to me, the place is almost tangible. I feel like it could exist, somewhere up in that amazing, fragile, beautiful area of North Queensland.

All of these books would never have made it to your kindle or bookshelf without a whole heap of help. To my beta readers, especially Rebecca, who's unfailing support keeps me going, thank you for keeping me on the straight and narrow and helping me figure out some of the more tricky American phrases that I will never understand.

To my wonderful ARC team, who are essential to an Indie Author like me. The way you encourage me, endorse the books that you love with your reviews, and help other people find my stories is priceless.

Big thanks to my editor, Tanya Saari for putting up with my total inability to understand the comma.

To my husband and my two beautiful sons. Thank you for your unconditional love.

And last but definitely not least, I'm so very grateful to all the readers who have bought and enjoyed my books. Thank you from the bottom of my heart.